INVERCLYDE LIBRARIES

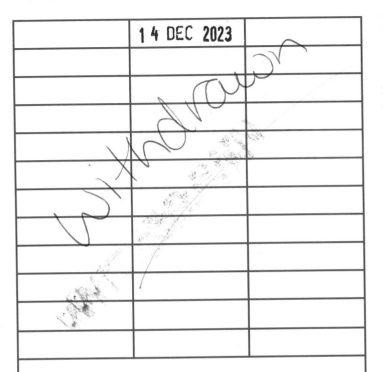

	1 4 DEC 2023	

This book is to be returned on or before
the last date above. It may be borrowed for
a further period if not in demand.

For enquiries and renewals Tel: (01475) 712323
www.inverclyde.gov.uk/libraries

First published in Great Britain in 2023 by Boldwood Books Ltd.

Copyright © Sarah Bennett, 2023

Cover Design by Alice Moore Design

Cover Photography: Deposit Photos and Shutterstock

The moral right of Sarah Bennett to be identified as the author of this work has been asserted in accordance with the Copyright, Designs and Patents Act 1988.

A CIP catalogue record for this book is available from the British Library.

Paperback ISBN 978-1-80483-320-9

Large Print ISBN 978-1-80483-319-3

Hardback ISBN 978-1-80483-321-6

Ebook ISBN 978-1-80483-318-6

Kindle ISBN 978-1-80483-317-9

Audio CD ISBN 978-1-80483-326-1

MP3 CD ISBN 978-1-80483-325-4

Digital audio download ISBN 978-1-80483-322-3

Boldwood Books Ltd
23 Bowerdean Street
London SW6 3TN
www.boldwoodbooks.com

For Bree x

PROLOGUE

Hope's phone pinged, breaking her concentration. Not that she minded the interruption – she'd been wrestling with the estate's rental accounts for the past couple of hours and was near cross-eyed from staring at her computer screen. A long-term tenant was retiring and had asked for a final account to be drawn up, and Hope had made the mistake of deciding she might as well do the rest at the same time.

Looking after everything to do with the various rental properties on the sprawling Juniper Meadows estate was normally her Uncle Ziggy's responsibility, but he was away for a few days and Hope was looking after things in his stead. She clicked save on her file, then sat back, rubbing her tired eyes.

It would probably have taken Ziggy a few minutes to do what had taken her a couple of hours. As the managing director of the estate, he knew everything inside out and back to front. Unfortunately, that meant a lot of the information Hope needed was in his head, which she very much hoped was currently resting easy on a sun lounger by the pool in his hotel in Portugal. She smiled to herself at the thought. Ziggy lived and breathed Juniper Meadows and was probably fretting over not being there. He'd been pushing himself too hard and the rest of the family had united and ambushed him with the tickets. It was only a week, knowing he'd baulk at being away any longer, but there was a lull in events at the estate and they'd wanted him to recharge his batteries a little before the trifecta of Halloween, Bonfire Night and Christmas.

Things had been tough over recent months after a disgruntled ex-employee had waged a sabotage campaign against the family and they needed to recoup as much of their lost income as possible. Hope was planning several promotions to boost the profile of the artisan gin distillery that she managed, including some seasonal recipes. Her mother and her aunt, Rowena, who was married to Ziggy's twin, Zap, were planning to run the first of what they hoped would be many art retreats at Stourton Hall, which had been converted into a luxury hotel and spa.

She pressed a hand to her suddenly fluttering stomach as she tried not to think about how much work the entire family had committed themselves to over the coming months. It was five weeks to Halloween so there was time to get all their ducks in a row. Hopefully.

'Everything okay?' Cam asked from the other side of the dining table.

Hope nodded. 'Just trying to get my brain around some of Ziggy's more creative accounting. A couple of the rental payments are lower than expected, that's all.' She knew he wouldn't mind if she offloaded some of her panic over her daunting workload, but Cam had enough on his plate.

Her boyfriend frowned at her over the tortoiseshell frames of his glasses. 'Something dodgy?'

'I don't think so. I'm sure it'll be something Ziggy has agreed to and forgotten to make a note of.' She rested her hand on the top of the stack of tenant files she'd lugged over from her car to the little haven that was the lodge she shared with Cam in the heart of the woods. She had a perfectly good office space above the distillery where her other uncle, Zap, concocted the award-winning gin flavours that had made Juniper Meadows a coveted brand amongst connoisseurs. But this was the final weekend before the autumn term started at the local university where Cam held a lecturing post in the archaeology department, and she wanted to make the most of him being around.

'I'm sure that's all it is,' Cam agreed. 'I know I'm still a relative newcomer here, but I can't think of anyone who'd try and do your family wrong.' His face fell as soon as the words left his mouth. 'Well, apart from...' He trailed off, giving Hope an apologetic look. She didn't blame him; the events of the summer still sat too close in everyone's mind. 'Have you still not heard anything from Amelia?' he asked.

Hope shook her head, her eyes straying towards her phone, where a long string of unanswered WhatsApp messages sat in the chat between her and her old friend. No one in the Travers family blamed Amelia or her mother for the awful things Keith, her father, had put them through, but their many assurances of that had hit a brick wall. Amelia had decided that the best thing for them all was for her to cut ties, and so far she'd shown no hint of changing her mind.

The messages all had a double blue tick to show they'd been read, so Hope continued to reach out. 'At least she hasn't blocked me.' Unlike her cousin, Rhys, who'd dated Amelia for a couple of years in their late teens. Hope could understand why he still felt a sense of responsibility towards their mutual friend, but he could be very high-handed when he was convinced he was in the right.

The last words Amelia had said to him before she'd blocked his number had told him exactly what she thought about his continued attempts to interfere in her life.

A tiny spark of hope flickered; perhaps the ping from her phone that had distracted her just now was a reply from her friend at last? Snatching up the phone, she looked at the notification. The happy spark was instantly snuffed out by a queasy feeling of apprehension. 'Oh.'

There must've been something of that uncomfortable feeling in her tone because Cam moved immediately to crouch beside her chair, a concerned hand resting on her thigh as he looked up at her. 'What is it?'

Hope felt her cheeks heat. 'I... umm... I set up a Google Alert about Ben and I just got a notification.' Of the many shocks and setbacks they'd been through, finding out she had an older brother she knew nothing about had been the one that had really knocked Hope off her axis. Her mother, Stevie, had done her best to explain and Hope had a huge degree of sympathy for the desperation Stevie must've felt as she made the impossible choice between leaving her little boy behind or saving the unborn child she was carrying. Safe behind the protective walls of the Juniper Meadows estate, Stevie had never stopped trying to get Ben back. It was only when he'd instructed her via a solicitor's letter on his eighteenth birthday that he wanted nothing to do with any of them that Stevie had finally given up.

Still, Hope couldn't help feeling like a part of her life had been stolen from her. She found herself lying awake at night, wondering what her brother looked like. Would he have the dark hair and blue eyes of the Travers genetics, or did he take after his father? *Their* father, Hope silently corrected herself. It was strange, really. Though she ached for a connection with the brother she'd never known, she felt nothing like that for the man who'd sired them both. She'd heard enough from Stevie about his coercive and controlling behaviour, which had turned their fairy-tale romance into a horror story within a matter of months, to know she had missed nothing by not having Benjamin Lawson Sr in her life.

Cam didn't say anything; he just pulled the empty chair beside him closer, sat down and held out his arms to her. Hope slid onto his lap and settled into the warm comfort of his body. Closing her eyes, she sent up a silent prayer of thanks for the odd circumstances that had brought him into her life. She knew that uncovering the ruins of what was turning out to be a substantial religious site had nothing to do with the troubles visited on her family, but more than one person in the village had mentioned old stories passed down about a curse connected to the ruins. She and Cam had read as much for themselves in the diaries of one of her many-times-great-grandfathers. He'd been the baron at the time and sought to repurpose the old stones to build a garden folly behind Stourton Hall, the family seat that was now a luxury hotel and spa. Even as she dismissed the gossip with a polite smile, a tiny part of Hope had wondered whether she should have just left well alone. No. If she hadn't gone digging, she'd never have met Cam and though it had only been a few months, she knew in her heart that he was the one for her. They weren't in any rush to formalise things between them. He had his career to think about, as well as devoting every spare hour to continuing with the work up at the dig. Things had slowed down on that front, first because of the police investigation into the reckless acts of sabotage caused by Amelia's father, Keith, and then September had arrived, and Cam and his team had returned to their jobs and studies after the summer holidays.

'It's silly, really. I don't even know why I did it.' She'd set up the alert on a spur of the moment whim while she'd still been trying to come to terms with Ben's existence. She'd originally gone online to search for him, had even typed his name into the search bar but something had stopped her from hitting enter. She'd wondered how she'd feel if the shoe was on the other foot and Ben knew about her and went poking around for information. Not that there was much of interest about her, but still, she had the usual social media accounts and she'd put out press releases and the like when the distillery had a new product launch, so stuff would pop up if someone searched for her. Her habit of tweeting too much during episodes of *Strictly Come Dancing* was there for all to see. Sitting down in front of the TV to watch it was something she, her mum and her aunt, Rowena, had always looked forward to.

The build-up for the latest series had already started with the usual press speculation about that year's contestants, but Hope hadn't been feeling it at all. Though they all put a brave face on it, the unresolved issue of Ben's existence and the way the older members of the family had conspired to keep it a secret from both Hope and Rhys had left a pall in the air whenever the family sat down together. There were other things, too. Other secrets that would need to be aired at some point. It was the only way they'd all be able to move on. Hope just wasn't sure how much she could deal with right now, so she hadn't pushed them on it. Not yet, at least.

Setting up the alert about Ben had been a compromise to herself. She wouldn't go poking around in the past, but if something came up about him in the future, she wanted to know about it. Make sure he was okay, even if it was from afar. 'I should've told you,' she said to Cam, putting her arms around his neck and giving him a hug of apology. 'After all my complaints about Mum keeping secrets and here I am doing the same thing.'

Cam pressed a kiss to her cheek. 'This is hardly in the same ballpark, sweetheart. It's only natural you'd be curious about him.'

She leaned back a little so she could meet his eyes. 'You don't think it's weird?'

He laughed. 'If you started hanging around outside his house or created a fake account to follow him on Facebook, then I'd be worried.'

Hope gave him a guilty grin. 'I was tempted to look him up,' she confessed.

'The fact you didn't shows a lot more restraint than many people might have managed.'

Was that a hint of a blush on his cheek? 'Cam? What did you do?'

Cam lifted one shoulder in a half-shrug. 'I might have checked out his Facebook profile.'

'And you didn't tell me?' Hope wasn't sure if she was disappointed or impressed at his ability to keep a secret like that. Then again, she hadn't mentioned the Google Alert to him so they'd both been a bit sneaky.

He held his hands up in surrender. 'I only did it once. I just wanted to make sure he wasn't a nutter who might hurt you or the family if he ever changed his mind about making contact.'

Hope knew she shouldn't ask, but she couldn't resist. 'What's he like?'

'From the couple of posts I scanned over, he's a keen park runner and given how many photos there are of him with a dog, he's definitely a Travers.'

Hope gave a little hiccup of a laugh as she glanced over to where her pair of black Lab puppies were sprawled near the door, snoring away. 'He'd fit right in here, then.' She couldn't keep the note of longing from her voice.

Cam touched a tender hand to her cheek. 'He's got your eyes, but his hair is blonde, not dark.'

She hugged the little nugget of information to her heart. 'It feels so strange, the knowing and not knowing.' She reached for her phone and handed it to Cam. 'Will you look for me? I just want to know he's okay.'

When Cam took her phone, Hope shifted back to her own chair so she wouldn't be tempted to look. Time seemed to stretch to unbearable slowness as he tapped on the screen to follow the alert link. The butterflies started to dance in her middle as she watched him. It made her think back to the summer when she'd asked him to use his database access to search her family tree and he'd uncovered Ben's existence via a birth certificate. That had been the trigger for all the upset. When would she learn to leave things alone?

It must've been five minutes later when Cam set aside the phone and reached for her hand, his kind eyes solemn. 'It's bad news, isn't it?' Hope could barely breathe around the lump in her throat.

Cam squeezed her hand gently. 'Ben's fine.'

The flood of relief she experienced seemed odd given her lack of relationship with her brother, and yet it felt like the most natural reaction in the world. 'Thank goodness.'

'The alert wasn't actually about him. I'm so sorry, Hope, it was an obituary notification in *The Times* for your father. There weren't a lot of details, just something about a short illness and information about the funeral.'

Hope stared up at him as she waited to feel something. There was nothing akin to the rush of sensation when she'd been worried about Ben, just a kind of blank numbness. She'd grown up believing her father was dead and she supposed she'd never fully adjusted to accepting he was alive. Setting that aside for now, she decided to focus on what was most important. 'Poor Ben. He must be devastated.' For all he'd treated her mother dreadfully, Stevie had been at pains to stress that Benjamin Sr had doted on their son.

Cam nodded. 'There's no mention of anyone else in the statement so I'm guessing he never remarried after your mother.'

'Let me see it.' Hope held out her hand and Cam gave her back the phone.

'I'll make some coffee.'

Hope watched Cam as he walked the short distance from the table to the coffee machine on the kitchen counter. It was an illusory offer of privacy given the open-plan nature of the lodge, but she appreciated his discretion nonetheless. Taking a deep breath, she turned her attention to the phone.

LAWSON Benjamin, following a short illness. Father to Benjamin. Funeral service at noon on 29th September at St Mary's Church, Brookham, RH3. No flowers please. All donations and inquiries to P. Exley & Sons.

The starkness of the statement struck Hope and she imagined trying to come up with a suitable form of words for her mother. She cut the thought off as soon as it started, because losing her was beyond Hope's comprehension. At least she would have family around to help her when such a terrible time came. Who did Ben have? Was he married? Did he have a partner at least? Someone he could lean on the way Hope had come to rely on Cam? God, she hoped so. When he returned with their drinks and sat beside her, Hope reached for his hand. 'Thank you.'

Cam's lips quirked in a quizzical smile. 'It's only a cup of coffee.'

Hope found herself smiling even past the ache inside. 'I mean for everything. I can't help wondering if Ben is dealing with all this alone or if he is lucky enough to have someone like you to support him.'

Cam nodded. 'I hope he does. I remember when my granny passed. Dad had such a faff with all the paperwork and formalities. The funeral director was great but that was the easiest bit. She didn't have much, and she left it all to him, apart from a token gift for me and my sister. Even so, it seemed to take forever to get everything tied up.'

'Mum hasn't shared much about their life together, but I can't imagine settling his affairs will be that straightforward.' His. She still couldn't bring herself to call him her father, had resolved not to give him that place in her life. But it would be different for Ben. 'Do you think I should reach out to Ben? I can't bear the thought of him dealing with it by himself.' She glanced at the funeral notice again. 'It's next week, there's probably not enough time for me to do anything to help, but I feel like I should at least be there.'

When Cam spoke, there was an almost painful gentleness in his words. 'He might not welcome you showing up. As far as you're aware, he doesn't even know you exist.'

'I know. But I can't just pretend it isn't happening. If I did go, I wouldn't make a fuss, just sit quietly at the back and see how things are for him. I don't expect you to come with me; I know next week is going to be busy for you.'

'It's mostly orientation for the new intake.' Cam shifted his chair closer until their thighs touched. Just the warmth of him next to her made her feel better. 'Besides, I'm not letting you face something like that on your own.'

Hope shifted from her chair until she could sit back on Cam's lap and put her arms around his neck. 'You really are the best thing that's ever happened to me.' She pressed a quick kiss to his mouth, then leaned back. 'Like I said, we'll be discreet. If he's got friends and family around to support him then we'll just leave him in peace.'

Cam nodded. 'And if he hasn't?'

'Then I think he deserves to know that he's not alone.' When Cam pulled her close, Hope settled against his chest with a sigh. Whether Ben chose to accept her or turned her away like he had the rest of the family? Well, that remained to be seen.

1

'Thank you for coming.' Ben Lawson shook hands with yet another grey man in a grey suit who'd offered him yet another platitude about his father. As he turned to the next person waiting to offer their condolences, he risked a glance along the line and felt his smile freeze at the sight of at least another two dozen people waiting to pay their respects. The chill autumn wind gusted through the open door of the church, bringing with it a smattering of icy rain and a swirl of dirty fallen leaves. The weather was as grim and dark as Ben's mood. How much longer would he have to endure this bloody pantomime? Fighting down the urge to check his watch, Ben twitched his mouth back into his best approximation of a smile and turned to the next person in the queue.

'Such a bloody shame,' Nigel Beecham said, not for the first time. He pumped Ben's hand up and down, his unpleasantly damp palm leaving Ben with the urge to pull away. No chance of that when Nigel clamped his other meaty fist on top of their clasped hands and squeezed. 'Don't worry, son, we'll give old Benny boy a send-off you can be proud of. I'm heading straight to the club now to make sure everything's shipshape.' The captain of the local golf club and one of his father's cronies, Nigel had caught Ben off guard with an offer to host a wake for him at the club and he hadn't known how to refuse.

'Thanks, Nigel, I appreciate it,' Ben said, lying through his back teeth. All he wanted was for these hangers-on to go away so he could jump into his car and escape back to London before the rush hour turned the M25 into a car park. An impossible thought that did nothing to lighten his mood. 'I'll be along when I can.' He gestured his head towards the mourners still waiting, hoping Nigel would get the hint and move on.

'Of course, of course.' Squeeze. Pump. Pump. 'Such a bloody shame.'

Piss off. 'Stick a pint behind the bar for me,' Ben said instead, hoping Nigel couldn't hear the grinding of his teeth. 'I'm going to need it.'

Nigel brayed out a laugh, abruptly cutting it off when he belatedly remembered where they were. His already florid face flushed the startling shade of a ripe plum. He opened his mouth as though he might start his 'bloody shame' litany over again, but Ben was rescued by the indignant snort of the woman next in the queue.

'Do move on, Nigel, for goodness' sake. I need to get back and let Lulu out or she'll be peeing all over my lino.'

Ben bit the inside of his lip, trying not to laugh as poor flustered Nigel released his hand and all but shot out the door. Feeling lighter for the first time since the news of his father's death had reached him, Ben turned to greet Amanda Bonnington, the retired head teacher of the local primary school. 'Hello, Mrs B.'

'Here, you'll want this,' Mrs Bonnington said, offering him a tissue to dry his hand. 'He always was a sweaty little beast,' she murmured under her breath as she waited for Ben to tuck the tissue in his pocket before she reached for his hand. 'I won't bother with all that useless flannel everyone's been spouting about how bravely your father bore his illness alone. I think it was unspeakably cruel of him to keep it from you rather than giving you a chance to come to terms with things.' She shook her head. 'Not the time or place, but you know I've always been one to speak my mind. The only person that matters today is you, my dear boy. You must let me know if there is anything you need.'

It struck Ben then that he'd been standing in this freezing doorway for a good ten minutes and she was the first person who'd shown any concern for his welfare. 'I'm fine, Mrs B, thank you. You know how my father was, always had to be in control of everything, even to the very last.'

She eyed him with that same sharp-eyed gaze that had cowed her pupils for over thirty years, and he had the feeling she could see right through his bullshit. Finding out his father had been ill for months and not spoken about it had been devastating. 'Hmm,' was all she said. 'Are you heading back to town tonight?'

Ben nodded. 'I need to get back to work.' That wasn't strictly true; his boss, Matthew, had granted him a couple of days' compassionate leave, but he couldn't bear the thought of rattling around his father's big house on his own. Not now he knew the old man had been struggling alone and in pain for weeks without so much as a word to Ben. 'I'll be down again next week to sort out the will and stuff.'

'Come for tea when you are back.'

It wasn't a request and Ben couldn't resist raising his hand in salute as he grinned down at the small yet still formidable woman. 'Yes, Mrs B.'

'Good boy.' Mrs Bonnington reached up and smoothed the lapel of his suit jacket before giving his chest a quick pat. 'You'll be fine.' He wasn't sure which of them she was trying to reassure.

'I'll see you next week,' he promised and with a quick grimace towards the awful weather, Mrs Bonnington tugged her hat down tighter and stepped out into the rain.

Thankfully, the rest of the queue moved quickly. Most were locals from the village, the rest former colleagues at the stock-broking firm his father had built from scratch and sold out of the blue twelve months earlier. From their shell-shocked faces, it was clear he'd spun them the same line about it being time to enjoy some of the money he'd spent a lifetime earning, and improve his golf handicap.

Having finally seen the last well-wisher out of the door, Ben looked around for the vicar, wanting to thank him for the service. He was one of the few people his father had apparently taken into his confidence and they'd planned the funeral down to the last hymn. All Ben had had to do was show up. He supposed he should be grateful, but he couldn't help wishing he'd had some input. He sighed, knowing he was being foolish to expect his father to have given him something in death that he'd never once granted in life.

It was only then that he noticed a trio of people standing off to one side. There was a strange tension amongst them, the body language of the young woman clearly saying she didn't agree with whatever the tall, dark-haired man beside her was murmuring. The other man, slender and bookish in glasses and a tweed jacket rather than a dark suit, was keeping out of it, his attention fixed on Ben instead. When he saw Ben had noticed them, he nudged the woman. She glanced up and Ben felt his breath catch. He knew her from somewhere, though his mind couldn't seem to dredge up a name. There was something about the shape of her face, the way she held herself that felt deeply familiar. Realising he'd been star-ing, Ben moved towards them, holding out a hand in greeting. 'Hello, thank you for coming.' If they got speaking, perhaps he'd be able to remember.

The woman turned startled blue eyes up to him and Ben felt

his breath catch again. He knew those eyes, knew them as well as his own. As she tucked her smaller palm against his for a brief moment, there was another jolt of connection. 'Hello. I... I'm very sorry for your loss.'

'Thank you.' The words came automatically, the gears in his brain still frantically turning as he tried to place her. 'I'm sorry, but I can't remember when we've met before.' Ben gave her an apologetic smile. 'It's been a rough few days, and I'm a bit all over the place.'

'That's only natural given the circumstances.' It was the guy in the glasses who spoke as he stepped up beside the woman and offered his hand to Ben. 'My condolences for your loss.'

Ben shook it, still feeling at a disadvantage. 'Thanks. If you don't mind me asking, how did you know my father, exactly?'

The three of them exchanged a look before the woman took a deep breath. 'We didn't. We came here for you.'

Came here for him? Before Ben could put voice to his confusion, the dark-haired man muttered something about them making a big mistake then stepped forwards, thrusting out a hand. 'I'm Rhys Travers. I'm your cousin on your mother's side.'

'My mother?' Ben thought about the faded photograph sitting on the dressing table in his childhood bedroom, which, beside a handful of ghostly memories, was all he had to connect him to the woman who'd died when he was still a toddler. He wondered sometimes if those memories were even real or something he'd made up to try and ease the lonely ache in his heart. His father had never liked talking about her, so the photo was all he'd had to remind him he'd ever had another parent. He found his eyes drawn back to the woman in front of him. Those eyes of hers made sense now because surely she was some relation to him too. 'That's where I know you from,' he said, smiling in relief.

'I'm sorry?'

'I had a picture of my mother in my bedroom when I was growing up, which I suppose must've been taken around the same age as you are now. You look a lot like her, but that makes sense if we're cousins, right?'

The woman swallowed. 'Not cousins.' She held out a hand to Ben. 'Come and sit down a minute, please.'

Ben allowed her to lead him into a nearby pew, his earlier apprehension returning.

'We'll wait outside, Hope,' the man in glasses said, a pensive frown on his face. He placed a hand on Rhys's arm and steered him towards the door. Rhys looked like he wanted to stick around, only following when Hope – a pretty name, which suited the dark-haired woman – nodded.

She watched them leave, then turned back to face Ben. 'I'm sorry that we've dropped rather a bombshell on you like this. I just couldn't bear the thought you might be having to deal with every-thing on your own, that's all. Mum wanted to come, herself, of course, but we thought you might not be ready for that.'

Why would meeting her mum be any more of a shock than finding out he had any family on that side? 'It was very kind of you to think of me. I feel a bit awkward as I had no idea I had any other family. Dad was an only child, and I suppose I assumed the same must apply to my mother as he never mentioned anyone.'

Hope's dark brows drew together. 'I would've thought she'd have mentioned Zap and Ziggy in her letters, at least.'

'Who?' Ben frowned. None of this was making any sense. 'And what letters?'

'Our uncles.' Hope reached out a hand to him. 'Look, I can totally understand why you would be angry at her. I only found out about you a couple of months ago and I'm still struggling to forgive her for that. Mum has made a lot of terrible mistakes, but she only tried to do what she thought was best for both of us.'

There was something in the way she said 'Mum' as though she was... no, she couldn't be saying what he thought she was? Ben could hardly get his next words out. 'You... you said you aren't my cousin.'

Hope stared up at him, those blue eyes a mirror to his own swimming in tears. 'I'm your sister.'

'What?' His shout echoed around the empty church followed swiftly by the sound of feet clattering on the stone floor.

The vicar, robes flapping around his ankles, came hurrying down the nave towards them. 'Is everything all right?'

No, everything was very much not all right. Ben couldn't seem to catch his breath and he could feel his shirt beginning to cling to his back beneath his suit jacket. The cold wind still blew in from the open door and it promised relief. Some fresh air. He could think if he could get outside and get some air. Ben pulled himself together enough to remember he wasn't alone. Standing, he twisted his lips into a semblance of a smile. 'It's fine, thanks,' he assured the vicar. Feeling like he was moving on autopilot, Ben turned his fake smile towards Hope. 'Thanks for coming, but I really must get on. There's a wake at the local golf club and I have to show my face at least.'

She frowned up at him. 'Ben?'

'Sorry, I can't talk now.' Turning on his heel, Ben marched towards the door. There was no escape for him outside, though. He'd barely taken two steps into the blessedly cold air when Rhys and the other man straightened up from where they'd been lounging against the wall.

'Ben?' Rhys called out as he hurried past them.

'No!' He didn't stop, his eyes fixed on the wooden lychgate in the churchyard wall.

'Ben. Please, wait a minute!' It was Hope this time. Hope. *His sister*. Nope! His brain was still not anywhere close to being able to process that thought. He needed to get away. A couple of minutes and he'd be down the street and by the war memorial where he'd parked his car. He picked up speed until he was almost jogging. He could hear her heels clacking fast on the pavement as she tried to keep up. *She shouldn't be running when it's wet and there are fallen leaves everywhere; she might slip and hurt herself.* Torn between the need to get away and this sudden wave of unexpected protectiveness towards a woman he didn't know, Ben kept moving but slackened his pace. The footsteps slowed also but didn't stop.

His car was just a few metres away now and Ben saw something yellow on his windscreen. *You've got to be fucking kidding me...* The parking ticket was stuck right in the middle of the glass on the driver's side, meaning he'd have to peel it off before he could even think about driving. He'd never make it into the car before Hope caught up with him. His last chance of making a getaway ruined by an overzealous traffic warden. Defeated, Ben stopped and lowered his head.

'I'm sorry,' Hope said from behind him. 'I should've respected your wishes and not tried to contact you. I thought perhaps you might have changed your mind over the years, that you might need...' Her soft voice faltered on the word and trailed off.

Changed his mind? Straightening up, Ben turned to face her. She wasn't alone; Rhys and the other guy – it was really starting to bother him that he didn't know his name – were waiting a few feet further back. 'I don't know what you mean about my wishes and changing my mind. I didn't know you existed until about five minutes ago.'

Hope took a step towards him, seemed to stop herself and shoved her hands in the pockets of her black coat with a sigh. 'Mum showed me the letter you wrote when you cut ties. I should've left it be; I just thought...' Another sigh. 'I don't know what I thought.'

'I've never written a letter to her.' He couldn't bring himself to say 'Mum', so 'her' would have to do. It was all too surreal. There was a part of him that was convinced this was all some terrible mistake, even if that meant ignoring the evidence of his own eyes about the resemblance between them.

Hope rolled her eyes. 'Okay, Mr Pedant, the letter your solicitor sent to her on your behalf instructing her to stop contacting you.'

Solicitor? This was making less and less sense all the time. 'No, that's not what I meant. I've never contacted my mother in any way, shape or form because she died when I was a little kid. It's just been me and my dad for as long as I can remember.' She looked so shocked, Ben instinctively closed the distance between them. 'Do you think perhaps this is all some kind of big mistake? And perhaps I'm not the Ben Lawson you're looking for.' He said the last bit in an Obi-Wan Kenobi voice, the relief settling over him relaxing him enough that he was able to smile. That was it. She'd got the wrong person and this was all some big misunderstanding.

She didn't smile back. Not a Star Wars fan, he supposed. He tried again. 'Look, I really do think you've managed to get the wrong end of the stick here.' He glanced over his shoulder towards his car, then back down at her. 'I need to be getting along. I appreciate the sentiment that brought you here today, and there's no hard feelings on my part at all.' He offered her his hand. 'I hope you manage to track down your missing brother one day.'

Instead of taking his hand, Hope reached into the large handbag hooked over one shoulder and pulled out a plastic wallet. 'Take this.' She thrust it at him, leaving him no choice other than to do as she instructed. 'I should've found a better way to do this, and I'm really sorry I intruded on you today.' Hope took a step backwards. 'My details are on the card enclosed with everything else. I promise I won't bother you again, but know that if you ever want us, you have a family ready and willing to welcome you home.' It was his turn to stare in stunned silence as she turned on her heel and left without a backwards glance. The man in glasses folded a protective arm around her as soon as she reached him and the two of them carried on walking away. Rhys lingered for a long moment before he nodded once at the folder in Ben's hand, then turned to follow them.

2

_____

Ben watched them leave, completely perplexed by the entire encounter. What kind of person showed up out of the blue at a funeral and made such outlandish claims? He glanced down at the folder in his hand, then winced as a spatter of icy rain struck him in the face. The lull in the storm was over and by the time he'd managed to pull the parking ticket off his windscreen and get into the car, he could feel the dampness of his jacket through his shirt. With a shiver, he switched on the engine and cranked the heating up full blast. The radio came on automatically and he vaguely registered the news bulletin. It wasn't until the announcer did a time check at the end that Ben was reminded he had other priorities. He glanced down to find he was still holding both the parking ticket and the folder Hope had given him. With an exasperated sigh, he chucked them both over his shoulder and onto the back seat, then reached for his seat belt before putting the car in gear and heading towards the golf course on the outskirts of town.

It was just as well he'd taken the car, Ben thought to himself as he climbed back into the driver's seat three hours later, or he'd have been tempted to drown himself in a bottle of whisky as one after another of his dad's cronies bored him to tears with their not-very-amusing anecdotes. Every time he'd tried to slip away, another one had cornered him with a story about how 'Big Ben', which had been the excruciating nickname they all insisted on using, had wiped the floor with them all in the monthly medal competition, or reminding him he'd won the turkey trot last year and been presented with a massive 6kg Norfolk Bronze. It wasn't something Ben was likely to forget because they'd eaten leftovers for days and still filled the freezer with endless portions of turkey curry. His father had pulled out all the stops, getting a massive tree and hanging fairy lights around the front porch when they hadn't bothered with decorations for years. Had he known then how sick he was and been trying to create a special memory for Ben? God damn it, why hadn't he *said* anything?

He drove home on autopilot, his mind still occupied with memories of what had turned out to be their last Christmas together. It wasn't until he pulled up outside the house in the spot where he always parked that Ben realised where he was. He turned off the engine and found himself reluctant to move.

The house looked the same as always – two neatly trimmed miniature fir trees in pots on either side of the door, red velvet curtains framing the large picture window of the dining room on the left, the slatted wooden blind on the kitchen window tilted just so to block the sun on the right. Nothing was different and yet everything was. Ben placed his hand back on the car key still dangling from the ignition. He could head home as he'd originally planned. He turned on the engine and the radio filled the empty silence, the cheerful voice of the traffic announcer telling him the M25 was blocked with tailbacks of more than an hour already. Grimacing, he turned the engine off and shoved open his door. Though it had been nearly ten years since he'd moved out, this was still his home.

When he opened the front door, the first thing that struck him was the chill. His father had always been one for sticking on an extra jumper but Ben had felt the cold more keenly and so his dad would tweak the thermostat up on the days he knew he would be home for a visit. The second thing was the quiet. There should be classical music drifting into the hallway from the open door of his father's study, the scents of dinner cooking in the oven, the rich tomato of a lasagne or the meaty tang of a beef stew. With a sigh, Ben closed the front door and walked towards the study door. He rested a hand on it for a moment before reaching for the handle.

Locked.

Ben frowned, glancing back towards the little table by the door where his father's keys usually rested in a china bowl, but it was empty. Perhaps the cleaner had put them somewhere for safekeeping. Forgetting about the study for now, he headed into the kitchen, flipping on the light. The sight of the stainless-steel range evoked a flood of memories. His father had been a competent rather than an adventurous cook and had passed his skills on to Ben. From when he'd been too small to see and had to stand on the red plastic step his dad kept in the garage, Ben had loved to watch his father chop and dice and turn a pile of ingredients into something delicious. Sometimes he'd been given the all-important job of stirring the pot and it had always given him a little thrill to be so entrusted.

Shaking his head, Ben turned away towards the fridge, opening the door with more hope than expectation. The cleaner had already been and chucked away the perishables so he was left with half a dozen jars of pickles and sauces on the shelves in the door and a couple of cans of beer lining the top shelf. He grabbed a beer and a jar with a handful of cornichons still floating in vinegar and carried them over to the central island. His eyes strayed towards the pinboard on the wall and he considered whether or not to order a takeaway. There'd been a decent-looking buffet at the golf club. Nigel had certainly done his best to give his father a good send-off, but Ben hadn't been able to stomach any of it.

Deciding to investigate the freezer first, Ben choked on a half-laugh, half-sob as the first thing he saw was a plastic container neatly labelled 'Christmas curry'. Nine months and he'd still not managed to get through it all. Ben took it out and opened the lid, surprised to see it was less frostbitten than he might have expected. He popped it in the microwave and picked up his beer. There would be time for a quick shower before dinner and he wanted to get out of his suit.

He stripped off his jacket and hung it over the end of the banister before wrestling his tie off with one hand as he opened the door to the airing cupboard with the other. His plans for a shower fell by the wayside when he saw that both the heating and the hot water had been switched off. He flicked them both to constant and whacked up the thermostat before grabbing his jacket and heading into his bedroom. He'd visited often enough in the past that it made sense to leave a few bits and pieces in his wardrobe and the dresser.

Opening the top drawer, he pulled out a grey hoodie and a pair of sweatpants, then froze in the act of closing the drawer when he spotted the faded photograph of his mother. The clothing fell from his hand as he stared in the dim light spilling in from the hallway. Grabbing the frame, he carried the photo out onto the landing and sank down on the top step of the staircase, staring down at the image. His brain hadn't been playing tricks on him. It could be Hope standing there in a pretty sundress, one hand shielding her eyes as she laughed up at whoever was holding the camera – his father, presumably.

It was the only picture of her in the house. When he'd been old enough to question that and ask his father for family albums, he'd shaken his head and said he'd found it too upsetting and had got rid of everything soon after she died. A sick feeling lodged itself in the pit of Ben's stomach. If what Hope had claimed was true, then she hadn't died but had returned to her family instead.

Without Ben.

What else had his father lied about? With the photo still in his hand, Ben hurried down the stairs and back out to his car to retrieve the plastic wallet Hope had given him. He sat at the kitchen table and began to read, the half-cooked curry, his beer and his change of clothing all forgotten.

3

'I've made you some toast; what do you want on it?' Amelia Riley's mother called up the stairs.

Wincing as she caught a bit of her still-wet hair in the elastic band as she tied off the end of her plait, Amelia bent down to hunt for one of her shoes, which had somehow made its way under the bed. That would teach her not to kick them off, she supposed as she dropped to her knees and began to grope around with one hand. 'Not today, not today,' she muttered to herself. After weeks of being dangled on a string of promises, she was going to finally find out whether she was being given the transfer to the sales department. Sales was not her natural forte, but she had the potential to earn a lot more money through bonuses and commissions. And God knows, she needed the money. It was the end of the month so payday should feel like something to celebrate, but every penny was accounted for and she still had a mountain of debt to climb. *So much for that Friday feeling.*

'Amelia?' Her mum's voice sounded closer, like she'd climbed a couple of stairs.

'Just some butter, thanks!' she replied. She could eat it on the walk to the bus, her car currently off the road because she couldn't afford to get it through the MOT, never mind the monthly insurance premiums. She'd have to do something about it soon before someone complained about it being left in the car park behind the village hall. It had been embarrassing having to explain to Mr Beamish, the hall custodian, why she needed to leave the car there, but he'd been lovely about it. Still, someone would notice and say something about it. Someone *always* noticed those kinds of things and Amelia's pride would have to survive another blow.

It was amazing she had any left given the whole village knew by now that her father had waged a one-man vendetta of destruction on the Travers family over the summer after Rhys had sacked him from the estate farm for drinking on the job. She didn't blame Rhys for that, but it had been extra humiliating to have the man she'd once dreamed of marrying stand on the doorstep and apologise for doing it. She was never sure if her father's antics over the years had been the thing that had slowly poisoned her relationship with Rhys, or if they would've fallen out of love anyway as they grew up. It had been impossible for her to separate the two things and it was likely something she'd never figure out, but in her heart it was another thing she blamed her father for ruining.

She shoved the doom spiral of her thoughts away and forced herself to be positive. By next week that sales job *would* be hers and the company car that came with it. Once that was sorted, she could scrap her old one and no one would have anything to complain about. If she went all out, then her commission bonus could be enough to really make a difference to their current circumstances.

Mental pep talk finished, Amelia retrieved her shoe with a grin of triumph. She stood up then bent over to slip it on, only to spot that she'd managed to ladder her tights in the process. They were the last new pair she had and she'd been saving them for today. And just like that her mood took a nosedive. Yanking open her top drawer, she took one look at the tangle of black nylon snakes stuffed in the corner and pushed it shut again. Trousers it was, then.

She'd just reached the bottom of the stairs when the letterbox rattled, the sound enough to steal away any thought of an appetite. The postman only ever delivered more misery these days. She sent the little pile of envelopes a baleful glare, tempted to ignore them. But then she'd only sit at work all day fretting about them, or even worse, her mother would open them and hide them away somewhere. Daisy Riley didn't think it should be Amelia's responsibility to dig them out of the debt hole her father had got them both into, but what was she supposed to do? Walk away and leave it to her mother to sort out? Especially when her mother's only income was from a cleaning job up on the Juniper Meadows estate.

There was something faintly ridiculous about her mother being paid by Ziggy Travers for work Amelia was pretty sure the family didn't need doing in the first place, just so they could pay him back for the loan he'd given Amelia to help her consolidate some of her father's debts. She'd only accepted the loan because she'd thought the worst of it was his unpaid tab from the pub, the slate they'd run up at the local shop and a month or two of back rent. It was only once she'd started digging into things she'd realised the extent of the mess they were in. Her father hadn't paid any of the bills for more than six months, gambling away not only his wages, but every penny Amelia had given them towards her upkeep and more besides. As she'd turned their little cottage upside down, she'd found maxed-out credit card bills and proof of half a dozen so-called payday loans with interest rates so high, Amelia had burst into tears when she'd seen them. She'd spent every penny of her little savings pot – her escape fund, as she'd privately referred to it, though her dreams of going to art school and one day becoming a professional painter had faded long ago –

paying those off, but the credit cards were being staved off with minimum monthly payments and she knew that couldn't go on indefinitely.

If she spoke to Ziggy, she knew he'd clear the lot without a murmur and add the amount to the interest-free loan. But how could she possibly ask him for any more help after all the trouble her father had caused? The Travers had lost thousands of pounds, probably tens of thousands, when they'd had to close the estate and cancel all their camping and hotel bookings at the very height of the summer. The cost of the damage to their reputation was harder to calculate but they'd definitely taken a hit. Feeling particularly masochistic, Amelia had snooped around on TripAdvisor and in the comments section of the various Juniper Meadows social media sites. A few people had been sympathetic as they expressed their disappointment, but the majority of reviews she'd read had been full of vitriol and even a few threats of legal action. Amelia had no idea if anyone had followed through on those or if they were just ranting to let off steam, but it didn't leave a good impression for any future customers.

She'd just scooped up the little stack of envelopes when her mother appeared at the kitchen door. 'Oh, there you are, don't you look smart! The very picture of a professional saleswoman. Come on, love, your breakfast is getting cold.'

Once she'd got over the initial shock of her husband's arrest, Daisy had gone into full mother-hen mode, something Amelia found equal parts touching and infuriating. If her mother hadn't let Keith ride roughshod over her for so many years, perhaps things would never have got so bad. When she'd been a child, her parents had always been just that, two people whose entire beings existed to care for and raise her. As she'd grown older and had come to view them as actual people with their own personalities, hopes and fears, dreams and doubts, she'd wondered what had ever brought them together in the first place. They had so little in common other than the fact they were of a similar age and had grown up in the same village. Perhaps they'd started going out because their dating pool was somewhat limited, but even if she hadn't been disgusted and furious with her father, she struggled to see what it was about him that had attracted Daisy.

Looking back, she couldn't remember them being affectionate towards each other, though they'd never stinted on hugs and kisses for Amelia. It felt like she was the glue, the only thing that had kept them going long after they might have drifted apart, even if Keith's sense of responsibility had too often come second place to the many and varied perceived slights that had cost him this or that job. Amelia had come to dread the days when she got home from school to find him slumped in front of the television because that was when the drinking was the worst. Sometimes he was sad and sentimental, pulling her into his lap for cuddles as he lamented the way the world was against him; other times it meant frosty silences, slamming doors and the quiet sounds of her mother sobbing when she thought Amelia was safely asleep. So, even when Daisy's fussing around drove her mad, she let it go, knowing the deep sense of guilt that lay behind it all.

Setting the post to one side without looking at it, Amelia watched as Daisy bustled about buttering toast and flipping the kettle back on to re-boil before making them both tea. She set the plate and a mug before Amelia, settling into the seat opposite with only a mug on the mat in front of her. 'Are you not eating?'

'Not hungry, love,' Daisy said, shaking her head with a smile. 'I might fix something for myself later.'

Amelia doubted it. She'd noticed how thin her mum was getting, how often the excuse of not being hungry had been used to deflect her questions. She didn't know if it was because Daisy was trying to make their meagre shopping budget stretch further, or if she was unconsciously punishing herself. Either way, Amelia didn't like it. So far she hadn't found a way to tackle it that wasn't likely to end in a row, or tears, or most likely both. They were both so fraught and frayed at the edges that any hint of conflict would destroy the fragile peace between them.

Daisy nodded at the post. 'Anything interesting?'

Amelia had hoped to go through everything herself first, but too late. Bracing herself, she reached for the stack and shuffled through them. The first two were credit card statements and she set them next to her plate. She'd attempted to get the companies to transfer to paperless, but without knowing the passwords her father had set up they'd refused on the grounds of data protection. They were happy enough to take her bloody money, though. It was an old gripe, as was the way they'd recklessly offered large credit facilities and ignored the constant cash withdrawals against them until it was too late. The next one was a plain white envelope with only a first-class stamp and a local postmark. Intrigued, Amelia ripped it open and pulled out a single typed sheet of paper. Her eyes scanned automatically to the bottom and her stomach lurched as she recognised the signature of Eric Reynolds, their landlord.

She'd had a difficult conversation with him about the months of unpaid rent, but he'd agreed to let her increase the monthly payment and given her a year to pay off the balance. It was their biggest outgoing and swallowed up most of Amelia's regular monthly salary. The overtime she'd managed to persuade her boss to give her and her mother's cleaning money had to stretch to cover everything else. If she got the sales position, it would give them a tiny bit of breathing space. *Stop counting chickens...*

Turning her attention to the letter, she read over each paragraph, her sense of despair and disbelief growing with every word.

*Must appreciate my own situation… too good an offer to turn
down… if you can match the offer then let me know…*

'What is it, love?'

Amelia let the piece of paper drop, not caring when it landed
on top of her toast. 'Eric is selling the cottage.'

Daisy's face turned sickly pale and she swallowed hard. 'But I
thought he'd agreed to let us pay off the back rent.'

'That was before a visitor to the area put it about with the local
estate agents that they were looking to buy a property. Eric claims
he fell into conversation with John Bradley and he told him this
potential buyer's preferred location was Stourton-in-the-Vale.'
Amelia let her cynicism coat the words. John Bradley owned a
string of estate agencies across the county and specialised in the
rural market. He'd grown rich on the never-ending demand from
Londoners desperate to snatch up a slice of the picturesque
Cotswold countryside, which was a convenient weekend dash up
and down the M4 corridor.

'You think Eric was looking for a reason to sell?' Daisy sounded
close to tears as she reached out and retrieved the letter to read for
herself.

'Wouldn't you be, in his position? Dad wasn't exactly a model
tenant after all. He's probably relieved to have an excuse to get shot
of us.' That didn't mean she would forgive Eric for smiling and
patting her hand sympathetically as he'd promised her they could
sort it all out and not to worry about anything. She realised now
he'd been fobbing her off. It was much easier to evict a tenant for
unpaid rent, especially when they were on remand awaiting trial
for a serious offence.

'Oh God,' Daisy gasped. 'He says we've got until the end of the
month to pay the full back rent or to come up with a mortgage
offer that covers the amount the buyers have put in.'

Amelia shoved her chair back and grabbed her plate. The letter from Eric had stolen what little appetite she'd had. As she pressed her foot to the pedal on the bin and tried not to feel guilty about the wasted food, a sense of righteous fury rose up in her. She'd done her bloody best to sort everything out, but she was at breaking point. 'Well, he can shove his back rent up his arse now, can't he?' she snapped as she slammed the plate down on the side and spun to face her mother.

'Amelia!' Daisy gasped at the unfamiliar crudeness.

'I'm sick of it! It doesn't matter what we do, how hard we try to make things right, all we're doing is digging the hole deeper!' Amelia marched over to the table and grabbed the unopened credit card statements. She ripped them in half, the tearing sensation so good she did it again and again until they were little more than bits of confetti. Gathering the pieces, she marched over to the bin and tossed them in on top of her cold toast. 'If Eric wants the money he's owed, he can bloody well sue Keith for it. Same goes for the vultures at the credit card company and everybody else he owes. I'm done! I'm absolutely, completely and utterly done with the whole damn mess.'

4

Amelia snatched up her handbag and stormed out of the cottage, still riding her wave of anger. She made it all of ten steps down the street before the tears started. 'Stop it, stop it, stop it,' she muttered to herself as she tried to ignore the wetness trickling down her cheeks. She'd sworn she wouldn't shed another tear over that useless arsehole she had the misfortune to call her father, but if she didn't let it out somehow, she didn't know what she'd do. If she screamed to vent the frustration, she might never stop.

She got as far as the corner where her little street turned onto the main road through the village just in time to see her bus pulling away from the stop outside the pub. The next one wouldn't be for an hour, by which time she'd be late for work and that would put paid to any chance of getting the sales job, wouldn't it? It was the last straw and what little bit of fight had been left in Amelia seeped out of her. Sinking down onto the stone wall behind her, Amelia folded in two and began to sob in earnest. This was it, she thought to herself as she made no attempt to stem the tears. This was rock bottom. Nothing could be worse than this. Not one thing.

A horn beep-beeped and Amelia managed to raise her head enough to look up as a black Range Rover with a familiar swirling logo on the door pulled up next to her. As the imposing bulk of Rhys Travers climbed out of the driver's side like Neptune rising from the waves, Amelia choked out a strangled laugh. Rock bottom? There was no such thing in her cursed existence, it appeared.

He didn't speak, just walked around to the passenger door and opened it. Crossing his arms, he leaned against the side of the car and stared at her. Outrage at so presumptuous an action was enough to stem the flow of her tears. Fumbling in her pocket, Amelia pulled out a tissue, wiped her eyes and blew her nose. It wasn't like she had anything in the way of dignity left. 'Remember when I told you to go away and leave me alone?' she snapped at him.

'I remember.'

God, he was as stubborn as a rock. 'Nothing's changed.' Apart from the fact she'd missed the bloody bus and was going to be late for work, oh and the small matter of where she and her mum were going to live after Eric gave them the boot at the end of the month.

'Not for you, perhaps.'

Now, what was that supposed to mean? She narrowed her eyes at him, wondering what kind of trick he was about to pull on her. 'I don't need your help,' she insisted, refusing to be drawn into asking, even though he'd piqued her curiosity.

'Of course you don't. It's not like your car's been sitting in the corner of the village hall car park for the past month for any good reason other than you've taken a fancy to riding the bus.'

Trust him to have noticed. 'Are you going to get to the point or did you just stop to make the shitty start to my day ten times worse?'

Rhys grinned and she remembered too late how much he liked

it when she showed a bit of backbone. It only lasted a moment before his expression grew serious. 'I need to talk to you about Hope.'

Hope? Amelia felt a stab of guilt at the way she'd pushed not only Rhys away, but her best friend, too. She hadn't had any other choice. If she'd maintained contact with one member of the Travers family, the rest of them would worm their way back in with their kindness and generosity, or bossiness in the case of the man in front of her. Her resolve wavered. Cutting herself off from them had been for their sake, not for hers, but if Hope was hurting... 'Why? What's wrong with her?'

Rhys pointed to the open door. 'Get in and I'll tell you.'

Amelia scowled. 'If this is some ploy to get me to accept your help then you can get stuffed.'

He gave a long-suffering sigh and she could all but hear his back teeth grinding. 'I'm going into town anyway and I'm pretty sure I saw the bus going around the corner just now so you're going to be late for work. Unless you've had a change in career and you're now the village banshee and that's what all the howling and wailing was about when I pulled up.'

Amelia's cheeks started to blaze as she wondered how many curtains were twitching as her neighbours enjoyed the show she was putting on. That insistent little voice reminded her that the sales job was still up for grabs, and right now Rhys was the only chance she had of making it into work on time. 'This isn't me accepting help from you,' she muttered as she stomped over and climbed up into the high seat of the Range Rover. 'I'm just worried about Hope.'

It was a miracle when her tongue didn't turn black and fall out of her mouth after such a whopper of a lie, but she kept her face averted as she tugged on her seat belt. *Just this one time.* She would find out what was wrong with Hope and then go back to ignoring Rhys again.

'God forbid!' Rhys closed the door none too gently and she could've sworn she caught him rolling his eyes as he did so. She knew she was being petty, but she didn't know how else to keep him at arm's length, not when it would be so very easy to collapse against the warm, familiar bulk of his chest and sob out all her worries and woes.

Though the windows of the car were tinted, Amelia still slid down in her seat and ducked her head as they drove past the village store and Bill Walker paused in the act of tying his dog, Paddy, to the railing outside to study them with interest. Bill had a heart of gold, but nobody sneezed in the village without him knowing about it. He'd be perched on his regular stool at the bar of The Stourton Arms later, telling anyone who came within ten feet of him that he'd spotted her out and about with Mr Rhys and speculating about whether they were courting – his word, not hers – again.

'Well, that was unfortunate timing,' Rhys deadpanned, his thoughts obviously an echo of her own.

'Maybe he didn't spot me,' Amelia said, knowing it was wishful thinking.

'I'm sure he didn't, what with the subtle way you squirmed about and did everything to draw his attention to you.'

'I...!' Amelia clamped her mouth down on the urge to argue with him. More as a distraction than anything else, she dug in her pocket for her phone and sent a quick text to Caroline, her line manager.

Missed the bus but getting a lift in so I'll hopefully be in town in time to hit Starbucks. Do you want me to grab you something?

While she waited for a reply, she turned her attention back to the reason she'd accepted the lift in the first place. 'You wanted to talk to me about Hope.'

Rhys was silent for a long moment as he steered the Range Rover expertly along the winding back lanes. It was only when he'd reached the junction for the main road and had to pause for the rush-hour traffic to thin that she sensed him turn towards her. 'Did she tell you about Ben?'

Amelia wrinkled her brow as she tried to recall the name. She cast a quick glance towards Rhys to find his attention was fixed on her, not on the stream of traffic passing in front of them. 'Is that the young lad who was working on Cam's team? The one with the awful father?'

Rhys shook his head. 'No, that was Scott.'

He took a deep breath and there was something so serious about his expression that Amelia found herself reaching out to touch his arm. 'Rhys?'

'We found out over the summer that Hope isn't Stevie's only child. She had a son not long after she was married, but she had to leave him behind when she ran away from her husband and came home. He died a couple of weeks ago, Hope's father, I mean, and we went to the funeral yesterday. She told Ben who she was, but he didn't want to know. I'm not sure he believed her, if I'm being honest.'

Amelia dropped back into her seat, feeling like all the stuffing had been knocked out of her. 'Are you serious?' she asked, unable to take it in.

Rhys nodded. 'Deadly.' A loud beep startled them both and Rhys held up a hand in apology to whoever had pulled up behind them and turned his attention back to the traffic. At the first sign of a gap, he accelerated, the smooth engine of the big car responding in an instant so they were soon up to speed with the moving traffic.

'But how did you hear about the funeral?' She shook her head. The how and the why could wait. 'Is Hope okay?' It was a stupid question; how on earth could she be okay when faced with something so life-altering?

Her phone began to ring and she glanced down at the screen. 'Damn, it's my boss, hold on.'

'Amelia, I got your message. Is everything okay?' Amelia bit back a sigh, wishing she hadn't bothered with the text. Her boss, Caroline Harper, had a sixth sense for when Amelia was having a problem. And just lately, she'd been having nothing but problems.

'Hi, Caroline. Yes, everything's fine! I got in a bit of a tizz wanting to make sure I was all prepared for today and ended up making myself late. Luckily a friend was passing and offered me a lift so it's actually working out much better because I'll be in town sooner than I expected so I thought I'd grab us a coffee. A bit of a treat to start the day.' Goodness, what an absolute babble! If Amelia had been trying to allay Caroline's suspicions, that was a terrible way to go about it.

There was a painfully long pause followed by a gusty sigh. 'Oh, Amelia. I don't know how to tell you, but I overheard Tim and Nathaniel talking just now in the kitchen.' Caroline sounded like she wanted to cry. She was one of the few people to whom Amelia had told the whole, horrible truth about her father. She hadn't seen any way to avoid it, especially when his arrest had been reported in the local papers. Caroline had shielded her from too many questions from nosy colleagues and been happy to give her as much overtime as she could handle.

Amelia felt the world fall out from under her as she understood what it was Caroline was trying to tell her. 'I'm not getting the sales job, am I?'

'No. I'm sorry.'

'Did they say why?' When Caroline remained silent, Amelia let out a strangled laugh. 'It's something to do with my dad, isn't it?'

'They just don't think it's the right position for you, that's all.'

Amelia didn't believe a word of it. 'Not the right position for the daughter of an arsonist and a thief, you mean? It's okay to keep me behind the scenes, but they don't want me in a customer-facing position, especially once the trial starts and people put two and two together.'

'I'm really sorry, and I hate that they think that way. I'll go and speak to Tim right now and tell him it's not acceptable.' Caroline would do it, too. Put her own job on the line to defend Amelia. No, Amelia couldn't allow anyone else get into trouble on her account.

'Please don't. At the end of the day, they have to think about the company's reputation, don't they?' Amelia closed her eyes. 'I could've really done with that extra money, though.'

'I know. Look, forget about the coffees and just get in as quickly as you can. We'll have a sit-down and go through the schedule over the next few weeks and I'll see what extra hours I can find for you.'

Amelia appreciated the gesture, but it was a drop in the ocean. Even if she followed through on her threat to leave her father to sort out his mess, she still had the immediate problem of where she and her mother were going to live. There was no way they'd be able to find another property in the village, so that would mean the end of her mother's cleaning job at the estate. And without the extra income the sales job would've brought in, Hope would struggle to afford to rent somewhere in town, which was likely the only place she'd be able to find a property at short notice. If it was just her, she could find a bedsit or a shared room, but what was she going to do about her mum? The weight of everything seemed to settle on her chest and she found it hard to breathe. 'I'll be in soon,' she managed to get out before she ended the call and pressed a hand to her suddenly racing heart.

She wasn't aware of the car stopping until the door beside her opened, sending a wash of cold air over her and then Rhys was crouching beside her, his big, comforting hand pressed against the one she had over her heart. 'It's okay, it's okay,' he soothed in that deep, familiar voice. 'Just listen to me and follow what I do. Breathe in... two... three... and out. That's it. You're doing great.'

It had been so long since she'd last had a panic attack, she'd forgotten the warning signs and allowed this one to ambush her. They'd started when she was still in school and had pushed herself too hard studying for her exams. That was when she'd still had dreams of escaping the humdrum life of the village and heading off to university to study fine arts. Rhys had encouraged her, even knowing it would take her away from him and shift their lives into entirely separate orbits. Even in the deepest throes of that first mad love they'd shared, he'd only ever wanted her to fly as high as her imagination and ambition would take her, had even encouraged her to speak to Ziggy about applying for one of the charitable bursaries the Travers family had established for local children to support their studies.

He'd always been there.

Amelia closed her eyes and focused on the gentle pressure of his hand on hers, the deep, regular cadence of his voice, and slowly brought her breathing back under control. When she opened them again, Rhys was close and she could see the deep lines etched into his brow, the dark shadows under his blue eyes. She'd pushed him away because she'd thought it was the right thing to do, but she realised now that for someone with a heart as big as Rhys's, that was tantamount to torture. 'I've hurt you,' she said softly.

Rhys stared at her for a long moment before he nodded. 'But you've been hurting yourself so much more. No one blames you for what Keith did, Amelia. It's high time you stopped blaming yourself.'

She thought then about how pale and thin her mother was, how she'd worried Daisy was punishing herself by not eating and she understood she'd been starving herself, but in a different way. Amelia had not been made to be alone; she was not someone who thrived in her own company, who enjoyed peace and quiet and couldn't wait for an evening out to end so she could go home. She needed people around her, needed her friends around her, and, God willing, would one day find someone to love her and be loved by her in turn. She'd thought she'd found that once with this lovely, kind man, but it wasn't to be. She cared about him, still, but there was nothing more to her feelings than that. 'I wish it was you,' she murmured, reaching out to cup Rhys's cheek.

Though he could have no inkling about what she'd been thinking, his face creased into a sad smile. 'I wish it was you, too.' He turned his head to press a quick kiss into her palm. 'Come on, let's get you to work – not that those bastards deserve you. I told you years ago they were taking advantage of you.'

As he stood up and closed her door, Amelia rested her head back against her seat and laughed softly. Rhys was always going to stick up for her – and stick his nose in her business. It was who he was, and she was damn lucky to have a friend like him.

5

'Ah, Ben, I wasn't expecting to see you quite so soon. I thought you'd want at least a few more days to recover from the stress of the funeral. Still, it's always good to get on with these things.' He made a show of checking his watch. 'I'm afraid I only have half an hour to spare before my first client, but Sally will be able to find a slot in my diary for us to go through everything properly. Would you like a drink? Sally? Can you get Ben a…' Dominic Proud raised a questioning eyebrow at Ben as he paused in the act of ushering him into his office. A near neighbour who also acted as their family solicitor, Dominic had known Ben since Ben was a small child.

Ben shook his head. 'Nothing, thanks, I'm fine.' Given what he had to say to this man over the next few minutes, Ben didn't think he could trust himself to be in reach of anything he could use as a weapon. He'd spent the entire weekend stewing over the contents of the file Hope had given him and it had taken all his willpower not to march across the street and hammer on Dominic's front door. Unable to wait a moment longer, Ben had shown up at his office bang on nine o'clock Monday morning, demanding to speak to him.

Brushing past him, Ben strode into Dominic's office. He eyed the paper knife resting on the leather blotter next to a heavy cut-glass inkwell and chose the seat furthest away from them. Was that the same inkwell Dominic had used when he'd signed the letter Hope had included in the folder she'd given him with such an enthusiastic flourish? The letter that had denied Ben the chance to know his mother; the letter that had betrayed everything he thought he'd understood about his father.

'Right, right, fair enough, probably drink more coffee than is good for me, anyway.' Dominic gave a weak-sounding chuckle as he rounded the other side of the desk and sat down in the plush high-backed chair. 'So, apart from the obvious, how are things with you? Other than the funeral, it must be four or five years since I last saw you. At your twenty-fifth birthday celebrations, wasn't it?'

The last thing Ben wanted to do was make small talk with this man, but he managed a curt nod. His father had invited him for the weekend and hosted a barbeque in the back garden. He'd got all Ben's favourite food in, and the champagne had flowed. His father had given this big, emotional speech about how proud he was of the man his son had grown into. Dominic had been amongst the people to come up to them afterwards and praise his father for doing such a fine job of raising Ben all on his own. Dominic's wife had had tears in her eyes as she'd told Ben how brave his father had been, moving to the village when he'd just lost his wife so that he could make sure Ben had the best life. He remembered feeling grateful at the time for all the sacrifices his father had made. Ben closed his eyes for a brief second. So many of his good memories would be forever tainted by the lies and secrets that had lain between them. And there would be more lies and secrets to come, he was sure of it. 'Can we get on with things, please?'

Dominic raised a hand to smooth the thinning strands of hair over his pate and gave that awkward little laugh again. 'Of course, as I said before I have another appointment shortly but I can run you through the basics of the will.' He pulled open the top drawer of his desk and pulled out a thick file. Opening the cover, he slid out a single document before going to replace the file in his drawer.

'You might as well leave that out as I'll be taking it with me,' Ben instructed him.

Dominic hesitated, and flicked a quick glance towards Ben before shutting the file away with an apologetic smile. 'I'm afraid that won't be possible. Client confidentiality, I'm sure you understand.'

'I understand that I am my father's sole beneficiary and therefore everything passes to me. I need to be able to understand his affairs fully, so I want a copy of every instruction he's given you and any and all correspondence you've sent on his behalf.' Ben bared his teeth in an approximation of a smile. 'I don't suppose you know what happened to my father's keys, do you? I've searched the house, but I can't seem to find them. His study is locked and it's the only key I don't have a copy of.'

Dominic swallowed hard. 'I'm the executor of your father's will and he left me strict instructions to dispose of the contents of his office. I took possession of the keys when I saw him at the hospital on the day he passed.'

'You knew he was in the hospital?'

The solicitor had the grace to look embarrassed. 'Your father didn't want you to see him like that. He didn't want those to be your last memories of him.'

'Surely that was my choice to make?'

Dominic raised his hands in a shrug. 'I did try to persuade him otherwise, but you know how stubborn he could be once he got an idea in his head about something.' He lowered his hands to the document on his desk. 'Shall we go through the will, then?'

Ben listened in silence as Dominic read through the contents. As he'd expected, he was the sole beneficiary of everything, including the house, but there was indeed an instruction to Dominic to dispose of the contents of the study apart from official documents such as birth certificates, the deeds to the house, insurance policies and the like. 'As I said...' Dominic paused to give what Ben supposed was meant to be a kindly smile. 'Your father has asked that I go through his papers. Perhaps we could arrange a convenient time for me to do that? I could do it one day next week, if you like. No need for you to be there.'

Ben shook his head. 'You're not setting foot on my property.'

The smile from Dominic was a little less friendly this time. 'Not technically your property until I've completed all the paperwork and had the deed transferred to your name.'

Time to stop pissing around and lay his cards on the table. 'You won't be completing any of the paperwork, I'm afraid. I'll be filing a complaint with the probate court to ask them to remove you as the executor.'

'What?' Dominic blustered, his face going red with outrage. 'On what possible grounds?'

Ben reached into the plastic wallet he'd brought with him and pulled out a sheet of paper. It wasn't the original Hope had given him, but a photocopy. Though he was raging inside, he didn't let a hint of his anger show in his voice as he began to read aloud in a monotone.

RE: Benjamin Lawson. I am instructed by my client to request that all further attempts at communication cease and desist. He has attained his majority and has asked me to state that he has no wish to have any contact with Ms Stevie Travers or any other member of his maternal family.

To that end, I am enclosing a number of items of correspondence previously sent by Ms Travers over the past eighteen years.

I trust you will honour my client's wishes, but should further contact be attempted, we will have no option other than to seek a legal remedy, which can only bring unnecessary distress to all parties involved.

When he had finished reading, Ben laid the photocopy on the desk in front of a white-faced Dominic and tapped the flamboyant scrawl at the bottom of the sheet. 'I believe that's your signature, isn't it?'

Dominic's mouth gaped open and closed like a goldfish. 'Where did you get this?' he demanded.

Ben stood up. 'My sister gave it to me.' He strode across the office, yanked open the door and then turned back to shoot the shaking man a smile that was all teeth and no warmth. 'By the way, I'll also be registering a complaint about your fraudulent actions with your industry regulator, and I'll be encouraging my mother and my sister to do the same.'

'Now wait just a minute! You need to give me a chance to explain.' Dominic rushed across the office and grabbed Ben by the arm.

Part of him wanted to shake the lying little weasel off, to storm out and never look back. But then he wouldn't get answers to the questions bouncing around in his head like lottery balls just before a draw. 'You've got five minutes.' They resumed their seats and Dominic fiddled around, straightening things on his desk, adjusting the cufflinks at his wrists. Anything to avoid meeting Ben's eye. 'Four minutes.'

Dominic's head shot up, his eyes wide. 'Yes. Sorry, I was just trying to work out where to start.'

'The beginning is usually the best place. And don't think about leaving anything out.'

It took considerably longer than four minutes for Dominic to bluster his way through an explanation, starting with how he and his wife had popped across to say hello when they'd spotted the removals van the day he and his father moved in. 'Chessie brought you back to our house, do you remember?'

Ben shook his head. 'Can't say that I do.' Everything from those early days was a blur.

Dominic gave him a sickly smile. 'Yes, well, you were only little and it must've been a very confusing time for you. Your father told us about losing his wife... your mother, I mean.'

'Only he didn't lose her, did he? She ran away from him for reasons I can't get my head around.' Reasons he didn't want to dare contemplate.

'Indeed.' Dominic straightened his already straight blotter, then clasped his hands together tightly and rested them on the desk. 'I didn't know that at the time. I only found out after I'd already been working for your father for several months. He engaged me to help him set up his new business. He turned his back on everything after your mother left, couldn't bear people to know the truth about it so he built this nice little fictional world for the two of you. The caring, grieving widower and the poor, sad little kid. Everyone was eating out of his hand.' Dominic gave a bitter laugh. 'Half the women in the village propositioned him at some point or another, thinking all he needed was the love of a good woman to make everything right again. He was happy enough to shag one or two of the really desperate ones, but only if they had a ring on their finger. Even had a crack at Chessie once, though she turned him down flat.'

Ben had told Dominic he'd wanted the whole truth, but details of his father's private life were too much. 'I'm more interested in your arrangement with him. Why did you keep working for him when you found out the truth? If you knew he was lying to everyone, why didn't you tell him to find another solicitor?'

'Do you think I have the luxury of turning away a client if I find out something unsavoury about them?' The look Dominic shot him was one of pure contempt. 'Are you really that naïve? Well, I suppose when you've been spoiled your whole life, it's easy to have a rosy outlook on things. But not everyone's had daddy's money to bankroll them, have they? How is the flat in London?' There was a nasty edge to Dominic's tone now, a spiteful glint in his eye, and Ben had the feeling he was seeing the real person beneath the obsequious façade he'd grown up with. 'Yes, I know all about him buying that for you because I dealt with the conveyancing. Just like I dealt with every other legal aspect of your father's life.'

'And got paid handsomely for it, as well.' Dominic's lips compressed and then the real reason the solicitor had gone along with all of this dawned on Ben. 'Just how much over the odds did he pay you?' No wonder he didn't want Ben getting hold of his father's client file.

'Your father and I came to a mutually acceptable fee scale. There's nothing wrong with that.'

Ben laughed. 'You let him buy you, you mean! What is the going price for a man's personal integrity these days?' He waved the question off as soon as the words were out. 'Never mind, I don't want to know. Well, whatever it was, I hope it was enough for you to keep Chessie in the style to which she's become accustomed because I won't rest until you are put out of business.' When Dominic's mouth fell open, Ben leaned forwards. 'Oh, did you think I was joking about reporting you to the regulators?'

Dominic glared at him. 'If you do that, then it won't be long before everyone finds out the truth. Do you want people around here to know how your father lied and manipulated them all these years?'

Ben had heard enough. 'I couldn't give a shit. Dad's dead so his reputation doesn't matter, and I'll be out of here as soon as I can get everything settled and the house sold.' He stood up and marched out, not breaking stride as he called out loud enough for the staff in the outer office to hear him, 'You've screwed the last penny out of my family, Dominic. You'll be hearing from *my* solicitor very shortly.'

* * *

Two hours later, Ben was standing on the doorstep of his father's house watching as the emergency locksmith backed his van into the driveway. He'd been so furious as he'd left the solicitor's office, he hadn't remembered to get his father's housekeys back. Given the bombshell he'd dropped on Dominic, he doubted he'd be in any mood to cooperate, so he'd decided to take alternative action. 'Thanks for coming out so quickly,' he said, shaking the man's hand and ushering him inside. The locksmith made a show of wiping his feet on the doormat before he set his toolbox down. 'Whole house, you said? Windows too?'

Ben hadn't considered that. He tried to picture Dominic climbing in through the big bay window and almost laughed. Still, better to be safe than sorry. 'I can't remember whether my father had a key to the window locks on his ring, but I can't take the risk, I suppose.'

The locksmith shook his head. 'It'd knacker any insurance claim if someone was to break in, even if they didn't use a key. You don't have to worry about that today as it's not like they can use the key to get in from the outside anyway. If you're handy with a screwdriver, you can nip down the DIY store and buy replacement handles for the windows and fit them yourself. There's loads of videos showing you how to do it on YouTube; I'll send you a link to a couple if you want?'

Ben was impressed with the man's honesty because he could've charged to do the work himself and Ben would've been none the wiser. 'Oh, that's handy to know, thanks. I'll have a look at the videos and let you know what I think. Come on, I'll show you around.'

After a full tour of the house, they returned to the hallway and Ben paused next to his father's study door. 'Can I add this door to the list please? I think the only key for it was on the same ring that's gone missing and I need to dig out all the paperwork and start going through it.'

The locksmith studied the door for a minute. 'Yeah, shouldn't be a problem.' He turned to Ben with a sympathetic smile. 'My mother-in-law died last year and we had a bloody nightmare going through all her stuff.' He shook his head. 'We knew she was getting a bit forgetful, but we had no idea how bad she'd got. She started hoarding every bit of post that came through the door – all the junk mail as well. Never seen so many takeaway menus in my bloody life.' He shook his head again. 'Terrible business, you have my sympathies, mate.'

'Thank you.' Ben took a step backwards, supposing he should be grateful that at least his father had still been in possession of his full faculties when he died. Then again, maybe not because that meant he'd gone to his grave determined to deprive Ben of the truth about his mother forever. He couldn't think about that now; he had to focus on the problem at hand. 'You won't need me hanging over your shoulder, so I'll leave you to it. I'll be in the kitchen, so give us a shout if you need anything. Do you want a coffee?'

'Tea if you've got it? White and one sugar, please.'

'Sure thing.'

Once he'd made them each a drink, Ben settled at the kitchen table with his laptop and logged in to his work emails. He'd taken a week off to try and get on top of as much as possible, but realised he'd jumped the gun. Other than getting the locks changed, there wasn't much else he could do until he got the situation with Dominic sorted out. Yes, he wanted to punish the man for his duplicity but the person he really wanted to direct his anger at wasn't here any more. If Ben followed through on his threats of complaining to the probate court, it would likely be weeks if not months before they took any action, meaning he'd be stuck in limbo.

He glanced towards the open doorway where the locksmith could be heard whistling between bouts of drilling. He needed to get into the study and get to the bottom of everything. If he found enough proof, perhaps he'd be able to force Dominic to step aside without the need for legal action. Knowing his father, there'd be copies of every interaction between the two of them, including the letter he'd instructed Dominic to forge on Ben's behalf. Unless he'd destroyed them all already, but then why would he need to keep Ben locked out until Dominic could go through everything? Surely his father must've realised Ben would be suspicious about why he didn't want him to have access to his private papers. Then again, when was the last time Ben had challenged his father on anything? In his heart, he knew that none of this was his fault, but he couldn't deny he'd let his father have his way more often than was sensible. Avoidance had always been his style, though. With his dad, with his work, when things got tricky with a girlfriend. With his whole damn life, Ben had taken the easy way out.

'Front door's sorted,' the locksmith said, walking into the kitchen, carrying his empty mug. 'And the back patio doors too.'

He set the mug down and nodded towards the door leading from the kitchen into the garage. 'I'll do this one next, if that's all right, and then at least the ground floor will be fully secure.'

Ben followed him to the door, opened it and turned on the light. His father's racing-green Jaguar filled one side of the space. The other half of the double-width garage was given over to storage. Most of it was tools and stuff for the garden. Ben felt a pang of sadness as he spotted the Christmas tree, still in its original box, sitting on one of the shelves next to a clear plastic crate filled with decorations. His father had never been particularly sentimental, but in amongst the shiny gold baubles were Ben's own efforts at making decorations dating back to when he'd been at primary school.

Art had always been his favourite lesson and he'd shown a natural aptitude for it. He'd even harboured dreams of doing something artistic for a living, but his father had scotched that idea and pushed him towards a career in finance, even hiring a maths tutor to ensure Ben had passed the requisite exams. Art was just about acceptable as a hobby, but it wouldn't pay the bills nor build the robustness and ability to work as part of a team as sports did. Well, that had been his father's philosophy. Ben had known he was never going to be permitted to do what he wanted when he came home full of excitement about an art summer school his teacher had given him details of, only to find his father had already signed him up for rugby camp with the local club.

He didn't mind rugby, even if some of the more boisterous behaviour of his teammates had annoyed him. He had the natural speed and stamina to be a decent fly-half but winning a match never gave him the same thrill as creating something out of nothing with just a blank piece of a paper and a pencil. Ben glanced towards the large cloth-covered mound in the corner where his potter's wheel and other art stuff was stored. University had given him some freedom away from his father's watchful gaze and he'd signed up to every art club going. Though he loved painting and drawing, pottery had spoken to him in a visceral way. There was something about taking a formless lump of clay and turning it into something beautiful as well as practical. When he'd come home at the end of term with a pile of dirty washing and a set of mugs he'd hand-thrown, fired and decorated, his father had relented and bought him his own wheel for Christmas. He'd baulked at the suggestion Ben might transfer from his economics course to an arts-based curriculum, threatening to cut Ben off completely if he dared try and throw away his future. He'd have done it too, so once again Ben had relented under the pressure and knuckled down to his studies.

His flat in London was too small for him to have a decent work-space, and the light was terrible, so his wheel and his other things had stayed under cover here in the garage. When the urge to create something got too much, Ben took himself off to a few evening classes but it was never the same.

He could do what he wanted now.

The reality of it struck him like a hammer blow and Ben had to reach out to steady himself against the wall. He wasn't answerable to anyone but himself. He could put in his notice, wait for the probate to clear, sell the house and find himself a little bolthole and build a proper studio space. The commuter belt south of London had some of the highest property prices in the country. If he wasn't fussy about where he moved to, he could live well enough on the proceeds from the house as well as whatever liquidating his father's various investment portfolios brought in.

He could even go back to school if he wanted. He could stop following his father's dreams for him and start following his own. Finally live life on his own terms. The thought was enough to make him giddy and if the locksmith hadn't been there, Ben would've thrown back his head and laughed from the sheer relief bubbling inside him.

'You all right, mate?' The concerned question from the locksmith brought Ben back to himself and he offered the other man a weak smile as he tried to corral his wildly shifting thoughts.

'I'm okay.' He laughed. 'Well, you know what I mean.'

'Of course. I won't be too much longer here, then I'll sort that door for the study out for you. Another hour tops and I'll be out of your hair for the day.'

Ben nodded. 'Cheers. Well, I'll leave you to it. I did promise I wouldn't hover.' He cast a final glance towards the cloth-covered potter's wheel.

'Look, it probably seems insurmountable at the moment, but give yourself a bit of time to sort things out rather than going rushing in trying to go through everything all at once.'

'You should be a counsellor,' Ben said, with a genuine laugh. 'Because you've offered me more sensible advice in the past hour than anyone else I've talked to since my father died.'

The locksmith blushed, but there was a pleased smile on his face as he waved Ben's comment away. 'Nah, mate, just sharing what I've learned along the way.'

'Well, I appreciate it. I don't have anyone else to talk to about this stuff so it all goes around in my head. I'll make us another drink, shall I?' As he wandered back into the kitchen, Ben was struck by the fact that what he'd said was no longer true. He did have people he could reach out to. He had a sister – a bloody sister, for God's sake, and a cousin too. *And a mother.* Ben pushed that thought away as he reached for the kettle. He wasn't quite ready to deal with that yet.

By the time he'd drained the last of his coffee, the locksmith had finished with the study door. It had been an easy case of popping the lock and as Ben wasn't worried about locking it again, it hadn't taken more than a couple of minutes to sort out. As he watched the locksmith pack away his tools, Ben was caught between admiring the neat, methodical way the man went about everything and a sudden burning desire to have the man gone because all he could think about was what lay beyond the now open door. He suppressed the feeling, forcing himself to lounge against the opposite wall in a faux relaxed pose so the guy didn't feel rushed. He'd been kind and generous from the moment he'd arrived and Ben owed him courtesy for that. When the locksmith finally straightened up and slung his bag over one shoulder, Ben offered him his hand. 'I really appreciate everything you've done for me today.'

'Hey, it was no problem.' They shook hands. 'I'm sorry again for your loss and don't forget what I said about giving yourself a bit of time, yeah?'

Ben nodded. 'I won't forget. Ping me over your invoice as soon as you're ready and I'll get it paid straight away.'

The locksmith smiled. 'My wife sorts the paperwork out so it'll be a day or two, but I appreciate that. I wouldn't stress too much about those window locks, but best to get them sorted when you can. You know what bloody insurers are like.' He rolled his eyes and Ben had no doubt he'd dealt with plenty of unhappy customers who'd been shafted for something trivial on top of dealing with the trauma of a break-in and the like. It occurred to him then that this man must deal with people in some form of crisis or another pretty much every day. Little wonder he'd developed a finely tuned sense of empathy.

'Will you send me a quote for replacing them?' He'd had a quick look at the YouTube video while waiting for him to finish and could probably do it himself but he really didn't think he could be bothered with the faff. Besides, he was happy to send a bit of extra work this man's way after everything he'd done.

The locksmith smiled. 'I'll be happy to. I'll get a price for you and send it with the invoice. If you decide to go ahead let me know and I'll check my diary and find a time to fit you in.' They shook hands again at the threshold and Ben waited in the doorway to wave him off.

The moment Ben shut the front door and turned around, the house took on that horribly empty feeling again. Straightening his shoulders, Ben marched straight into his father's study and sat down in the tall-backed chair behind the desk. The scent of his father, the scent of a thousand memories, filled his nostrils and he had to close his eyes and brace his hands against the worn leather of the blotter to fend off the assault of them. By the time he was able to open his eyes again, his vision was blurred with tears and he fumbled in his pocket for a handkerchief to blot them away.

Leaving the crumpled square of cotton on the desk in front of him, Ben reached for the top drawer on the right-hand side and had pulled it open before he could second-guess himself. A disappointed breath gusted from his lungs. He hadn't known what he was expecting to find, but this jumble of cheap biros, paperclips, discarded Post-it notes and a box of staples spilling its contents all over the place was the last thing he expected. His eyes rose to survey the painful neatness of the desk. The blotter set exactly in the centre, the single fountain pen laid neatly against the top edge of the closed day-to-a-page diary, the phone at the perfect distance to be answered on the first ring. His focus widened to take in the rest of the room. The pair of bucket chairs on the other side of the desk equidistant from him, like the three corners of an equilateral triangle. Along the back wall, the heavy wooden bookcases filled with ranks of straight-spined books, placed in precise alphabetical order. Even the curtains hung on either side of the windows in parallel lines, not a crease or a fold out of place.

He glanced back down at the messy drawer. It was a side of his father he'd never seen before, and Ben wasn't sure he liked it. Was this what had really been going on behind that perfect façade his father presented to the world? One he had been so desperate to maintain he'd constructed the worst possible lie and stuck to it for years to preserve his reputation? Was that why his mother had left, because she couldn't live up to his exacting standards? Ben shoved the drawer closed with a bang. No matter how hard he tried to ignore it, thoughts of Stevie kept creeping back in. He clasped his head in his hands, pressing hard against his temples as though if he applied enough pressure, he could squeeze out the unwanted thoughts. He wished Hope had stayed away, had left him well alone in happy ignorance. Well, not happy, but anything would have been better than this lurching from one emotion to another. For a moment he could almost sympathise with his father's choice to reinvent his life. If Ben tried hard enough, maybe he could push everything down and forget about it as well. He pictured the messy chaos of the now-closed drawer and knew he wasn't going to be able to fool himself any better than his dad had done.

No, hiding from the truth was not the way. Bracing himself for what else he might find, Ben reached down and tugged open the next drawer.

6

The following Thursday evening, Amelia pushed open the door to The Stourton Arms, wondering if she was making a mistake. She'd hesitated over the weekend, knowing that if she reached out to Hope there was no closing the door on their friendship again. All the reasons why Hope and the rest of the Travers family would be better off without her around hadn't gone away, but at the end of the day she couldn't leave her to deal with something so earth-shattering on her own. She'd sent Hope a message on Sunday evening and they'd agreed to meet for a drink later in the week.

A movement on the right caught her eye and she turned to see Hope waving at her from a table tucked into the big bay window. Oh well, it was too late to back out now. Plastering a smile on, Amelia crossed the bar and hesitated as Hope bobbed up from her chair. They shared an awkward look for a moment before they both laughed and Hope flung her arms around Amelia. The familiar touch was a balm to her frazzled soul and Amelia returned the warmth of the embrace with enthusiasm.

'I'm so glad you came!' she burst out just as Hope said, 'I'm so glad you messaged me!'

They laughed again and the tension of the past few weeks seemed to melt away. 'I shouldn't have pushed you away,' Amelia said, reaching out to clasp Hope's hand. 'I'm sorry.'

'It's all right,' Hope reassured her and then she grinned. 'It's not actually, I'm still bloody furious with you for shutting me out like that, but I'll get over it.' She stood up. 'I'll grab us a bottle of wine while you work on another apology.'

She was halfway to the bar before Amelia could even think about trying to stop her. Though what would be the point when they both knew the absolute dire straits that were Amelia's finances. Any protest lodged would only be for pride's sake.

Hope returned a few minutes later with a bottle of wine in a metal cooler, two glasses and a menu. 'I wasn't sure if you'd eaten or not, but I got caught up in a Zoom meeting with a new supplier so didn't have time to grab anything before I came to meet you.'

Amelia wondered if that was true, or if that was the excuse Hope had come up with to try and buy her dinner as well as a drink. 'The traffic getting onto the ring road was awful so the bus was nearly half an hour late dropping me off,' Amelia admitted. 'I only had time to grab a slice of toast in between jumping in the shower and coming out to meet you.'

'I'm not in the mood for anything too heavy. Why don't we get one of the sharing platters?' Hope suggested, tapping the bottom item on the starters section of the menu. 'And maybe a bowl of chips?'

'Sounds good to me.'

Hope returned to the bar to place their order while Amelia reached for the wine and poured them each a drink. 'Cheers,' Amelia said as she handed Hope a glass. 'And I'm sorry again for cutting you off so abruptly. I just got overwhelmed by...' She waved her glass vaguely as she tried to think of a way to sum up the awfulness of the past few weeks.

'Everything,' Hope suggested, with a gentle smile. 'I do understand why you felt like that, but that's twice I've let our friendship go against my better judgement and I won't let it happen again. You're stuck with me, I'm afraid.'

Amelia laughed. 'People think you're so sweet, but you're actually quite scary when you get that determined look in your eye.'

Hope tossed her plaited hair over one shoulder and swaggered her shoulders. 'Don't you forget it!' They both grinned before Hope's expression grew serious. 'So, umm, Rhys might have mentioned things weren't going too well for you at work.'

Amelia groaned. 'I didn't reach out to you because I wanted to cry about my latest misfortunes. I'm more worried about you. He told me about Ben.' She'd meant to ease into the topic, but the last thing she wanted was for this meeting to turn into yet another pity party for herself so she just blurted it out.

Hope nodded. 'He said he'd told you.' She puffed up her cheeks and blew out a long, frustrated sigh. 'It's so hard, Amelia, knowing he's there on his own trying to sort everything out and I want so much to jump back in the car and drive down there to help him.'

'That's because you're used to having people around you to lean on so it comes naturally to you to reach out when you see someone else struggling.' Amelia had grown up understanding she only had herself to rely on. Intellectually, she knew that wasn't true, that she had many kind people around her like Hope, like Caroline at work, but deep down inside she kept waiting for that safety blanket to be whipped away, leaving her out in the cold once more. She wondered if she'd pushed both Hope and Rhys away because she'd expected they would turn their backs anyway. A preemptive strike where she could pretend it had been her choice to make.

Hope shook her head. 'You always make it sound like I grew up in some perfect idyll, like I had everything easy.'

'It looked pretty bloody easy to me.' The words were out before Amelia could stop them and she hated the ugliness of them. She reached out a hand to Hope. 'I'm sorry, that was mean of me.'

Hope stared down at her proffered hand for a long time before she placed her own down against Amelia's open palm. 'I am aware of the monumental amount of privilege I grew up with.'

Amelia curled her fingers around Hope's. 'I know you are. You can't help being born into your situation, any more than I can.' She sighed. She was like one of those poor neglected dogs from Battersea, always biting at a hand only ever extended in comfort. 'I used to pretend sometimes that we'd somehow got swapped at birth, that one day your family would wake up and realise the mistake and I'd be taken to live on the estate – which doesn't even make sense given our birthdays are six months apart.'

'Oh, Amelia. Were things really that bad even all those years ago?'

Amelia nodded. 'Yes. I don't know why my parents ever got together in the first place, because they never seemed happy. Dad would go through small phases when it felt like he'd got himself on track and those weeks and months were like a breath of fresh air because he'd be fun to be around. Mum, on the other hand...' Amelia trailed off, wondering if she'd ever known a time when she could say Daisy had been happy. Oh, she put a good face on things, especially for birthdays and holidays. There were plenty of photos in the album that a stranger would look at and see a perfectly normal family having a good time but on the few occasions when Amelia could bring herself to look at them, she could sense a shadow hanging over Daisy as if she was always wishing herself somewhere else. 'I think if she hadn't fallen pregnant with me, Mum would've lived a whole different life – a much better life.' She wasn't an idiot and her birthday being less than six months after her parents' wedding anniversary had been a dead giveaway.

'She made her choices.'

There was a whip-sharp edge in Hope's voice that shocked Amelia. 'I know that.'

'Do you?' Hope raised an eyebrow. 'Because it sounds to me like you're taking the burden of their unhappy marriage on your shoulders, just like you do everything else.'

Amelia bristled, tugging her hand free and wrapping it around her wine glass as though there were any comfort to be found in alcohol. 'You make me sound like a martyr.'

Hope gave her a long look. 'You had other choices, too.' When Amelia opened her mouth to issue a hot protest, Hope held up her hand. 'All I mean is that you could've put yourself first, taken one of Ziggy's scholarships and gone to art school. But that's not in your nature. You saw how bad things were at home and you've done everything in your power to try and fix it.'

Amelia crumpled in on herself. 'But I didn't fix it, did I?'

Sliding around on the bench seat beneath the window, Hope put an arm around Amelia's shoulders. 'You couldn't fix it because it wasn't your problem to fix. You can't help someone who doesn't want to help themselves.'

Amelia stared at her glass. 'Keith was never prepared to help himself.'

Hope squeezed her gently, then let go and shifted back to her seat. 'And I'm sorry to say it, but your mum didn't do anything to sort things out either. I think it's time you put yourself first for a change.'

'You're right, I know you're right. The thing I hate the most is how much of a waste of time it feels right now.' Amelia told Hope about the letter from the landlord.

'Oh, God, that's awful! He can't just turn you out like that!'

Amelia shrugged. 'I think he probably can. The tenancy agreement is in Keith's name and I'm sure there'll be something in the fine detail about subletting or whatever.'

'But you're his family, not his bloody tenants!' Hope was practically spitting with rage, even though she remembered to keep her voice down so as not to draw the attention of the few other locals who'd popped in for a quiet drink.

Amelia shrugged, neither willing nor able to argue the point. 'I can't afford to fight him over it, so I'll just have to do my best to find us somewhere else to live.' She took a quick sip of her wine, thinking about her fruitless trudge around the letting agencies in town at lunchtime. 'If I'd managed to get that sales position at work then things wouldn't be so bleak.'

Hope shook her head. 'After all the hard work you've put into that firm over the years, the least they could do is have your back when you need them.'

'It's a business, not a charity.' She thought again about just how sheltered a world Hope had grown up in. There were very few companies as caring and altruistic as the way Ziggy and the rest of the family chose to run the estate. 'And they're responsible for lots of jobs, not just mine.' It still really hurt that she'd been passed over, but Amelia was too practical not to see the reasoning behind it. 'Once the trial starts next year, it'll be all over the papers.' They hadn't been given a firm court date yet, but the solicitor appointed to represent Keith had told them it would be months before they got a date due to the current backlogs. 'You only have to look at the way people speculate any time there's so much as a whiff of tragedy or scandal around a news story to understand why they would want to keep me in the background as much as possible.'

'Well, I think they're a bunch of selfish bastards and they don't deserve you. You should tell them to stick their job and go and work somewhere else.'

Amelia rolled her eyes. 'Because I can just walk into any job tomorrow. Look, if that was possible then I'd be out of there like a shot, but you and I both know that life doesn't work like that.'

Hope nodded. 'I know.' She reached for her drink, then sent her a long, speculative look over the rim of her wine glass. 'I can't do anything about your job worries, but what if I told you I have a possible solution to your housing crisis?'

Amelia almost choked on her wine at that. 'Don't even joke about it, Hope, please.'

Hope set down her glass. 'I'm not joking.'

A tiny spark of something sprang to life inside her, but Amelia ruthlessly crushed it before it could grow. Life didn't just hand things to you on a platter – well, maybe it did if you were fortunate enough to be the granddaughter of a baron, but fortune did not favour the likes of Amelia Riley. Folding her arms, she sat back in her chair and stared at Hope. 'So, what's the catch?'

Hope shook her head. 'There's no catch. The housekeeper for the hotel retired a few weeks ago and has moved to Yorkshire to be near her daughter and her grandchildren. Her replacement didn't want to live on the estate, so we have an empty cottage. It needs redecorating and there's a few little maintenance jobs Rhys wants to do, but if you want it, it's yours.' Hope named a rental price that was less than half of what they were currently paying.

'That's ridiculously cheap!' Amelia protested. 'I don't need your charity, Hope. I already feel sick about how much I've got to pay back to Ziggy as it is; I can't afford to be any deeper in debt to your family, physically or metaphorically.'

Hope frowned. 'It's not charity. It's the same rate everyone else pays. We don't look to make a profit from our tenants. The rents go back into a central pot, which we use for the upkeep and maintenance of the estate cottages. It's not like we have mortgages or anything else to cover on them. If you want to pay more than that then you'll have to take it up with Ziggy because he's the one who sets the rents.'

'Which would be a self-dooming act because it would mean taking even more time to pay off what I owed him! Talk about a catch-22.' Amelia sighed. 'It still feels like I'd be taking advantage.'

Hope reached out and took her hand. 'It doesn't have to be forever. We could set a time limit if you wanted – six months, maybe a year, whatever you'd be comfortable with. You can use the saving you'd make on the commercial market to pay Ziggy back that much quicker and then you'd be free of that. Free of us completely, if that's what you wanted.'

Amelia couldn't bear the sadness in Hope's voice. 'You know that's never what I really wanted. I just couldn't cope with the humiliation of what Keith had done. I wasn't thinking straight, I see that now, but at the time it felt like it was the only way to shield you and the rest of your family from any more trouble.'

'I understand why you did it,' Hope said in a soft voice. 'But I've been so very worried about you.'

Guilt twisted Amelia's insides. She'd been so caught up in the stress and worry of her own problems that she'd not spared a thought for anyone else. She'd been so sure she was doing the right thing by shutting Hope and Rhys out, but all she'd done was make herself more of a burden to them because she'd refused to speak to them.

'I'm really sorry.'

'Everything all right, girls?' They both glanced up as Iain, the landlord, arrived bearing a platter covered in mezze bits and a bowl of crisp, golden chips.

'All good, thanks,' Hope answered with a smile, and Amelia could only admire the smooth way she was able to mask her feelings and switch on the charm.

Taking the two pairs of napkin-wrapped cutlery that he pulled out of his apron and offered to them, Amelia did her best to imitate Hope's smile. 'This looks great, Iain.'

Iain smiled, looking pleased with the compliment. 'You need a refill?' He nodded towards the ice bucket.

They'd only had a glass each, and not even finished those. Amelia never drank at home, but she'd refused to give herself yet another hang-up to do with her father so enjoyed a glass or two of wine when she was in a social situation. 'Not on a school night,' she said to Iain, giving him another smile that felt more than halfway genuine this time.

'No problem.' Iain paused, then placed a gentle hand on her shoulder. 'It's good to see you out and about, lovie. We've missed your smile around the place.'

A lump formed in Amelia's throat as she reached up and touched his hand on her shoulder. It wasn't only the Travers family she'd cut herself off from: the village was full of friends. Poor Iain had copped more trouble from her father than most, but he'd never once made Amelia feel anything less than welcome, even after he'd barred Keith from the pub. 'I'll try and be less of a recluse in future.'

'Good girl. Give us a shout if you need anything else.'

Amelia waited until he'd returned to his post behind the bar before she turned her attention back to Hope, who was dipping a chip into a bowl of creamy hummus. 'I'll have to talk to Mum about it.'

Hope nodded. 'Of course. Come up at the weekend and check it out to make sure it'll suit you both. There isn't much of a garden, but Mrs Knowles has left a lot of her pots because it was too much hassle to move them and Denny has been popping around to water them to make sure they don't die.'

'Denny lives next door?' She knew him a bit as he was one of the other farmhands that worked for Rhys and had been persuaded by her father to come around for a drink or a barbeque now and then when he'd been in one of his good phases. Denny had always been polite, but he seemed the type who preferred to keep himself to himself. A neighbour you could call on if you needed help with something, but not someone who wanted to be your best friend. That would suit Amelia just fine.

'Yes, and Carrie-Ann is on the other side. She spends most of her time in her workshop, though. Neither of them would be a bother to you,' Hope added with a smile as though she'd been able to sense Amelia's train of thought.

'And we definitely won't be a bother to them,' Amelia said. No doubt the neighbours they had now would be glad to see the back of the Rileys once and for all. She couldn't blame them for it.

'I don't want to be accused of offering charity again, but we've got a lot of events coming up in the next few weeks so if your mum wanted some extra hours, we could do with all the help we can get. It might be at short notice and at irregular times but with you both living on the estate it'd be much easier to get her to fill in, if that's something she'd be willing to do.'

'I'll see what she says.' The extra money would be welcome, but Daisy wasn't doing well, no matter how hard she tried to put on a brave face for Amelia.

'No pressure.' Hope seemed to hesitate, then spoke in a rush. 'I'd have some evening work for you too, if you want it. Nothing fancy, a bit of stewarding for stuff like the Halloween weekend and Bonfire Night. We'll be opening it up to anyone in the village so it's not a special favour or anything.'

Gosh, that dig she'd made to Hope about charity had really struck a nerve. 'That sounds great, count me in for whatever you need.'

Hope heaved a sigh of relief. 'That's good, that's great, and it'll be really convenient what with you living right there.'

It didn't escape Amelia's attention that Hope was already talking about the cottage like it was a done deal. As she picked at a bowl of olives, Amelia realised she was mentally already more than halfway there herself. If they were safe behind the protective walls of the estate, both she and her mum would be shielded from the worst of the fallout that was coming down the line once Keith went on trial. No one would be able to doorstep them. She wouldn't have to face walking down the street and wondering if people were talking about her, were judging her or looking down their nose at her.

It was a powerful message from the Travers family, too, to have both her and her mum living on the estate when it had been the scene of the worst of her father's misdeeds. Their opinion still counted for a lot in the area. There wasn't any more to be said about it tonight. As much as it felt like she could finally see a light at the end of the long, dark tunnel, Amelia would not rush into anything.

She picked up the bowl of chips and added a few to her plate, along with some meat and cheese from the platter. Spearing a chunk of cheese, she pointed it towards Hope. 'Enough of all that for now – I want you to talk to me about what happened with Ben. Rhys said you went to the funeral. That must've been tough for you, even though you'd never met your dad.'

Hope's phone beeped suddenly and she cast it a quick glance. Amelia watched as her eyes widened. 'It's him,' Hope whispered. 'He wants to know if I'm free because he wants to call me.'

Amelia edged her chair closer before replying in the same low tone. 'It's who? Ben?'

Hope nodded.

'Have you heard from him since the funeral?'

'Not a word. I gave him my contact details, but I wasn't sure I'd hear from him. Certainly not so soon...' She looked up at Amelia, eyes still wide. 'What should I say?'

'Tell him you're free, of course!' Amelia stood up. 'Look, I'll give you some privacy—'

Hope placed a hand on her arm. 'No, stay.' She swallowed hard. 'Please?'

'Okay.' Amelia sank back into her seat. 'But if you want me to leave at any time, just wave at me or something and I'll go.'

'Thanks.' Hope picked up her phone, sucked in a deep breath and put it down again. 'What if he's only calling to tell me to leave him alone?'

'Why would he do that?' Amelia reached for her friend's hand and gave it a squeeze. 'If he didn't want to speak to you, he would surely have kept silent and you'd have got the message.'

Hope covered her face with her hands briefly. 'God, I'm really overthinking all this, aren't I?' When Amelia didn't say anything, Hope gave a little laugh. 'Point taken.' Amelia watched as she picked up her phone and tapped a quick reply. Less than a minute later, the phone rang. 'Ben?'

Amelia rose silently and lifted her chair, setting it down a couple of feet further away. She wanted to be there to support Hope, but she also didn't want her to feel like she was eavesdropping. She picked up a chip, bit into it and set it down quickly when she realised they'd gone cold. Pushing the plate aside, she picked up her wine and took a sip as she half-listened to Hope exchanging awkward pleasantries. 'No, no, of course I don't mind you calling,' Amelia heard her friend say. 'I've been hoping you'd get in touch. How is everything?'

It seemed to be going okay, so Amelia pulled out her own phone and flicked open one of her news apps, more for something to distract her than out of any real desire to find out what was going on in the world. As ever, the leading headlines were a mix of the latest political rows, people's personal agonies wrapped up as public interest stories and entertainment gossip. She closed the app with a sigh and opened one of the match-three games she'd downloaded once she'd started taking the bus. They were mindless enough she could pick them up and put them down, but just frustrating enough to keep her coming back for one more level. She was still trying to reject the various offers to buy extra boosters when she caught Hope saying, 'Oh, Ben, none of that matters. None of this is your fault. Please, come home so that we can help you.'

7

'It's not my home.' The words sounded hoarse to Ben's ears, his throat raw as he forced them out.

'Not yet, perhaps, but it could be if you'd only give it a chance, give *us* a chance.'

Hope made it sound so easy. They didn't know anything about each other. What if they didn't get on? And he'd have to face Stevie, and he wasn't sure he was ready for that. He stared down at the fat file in the centre of his father's desk, the one he'd had to stop going through when he'd found a copy of the letter Dominic had sent, pretending it was from him.

He'd kept himself busy for most of the week doing what practical admin stuff he could, like logging into his father's various accounts and changing the passwords. He didn't know what information Dominic might have, but he damn well wasn't going to risk it. That done, he'd cleaned the house from top to bottom and had a couple of estate agents around. He wouldn't be able to put the house up on the market yet, but he wanted to know exactly where things stood.

Only after he'd exhausted every other task on his to-do list had

Ben returned to the file. There was more than enough evidence to prove Dominic's malpractice because his father had kept hand-written notes of everything the pair of them had discussed. It was all there in black and white. Somewhere deep inside, Ben had clung onto the hope that it was all some terrible misunderstanding, but in the run-up to his eighteenth birthday, his father had begun to panic that he wouldn't be able to keep Stevie from contacting Ben. So he and Dominic had cooked up the letter together, making it look as though it was Ben's choice to cut her off. No wonder he hadn't wanted Ben to see it.

Ben still wasn't sure why he'd reached for his phone, only he'd had a sudden need to try and explain himself to Hope. To make sure they truly understood it had been nothing to do with him. Talking on the phone was one thing – going there and having to face everyone? 'There's still so much to sort out here.' It was an excuse and for a moment he hated himself for letting the fear rule him.

'Come to Juniper Meadows for the weekend.' Hope's tone was warm and persuasive. 'You can stay at the farmhouse, or I can sort you out a room at the hotel if you'd prefer that. Oh, hang on! There's a lodge next door to the one Cam and I are living in you can use. You'd have as much privacy as you need that way.'

Farmhouse? Hotel? Lodge? Just how big was this Juniper Meadows place? He'd have to get his laptop out and google it later. She made it sound inviting, though. Ben laughed, his throat still a little dry. 'You should be in sales.'

'Funny you should say that.' When Hope spoke again, her tone was more serious. 'Please come.'

'It's very short notice. I need to get back to London and back to work.'

'We've already lost so much time.' There was no mistaking the need in her voice, no ignoring the invisible tug of connection he felt towards her either.

'Okay. I'm not making any promises beyond this one weekend, though.' The words tasted like a lie on his tongue. He knew that if he took this step, there'd be no walking away afterwards.

'Oh, Ben, that's wonderful! And no one will put any pressure on you over anything, I swear! Look, I'd better go because I need to make sure the lodge is ready for you tomorrow. Will you text me on Saturday morning when you know your ETA?'

Her excitement was infectious, and Ben's cheeks stretched wide on a smile. 'Don't go to any special trouble on my behalf.' He checked his watch. 'I'd better go too, I... well, I'll see you on Saturday, I guess.'

'I can't wait! See you then.'

Ben stared at his phone for a long moment, already wondering if he'd done the right thing. He glanced down at the letter that had been his father's final attempt to deprive him of a relationship with his mother. Not just his mother – there was a whole family he knew nothing about. A sister. He thought about all the times he'd longed for a sibling to play with. It was too late for the sad, lonely boy inside him but Hope was right. They'd lost so much already. Too much.

It was time he started making his own choices instead of continuing to live with the fallout of those made for him.

* * *

He managed to distract himself for most of the next day, but sleeping was impossible. After tossing and turning, Ben found himself standing in the garage, the concrete cold beneath his bare feet. Before he could talk himself out of it, he whipped off the cover and stared at his potter's wheel. His hands itched to make something for the first time in weeks, but by the time he'd got himself set up it wouldn't be worth it. He looked at the narrow area he had to work with between the racks of neat shelving and the shiny monstrosity of his father's Jaguar. He'd have to move that for a start, and he didn't think the neighbours would appreciate being woken up if he started the engine. Once he had a bit more time, he would definitely start potting again. He shook the cloth out and was about to drape it back over the wheel when he spotted a small bag of air-drying modelling clay. It was probably no good, but Ben bent down to pick it up anyway.

Having re-covered the wheel, he took the bag into the kitchen and set it down on the counter. The seal hadn't been broken so there was a chance. He fetched a knife and slit open the bag, and was pleasantly surprised to find the clay still malleable. With a small smile playing about his lips, Ben cut a slice from the block and set to work.

Two hours later, his fingers were aching and his eyes were stinging from lack of sleep, but he had a delicate rose resting on a sheet of newspaper to dry. Feeling better than he had in days, Ben wearily climbed the stairs and was asleep the moment his head touched the pillow.

When his alarm went off the next morning, he felt as refreshed as if he'd slept for eight hours rather than four. Still buzzing, he showered, breakfasted and was on the road before seven, the fragile rose nestled on a towel on the back seat. The local roads were quiet and even the traffic on the M4 was sparse. Realising he was going to be early, he spent forty minutes nursing a cup of coffee in a motorway services. He needn't have bothered because his satnav decided to take him on a magical mystery tour of what seemed to be half the farm tracks in Gloucestershire. Calling them B roads felt like giving them too much credit, he thought to himself as he performed a seventeen-point turn and winced at the horrible scraping sound coming from somewhere underneath his car. A glance in the rear-view mirror assured him he hadn't left anything vital like his exhaust behind and he retraced his route towards a road he hoped would lead him eventually back to civilisation.

Ten minutes later, he was just about to pull into a lay-by with a food van parked in it when he spotted a large white sign telling him to exit at the next junction for Juniper Meadows. After that, it was easy. The signs were frequent enough that he was able to relax and enjoy the view. The trees were starting to turn, their leaves a mix of green and brown, which promised a truly spectacular display in a couple more weeks. The glimpses of fields beyond the drystone walls and hedgerows were furrows of deep brown or covered with rectangular bales of straw waiting to be collected for winter storage.

A black on white sign announced his arrival in Stourton-in-the-Vale and he allowed himself a little smile of wonder. He knew from the family tree Hope had given him that their family's full name was Stourton-de-Lacey-Travers and he also knew his grandfather had a title. But to have everything named after them? It was like another world. He'd grown up with the perks and privileges of a solid middle-class upbringing. Ski trips at half-term, summer holidays in the sun, whatever he'd asked Santa for under the tree at Christmas. The life that Hope must've known seemed like it was on another level again to that.

As he drove past thatched cottages that looked like they belonged in a cosy Sunday teatime drama, Ben's nerves started to get the better of him. He wondered what the locals really thought of Hope and the rest of the family. Were they popular? Or were they merely tolerated because folk knew which side their bread was buttered on? Well, he supposed he'd find out for himself at some point. Unless things went drastically wrong over the weekend, he'd already decided on the drive down that he was going to give things a proper chance with Hope, and yes, damn those butterflies, even with their mother.

As the miles had whizzed by, he'd found himself growing more and more curious about the woman who to all intents and purposes had abandoned him. He thought about the cards and letters Hope had handed him on the day of the funeral, which his father had intercepted and prevented him from reading, and then sent back to Stevie with the solicitor's letter allegedly from Ben, as though he wanted no reminders of his mother as well as no further contact from her. He remembered the desperate poignancy he'd felt reading those heartfelt messages that would have meant so much to the little boy who, for all his father's efforts to give him a good life, had never stopped missing his mother. No, he couldn't say Stevie had abandoned him, not completely, anyway. She was a victim of whatever cruel game his father had decided to play with them all, just the same as he was.

Though there were no other cars around, Ben flicked his indicator on out of habit as he drew level with another of the familiar Juniper Meadows signs with an arrow pointing him to the right. Turning off the main road, he made it all of fifty metres before pulling to a stop in front of an imposing stone archway spanning the width of the drive. A high wall in the same honey-coloured stone as the arch stretched in either direction as far as he could see. Black, wrought-iron gates stood open and there was a revolving pedestrian gate set off to the right-hand side. A large banner covered part of the wall advertising upcoming events including a Halloween Spooktacular and a Classical Fireworks Show running from Thursday to Sunday over the Bonfire Night weekend.

Ben checked his watch. He'd texted Hope from the services, and even with the unexpected detour he was still a bit earlier than the time he'd estimated. He stared down the driveway, awed at the size of the sprawling chestnut trees marching along each side in neat rows. He bet they'd look stunning in the spring, covered in blossom. He checked his watch again, wondering if he should wait or start making his way along the drive.

A tap on his window made him jump so hard he shot forwards in his seat. The safety mechanism on his belt kicked in, sending a jolt of pain across his chest as it restrained. 'Jesus Christ!'

Heart hammering, Ben turned to see an ashen-faced woman staring in horror at him through the glass. 'I'm so sorry! Are you okay?'

Ben lowered his window. 'Just a minor heart attack. What the hell are you doing sneaking up on me like that?'

Colour flooded her pale face and he didn't miss the protective way she folded her arms across her body as she took a step back. 'I wasn't sneaking! I was minding my own business when I noticed you parked here in the middle of the drive. I wanted to make sure you were okay, that's all.'

'I was just fine until you started banging on my window!' Ben snapped. He knew he was being unreasonable, but bloody hell, she'd given him the fright of his life. He sucked in a deep breath and forced himself to moderate his tone. 'Sorry. I'm okay, but thank you for checking on me.'

The woman gave him one more frown of concern before she turned away with a nod. She took maybe half a dozen strides down the driveway before she stopped dead and turned to face him. Her expression this time was something softer. 'Are... are you Ben by any chance?'

Ben rocked back in his seat. Who was this woman? How did she know his name? Had Hope and the rest of the family been gossiping about her long-lost brother? Oh God, what if this was yet another relative he didn't know about? The questions spun so fast through his head it was a wonder they didn't make him dizzy. 'Who wants to know?'

The woman held up her hands. 'Sorry, I didn't mean to make you feel uncomfortable.' She took a couple of tentative steps towards the car. 'I'm Amelia. Hope and I have been friends since we were little. I was with her the other night when you called; that's how I've put two and two together.' She pointed to her head. 'It's the blonde hair that confused me for a minute; I expected you to be dark like the rest of the family.' Her lips twitched up at the corners into a smile that turned her whole face from ordinary to beautiful. 'You found us all right, then, I see?'

Us. There was a friendly innocence to the word, an inclusiveness that made something inside him unfurl just a little. 'I had a couple of off-road adventures thanks to the satnav, but other than that it was a pretty straightforward journey.'

'Yeah, there's this one bit that catches everyone out. It's really frustrating and I know a few people have tried to get it corrected without success. Oh, does Hope know you're here yet?' She glanced over her shoulder as though she expected to see her friend coming up the drive towards them.

Ben shook his head. 'Not yet. I was just wondering if I should call her, or head on down when you—' He cut himself off to give her a wry smile. 'When you kindly enquired after my health.' Amelia laughed, that splash of colour highlighting her sharp cheekbones once again. She was very thin, he realised. Not slim, but thin, like she'd been unwell or not been taking proper care of herself. Dressed in jeans and a baggy jumper that covered her from neck to knees, it wasn't obvious at first. As he paid more attention, he noticed the dark shadows underneath her eyes, the way her nails were bitten almost to the quick. She glanced aside, her head dipping to hide her face and he gave himself a silent telling-off for staring. Feeling awkward, Ben cast around for something to say. 'Is it far to the house?'

Amelia glanced up at him through her lashes, a slight hint of her earlier smile showing she'd taken no offence at his inadvertent rudeness. 'It depends which house you're talking about.'

Ben laughed. 'Touché. I'd better call Hope and find out where she wants to meet me.'

'Okay. Well. I'll leave you to it. It was lovely to meet you, Ben, and I hope everything goes well today.' Amelia raised her hand in a little wave, then turned and headed back down the driveway.

Ben watched her for a few moments, before fishing his phone out and texting Hope.

I'm at the main gate. Should I wait here or come in?

He paused, then added:

I met your friend Amelia just now, she's nice

Now what had made him say that? He was just about to delete the message when a tiny image of Hope popped up beneath it, showing that she'd read it. A reply arrived a few seconds later:

She's the best! I'm at the lodge so it'll take me a few minutes to get back to my car. I can meet you at The Old Stable Yard car park. Just follow the signs x

From what he could recall from the Juniper Meadows website, The Old Stable Yard was a collection of workshops and artisan traders. It was on his mental list of things to check out, so the suggestion was fine with him.

See you there

Ben dropped his phone into the tray beneath the centre console and eased the car back into gear. Small signposts indicated a ten mile an hour speed limit, which gave him a chance to take everything in as he trundled along. It didn't take long for him to catch up with Amelia and he slowed to a crawl. 'Can I give you a lift? Hope's meeting me at The Old Stable Yard.'

8

Amelia lifted her eyes to the sky for a moment and Ben followed her gaze to take in the pale blue expanse. There was an edge to the air, a hint of a chill that would fade over the next couple of hours as the heat from the early autumn sun strengthened. 'It's a lovely morning for a walk, but as I'm heading to the café it would be silly to refuse, thank you.' She walked around the back of the car while he leaned across to pull the handle on the passenger door and override the automatic lock.

He waited until she was properly settled with her seat belt on. 'Okay?'

She turned to look at him, their faces just a foot or two apart. Up close, he had the full effect of her violet-blue eyes and the little spot inside him unfurled a little more. Had he honestly thought her ordinary? Even with her skin so pale and those purple-dark bruises under her eyes, she was... his mind groped for the right word. 'Pretty' was too conventional for her bold features, emphasised by the thinness of her face. *Striking*. He mentally tasted the word and found it fitted. She blinked suddenly and pulled back with a little laugh. 'Sorry!'

Ben eased himself back into his seat, an echo of her motion. 'Sorry for what?'

'I didn't mean to stare. I was just caught by how much you look like Hope. Which I suppose makes sense given you're full siblings.' She nodded. 'Yup, definitely a Travers.'

'I'm a Lawson, not a Travers.' Ben fiddled with his belt, not sure how he felt about being declared a part of the family who were still strangers. It had always been him and his dad, and even with all his anger and misgivings about everything his father had kept hidden, his defence was automatic.

'Yes, of course! I'm sorry.' Amelia sighed. 'I don't think I've apologised so much to someone in such a short space of time before. We really have got off on the wrong foot, haven't we? Let's get to the stable yard and then I can go back to minding my own business.'

Feeling abashed at her defensive tone, Ben opened his mouth to apologise, then settled for, 'Is it easy to find?'

Amelia nodded, keeping her gaze facing forwards. 'Straight down the drive until you reach the junction and then you follow the road to the right. It's not far.'

Christ, he really had done a great job of offending her. He'd have to watch his words a bit more carefully for the rest of the weekend or he'd be biting everyone's head off for saying something that put him on the defensive. He'd promised himself he'd come here with an open mind and look for common ground and here he was snapping at poor Amelia for what was, on reflection, an entirely innocent remark. If he decided to visit the estate on a regular basis, it wouldn't take long for word to get around about him, so everyone would be having a gawk. 'I should be the one apologising,' Ben said as he drove slowly along the tree-lined avenue. 'I don't like the idea of being the centre of attention once people find out about my connection to the family, that's all.'

Amelia made an indelicate sound through her nose, something

between a scoff and a snort. 'I wouldn't worry too much about the local gossips; you'll be a footnote compared to the main attraction, I can promise you that.'

Ben was about to ask her to explain her cryptic comment when the car cleared a low rise and the land fell away before them in a vista so exquisite, it looked like something from a movie. He braked without thinking, his eyes locked on the sprawling mansion dominating the valley below them. 'My God.'

'It never fails to take my breath away when I see it,' Amelia murmured softly.

'It's like time stood still here.'

'You think so at first,' Amelia agreed. 'But then you start to look closer and you can pick out signs of the modern world.' She pointed to the right, where a shiny red tractor was chugging through a field in the distance, ploughing the last of the hay stubble back into the earth.

'The family don't live in the Hall any longer,' Ben recalled. After he'd agreed to this visit, he'd spent a couple of hours on the estate website trying to learn as much as possible.

'No, they moved to the estate farmhouse when Ziggy took over running things and the family decided to convert the Hall into a hotel.' She glanced across at him. 'You should probably be talking to Hope about this, rather than me.'

'I prefer to get your take on things first, if you don't mind. Hope has a vested interest in putting the most positive spin on things.'

She visibly bristled at that. 'Hope is the most honest person I know.'

Ben sighed. 'I didn't mean that.' He scrubbed a hand through his hair. 'There's just a lot riding on this weekend.'

A soft hand touched his arm. 'They're good people. If they have any faults, it's that sometimes they try a bit too hard to do the right thing. For people with this kind of privilege at their fingertips...'

She swept her hand in a gesture that took in the rolling parkland before them. 'They are very down to earth.'

Ben let his gaze roam over the picture-postcard view before them. His father's house was one of the larger ones in the village and Ben had spent way too many hours of his summer holidays mowing the half-acre of back garden. He tried to imagine being responsible for something on the scale of the estate and found it was beyond his comprehension. He hadn't progressed as far at work as his father had expected him to for several reasons, mainly because he didn't have any enthusiasm for it. He'd been pushed towards promotion a few times, but he hadn't wanted to take on the responsibility for other people that came with a managerial position. He preferred to focus on the numbers. Numbers didn't have family emergencies like sick kids, or need motivating, or – God forbid – disciplining for not doing a good job. That didn't mean he wasn't a team player, nor that he wouldn't help out a colleague who was struggling. He just liked to turn off the computer at the end of the day and be able to forget about everything until the next time he walked into the office. 'Do you like your job?' The words were out before he realised and he was about to apologise when she replied.

'No.' Amelia's response was instantaneous and emphatic. 'Well, I mean the people I work with are mostly really nice, but it's not what I ever wanted to do.'

Ben was struck by how similar that was to his own situation and he wondered what had put Amelia on a path to a career she didn't enjoy. Maybe she had a pushy father who wanted a carbon copy of himself as well. 'What did you want to do?'

Amelia turned to stare out of her window. 'I always thought I'd apply for one of the estate bursaries and go to art school.' She wrapped her arms around herself as though she was protecting the girl who'd had different dreams once upon a time. She glanced back towards him. 'But drawing pretty pictures doesn't pay the bills.'

Ben gave a grim laugh. 'That sounds painfully familiar, only in my case it was pottery. Dad thought it was weird, even for a hobby, and kept pushing me towards more appropriate *activities* like rugby that suited his vision for me, I guess.' He put a sarcastic stress on the word 'activities'.

'Not a team player?'

He laughed again. 'Not so much that, just too much mud and testicle-squeezing for my liking.'

She laughed, a bright bubble of sound that seemed to fill the interior space of the car. 'I can imagine how that might be something of a downside.'

Ben grinned, delighted to have cheered her up as well as avoiding a conversational landmine between them for a change. 'I really hated the mud.'

She laughed again, and he felt like he'd won a prize. When it subsided, her expression softened into something a bit too close to sympathy. 'I take it you're not a fan of your job, either?'

He shook his head. 'I've just had a week off to sort things out at home and the thought of having to go back... well, let's just say it's not very appealing.'

'Maybe this can be a fresh start.' Amelia's eyes widened. 'I'm sorry! There I go overstepping the mark again.'

Ben held up a hand to stop her apology. 'It's fine. I can't pretend that life is going to carry on as it has been. Everything's different now.'

'Well, I hope you find a way forwards that brings you a fulfilling future.' Her gaze drifted towards her side window again and he wondered whether she was thinking of her own situation and how she might change things too. He wanted to dig, to find out more about her circumstances, about why she was feeling trapped in a dead-end job. She was young, free if the lack of rings on her hand were any indication – and yes, he had found himself checking for signs of a permanent romantic connection – so what was holding her here? She'd said something about art not paying the bills so maybe that had something to do with it. Were things really that bad in the local economy? Sure, she wouldn't have the same breadth of job opportunities as living in London offered him, but he doubted she had the same level of expenses either. He recalled the picture-perfect village he'd just driven through. A place like that with this estate and all its facilities on the doorstop would appeal to the weekend commuters; maybe things were tougher around here than appearances suggested. 'I'd better not keep Hope waiting.'

Amelia settled back in her seat. 'It's not far to the stable yard. Just follow the road until we reach the junction and take the road to the right.'

They finished the short drive in silence. Ben didn't mind and he was too busy trying to keep his mind on the road and resist the urge to stop every few yards and gawp at the scenery. He was glad he'd decided to stick a set of gym kit in with the rest of his clothes because he couldn't wait to be able to get out and explore the estate on foot. As both Amelia and Hope had said, the estate was well signposted and he was confident he would've found his way without their assistance. He pulled into the car park, which was empty apart from a handful of vehicles huddled together in one corner, and parked facing the long building opposite. The walls were the same honey-coloured stone he'd come to recognise, the roof dark-tiled rather than thatched. To the left sat a more modern building that had clearly been designed with a sympathetic eye to blend in. The wall facing into the courtyard was mostly glass and as he climbed out of the car, he could see tables and chairs scattered throughout – the café Amelia had mentioned. The right-hand side of the courtyard was dominated by a large building with a set of very tall double doors. More glass displayed an array of strange equipment, and a sign told him it was home to the Juniper Meadows distillery.

A couple walked around the side of the distillery and Ben recognised Hope and the man with the glasses who'd accompanied her to the funeral, who was trying to control two bouncy black Labrador puppies on leads. Hope waved, a broad smile wreathing her face, and Ben found himself smiling back as he raised his hand in greeting.

'I'll leave you to it, then.'

Ben spun at the sound of Amelia's voice. 'You're not staying to say hello?'

She shook her head with a smile. 'I'm seeing Hope later; I'll catch up with her then.' She waved towards the others before tucking her hands in her pockets and strolling towards the café.

Ben frowned at her abrupt departure before turning back to greet Hope. He offered his hand at the same time as she opened her arms and they stared awkwardly at each other for a second before Ben raised his arms just as Hope dropped them. They shared a laugh before Hope stepped forwards for a quick hug. 'You must've left at the crack of dawn to get here so soon,' she said as she stepped back to stand beside the man – her boyfriend, Ben assumed from their general body language.

'I wanted to be around the M25 before the traffic started,' Ben replied, then gave her a sheepish smile. 'I didn't get much sleep,' he admitted.

'Me neither.' Hope glanced up at the man. 'I bet you regret coming down this weekend.'

He stopped trying to control the puppies, who were tying their leads in knots in their excitement over meeting a new person, to grin at Hope. 'I never regret spending time with you, even when you toss and turn all night.' He gathered both leads in one hand and thrust the other towards Ben. 'It's good to see you again. I'm sorry we didn't have time for a proper introduction last time. I'm Cameron Ferguson. You can call me Cam; everyone does.'

Which was generous of him considering the short shrift Ben had given them. 'It's good to meet you, too. I should probably apologise for being rude to you guys last time we met,' Ben said as they shook hands.

'I think if a group of strangers showed up and dropped a bombshell like that on me, I would've had much the same reaction.'

One of the puppies started barking, which set the other one off. Cam bent down to try and shush them and Ben went down on his knees beside him. He'd grown up with dogs, but when their ancient cocker spaniel had died a few years back his father hadn't wanted to replace him and Ben's flat in London wasn't suitable for keeping anything bigger than a hamster. These two were full of joyful energy and he wanted to put them out of their misery at being restrained. 'Hello! Hello, then! Yes, yes, I'm happy to meet you too.' Ben laughed as the puppies began to try and clamber all over him.

'I probably should've warned you about the puppies,' Hope said as she crouched to join them, tugging one of the puppies back with a firm but gentle grip. 'Behave yourself, Sooty, or you'll give Ben the wrong impression about us.'

Her affectionate tone rather gave Ben the right impression about his sister as he watched her fuss and play with the ecstatic dog. 'And I bet you're called Sweep,' he said to the puppy who had propped himself up on Ben's knees. Bright button eyes seemed to gleam in delight as the little dog barked to tell Ben he'd guessed right.

'Not the most original names, I'll admit,' Hope said with a

smile. 'But they were the first ones that came to mind when I saw them.'

'I think they're great.' He meant both the names and the dogs. 'I love dogs and would have one of my own if I had more space.'

'That's just as well,' Cam said, giving Sweep's head a rub before he coaxed the puppy under some sort of control. 'There's another three you haven't met yet.'

Ben shot a surprised look at Hope. 'You have *five* dogs?'

'Between the family, he meant, not me personally! I can barely manage these two.' Hope pushed to her feet. 'I really must sign them up—'

'For obedience training.' Cam cut her off with a laugh. 'You've been saying that for as long as I've known you.'

Hope sighed. 'I know, I know! One of these days I might be able to find a space in my diary to actually do it.'

Cam stood up to give her a quick hug. 'Don't stress, darling, it'll all come good, you'll see.'

Feeling like he was intruding on something private, Ben remained crouching and turned his attention back to the puppies, who were more than happy to accept more strokes and fussing. It was only once Cam had stepped back and tugged the reluctant puppies with him that Ben straightened. He noticed then the faint strain lines bracketing Hope's eyes, the slight tension in the corners of her smile and he felt bad all over again for dumping himself on the family with little to no warning. 'We could've done this another time if you have stuff going on.'

Hope reached for him without hesitation. 'Don't be silly. Family always comes first, and besides, I was the one who told you to come down. Things have been a bit hectic lately, but if we waited for a quiet day then we'd never do anything. That's just the way life is around here.'

'You'll get used to it,' Cam said, giving his shoulder a friendly pat. 'I'm going to grab a coffee; can I get you guys something?'

'A hot chocolate, please,' Hope replied. 'It's a bit chilly this morning.' She rubbed her arms through the long-sleeved top she wore under a padded gilet.

'With all the works?' There was a teasing hint to the smile Cam shared with her, like he already knew the answer.

'But of course! What about you, Ben? Do you want something?'

Ben thought about the amount of caffeine already coursing through his system. 'A decaf cappuccino would be good, thanks.'

'I'm on it,' Cam said. 'Why don't you start the tour and I'll catch you up? Come on, you two. I bet Sandra's got some treats for you!' He addressed the last to the puppies as he began to lead then away.

Hope watched him go for a moment and there was no missing the goofy smile on her face. Ben felt pleased she had someone in her life who seemed so dependable and caring. The strength of feeling surprised him, as did the slightly protective surge that came with it that Cam had better live up to these first good impressions. He had no right to any kind of presumption over Hope's life, but telling himself that didn't make it go away. In a bit of a daze as he tried to sort through the jumble of emotions inside, Ben could only nod when Hope gestured towards the stable block. 'Shall we?'

Deciding to wait until he was on his own to try and sort his head out, Ben did his best to push everything to one side and focus on the here and now. He'd come to find out more about the estate as well as the family, after all. He fell into step beside Hope. 'Are these all independent businesses?' he asked as they stopped in front of the first workshop, belonging to a silversmith who specialised in jewellery.

Hope nodded. 'They pay rent, but we've tried to keep it at a reasonable rate.' She glanced up at him. 'This part of the world has become ever more desirable so we are doing what we can to give opportunities to people who were born here to stay within the community if they want to.'

So, it was as he'd suspected and times were tougher around here than the idyllic countryside might suggest. 'Amelia said something earlier about the estate offering bursaries. Is that part of this?'

'Yes. Both Carrie-Ann and Jason were beneficiaries.' She pointed first at the silversmith's and then at the leatherworker's next door. 'We try to encourage recipients to come back after their training, but it's not a requirement and not everyone who's joined us here is a local.' Hope gestured towards a unit further along the row that bore a sign saying 'Alhambra Rugs'. 'Eduardo was born in Granada in Spain and was taught to weave by his grandmother. He was on a backpacking holiday about three years ago and camped on the estate for a week and just kind of never left. You'll see a couple of his rugs when I take you over to the lodge later. They're a lovely splash of colour.'

'The rest of the family don't mind about me not staying at the farmhouse?' Ben had been relieved by the offer of using one of the lodges on the estate, but he didn't want to start off on the wrong foot with anyone.

'Not at all. They just want you to be comfortable.' Hope took a deep breath. 'I'm not sure how to ask this so I'm just going to come out with it. How do you feel about meeting Mum this weekend?'

Ben turned away from her and continued to study the stable block while he wondered what to say. He should've known from their previous interactions that Hope wasn't one to avoid the tricky conversations, but she'd blindsided him by coming right out with it. 'I... Honestly, I don't know how I feel about it... about her.'

He felt a gentle touch on his arm, and he glanced down at the woman beside him. 'I only asked because she wants you to know that if you're not ready to talk to her yet, she'll keep out of the way.

She'll be up at the hotel for most of the weekend anyway because one of the reception staff has called in sick and it was too late to find a replacement.'

It would be easy to accept the offer, to ease into things with the rest of the family, maybe just hang out with Hope and Cameron this weekend and try and get his bearings, but that would just be putting off the inevitable. 'Maybe if I could meet her without everyone else around the first time?'

Hope squeezed his arm. 'I think that might be a good idea.' She sighed. 'I'm still so confused about everything.'

In the whirlwind of the past few days, it was easy for Ben to overlook the fact he wasn't the only person who'd been deeply affected by all of this. Whatever their mother had been guilty of, their father had been just as bad – maybe worse because what could he have done that would make his pregnant wife leave him and their child and hide away for the best part of twenty-five years? Ben mentally shied away from that. Perhaps there were some things that were best left in the past. 'We'll work it out.'

'Will we?' Worried blue eyes so like his own stared up at him.

'It'll take more than a weekend, but we'll get there.' He raised a tentative arm and Hope settled against him, her arm coming around to circle his waist. They stood like that for a long moment and Ben could only wonder at how comfortable it felt to be with her.

This is my sister.

He'd never given much thought to the nature vs nurture arguments but there was no denying the sense of connection. The possessiveness he'd experienced came roaring to life and in that moment he thought he might do anything for her. Needing a distraction from the intensity of these strange feelings, Ben turned his attention back to the stable block. 'Are all the units occupied?'

Hope straightened up and Ben let her go, thinking a bit of

distance wouldn't be a bad thing for either of them. This all had to be as hard for her as it was for him – although she was doing a better job of hiding it. 'There are three empty units at the moment. I've got interest from a florist who is struggling with a recent rent increase on her shop and I think she'd make a really good fit. As for the others?' Hope shrugged. 'There's a Christmas shop in Lechlade and I'd really love it if they would open a temporary outlet in the run-up to the holidays. I've reached out to them, but they haven't committed to anything yet.'

Ben nodded. 'That would definitely be a draw.' He turned in a slow circle, taking in the whole of the stable yard area. 'You'd even have room over there to set up a little Christmas market.' He pointed towards an empty paddock behind the café that didn't seem to be used for anything.

Hope grinned. 'You must be a mind reader because that's exactly what we've got planned. We're trying to ramp things up this year, recover some lost revenue from over the summer.'

She didn't elaborate, and though curious, Ben didn't feel like it was his place to enquire further. 'Christmas markets have been growing more popular over the years; I'm sure it'll pull in the visitors.'

She nodded. 'I hope so, and fingers crossed it'll give our traders a boost too. We've got plans to create a Christmas light trail through the woods as well. We're trialling a similar thing over Halloween – though hopefully with more frights than fairy lights.'

'I got you extra marshmallows,' Cam called out from behind them and they both turned to find him brandishing a couple of takeaway cups. He dished out their drinks, then shot an apologetic smile towards Ben before saying, 'Umm, Amelia said you don't need to worry about meeting her later. She's happy to grab the keys to the cottage and have a look around for herself.'

Cottage? Ben's ears perked up at that. Was Amelia thinking of moving onto the estate for some reason? She hadn't mentioned anything on their short drive about her reason for visiting today – not that he had any right to know her business – but still it was interesting enough to file away with the other little puzzle pieces he was collecting about her.

Hope clapped her free hand to her forehead. 'Oh bloody hell! I was going to collect them from the safe in Ziggy's office and then I completely forgot.'

'I guess that's probably my fault for calling out of the blue and gatecrashing this weekend,' Ben said, feeling a bit awkward about the way he'd jumped on Hope's invitation at such short notice. 'I didn't mean to mess up your plans.'

'Oh, shut up,' Hope chastised him, the teasing tone taking any sting out of her words. 'As if I wasn't thrilled to drop everything and see you!' Her smile warmed him as much as their earlier brief hug. *Steady now*, he warned himself. It wasn't only himself he needed to protect; Hope was so open and eager for things to work out. He needed to be a bit more cautious about the way he approached things this weekend, not just plunge in headfirst. He hadn't even seen their mother yet. If he couldn't find a way to forgive her for abandoning him, then it would be game over.

'I can show Amelia around,' Cam offered. 'If she has any questions, you can go over it with her later.'

When he saw Hope considering it, Ben seized the opportunity to give them both breathing space. 'Hey, surely it would be easier if Cam showed *me* around a bit and then you can do whatever you need to do with Amelia and catch up with us later.' He turned to Cam, keeping his voice casual, trying not to sound like he was eager to get away from Hope for a bit. 'If you don't mind, that is?'

'Fine with me.'

Ben sighed in silent relief when Hope agreed, though he didn't miss the sharp look she shot his way. He pretended not to notice.

Some distance from her would give him a chance to get his head sorted out. If he was subtle about it, he might be able to glean more info from Cam about the rest of the family while he was at it and really see what he might be letting himself in for before he rushed into a commitment he wouldn't be able to easily untangle himself from.

And, of course, there was still the question of his mum. What *was* he going to say to her?

9

When the café door opened a few minutes later, Amelia was surprised to see Hope rather than Cam walking in. Abandoning her half-drunk tea, she crossed the room and gave her friend a quick hug. 'What are you doing? I thought Cam was going to make it clear that I was happy to check out the cottage on my own?' The last thing she wanted was to steal precious time away from Hope and Ben.

'It's fine, really. He's going to show Ben around and I'll catch up with them afterwards. You're bound to have questions so it's just easier this way.' Her eyes darted to one side and Amelia got the impression she wasn't being completely truthful with her.

'Is everything okay?'

'What? Oh yes, everything's great. I just need to call in at the farmhouse and grab the keys from Ziggy's office because I completely forgot this morning. I swear I'd forget my head if it wasn't screwed on these days!' The words tumbled out on top of one another.

It was unlike Hope to be this jittery, and Amelia tugged her down onto the nearest chair and dragged another up close to it.

'What is it? What's wrong?' The café was empty apart from Sandra, who was behind the counter with her back to them. Still, Amelia kept her voice as low as possible. 'Did something happen with Ben?'

Hope opened her mouth as though to issue another volley of protest and then snapped it shut. Her shoulders slumped and her slightly manic smile collapsed into a worried frown. 'I can't do it!'

'Can't do what? Can't spend time with Ben? But I thought you wanted him here?'

Hope's next words were an anguished whisper. 'I do, I do, but I'm worried about coming on too strong! I can't afford to let myself get carried away like that – not when so much is still up in the air. What if he spends the weekend getting to know us and then decides he doesn't want anything to do with us after all? I'll have exposed not just myself, but all the rest of the family to untold heartache. What was I thinking of, inviting him to come here without properly considering the consequences? And what about Mum? What if he loses it and shouts at her or something?' Tears welled in her eyes. 'I know he has every right to be angry with her, *I'm* angry with her, but you didn't see her that day when she told me about him. Her heart was breaking, Amelia; I think it's been breaking since the day she left him behind.'

'Oh, sweetheart, come here.' Amelia put her arms around Hope's shaking shoulders. 'Why would he have agreed to come if he only wanted to hurt you?' She hadn't spent a lot of time with him, but there'd been nothing about Ben's manner to suggest he was capable of inflicting that kind of deliberate cruelty. 'He was a bit stressed when I met him earlier, but he was more worried about getting caught up in local gossip. He seemed like he genuinely wants to be here. He certainly must've left home at the crack of dawn to get here as early as he did.'

'Do... do you think so?' There was a wobble in Hope's voice, but she seemed a little calmer.

Amelia fumbled in her pocket with one hand and fished out a clean tissue before easing back so she could look at Hope. 'Here, now, dry your eyes and take a deep breath.' The tip of Hope's nose was red and there were tear stains on her cheeks, but if she could get herself back under control, she could put the redness down to the cold bite in the morning air. When Hope had done as she told her, Amelia took both her hands in hers. 'It's a lot to deal with. You need to stop worrying about Ben and your mum and everyone else and think about how all this is affecting you as well.'

'I didn't expect to feel this way,' Hope admitted. 'Not so quickly, but the moment he hugged me it was like this instant connection. I found myself wanting to touch him, to keep checking he was really there. I think I might have freaked him out because as soon as Cam reminded me about you needing your key, Ben was practically pushing me away, saying he was happy for Cam to show him around.' Hope glanced over her shoulder towards the door. 'I think I've blown it already.'

Amelia couldn't help a slightly exasperated laugh. 'Hope Travers, will you listen to yourself?' When her friend turned back to face her, Amelia put her hands on each of Hope's shoulders and gave her the gentlest of shakes. 'You need to stop panicking and start using that very sensible, very rational brain of yours. Everything is going to be fine. Ben is probably as worried as you are about messing things up, so you are both going to take a few missteps along the way. Now, let's deal with the most important thing first. Did you ask him about meeting your mum?'

Hope nodded. 'He said he doesn't know how he feels about her.'

'Which is completely understandable,' Amelia said. 'And it'll probably be really difficult for both of them but I think you're going to have to let them sort that one out themselves.'

Hope glanced over her shoulder once more. 'You're right, I know you're right, it's just...'

'You want to fix everything.' When Hope opened her mouth to protest, Amelia gave her a quick hug. 'That wasn't a criticism!' She sat back and let Hope see the sincerity in her eyes. 'You have the biggest heart of anyone I know and that's a good thing, but not everyone or everything is your responsibility. Not your mum, not Ben, not me.' She added herself to the list almost as an afterthought, but it was true. Hope would take on all her burdens if Amelia let her – she was very much like Rhys in that regard. If Amelia didn't stand her ground, there was a risk they could ruin their friendship in the same way Rhys had stifled her love for him with his overprotectiveness.

'So I shouldn't have offered you the cottage, then?' There was a hint of the old Hope in the slightly teasing way she said it, and Amelia was relieved that the worst of her panic seemed to be over.

'Ha! Well, I'll let you know about that after I've seen it. Come on, let's go and then you can get back to what's really important.'

As they stood up, Hope grabbed Amelia's hand and gave it a squeeze. 'You're important. To me, to all of us. I can't lose you again; I won't.'

Amelia felt a catch in the back of her throat, knowing how lucky she was to have Hope in her corner. 'I'm not going anywhere, I swear. But you have to promise to let me work things out for myself.'

Hope looked like she was going to protest, but then nodded instead. 'I'll do my best not to overstep the mark. You must tell me if I do.'

'That's all I ask.' They both rose and Amelia put her arms

around Hope. 'You are my best friend in all the world, and I don't want you to ever think that I don't appreciate you.'

Hope pulled back and this time her smile reached all the way to her eyes. 'But back off, huh?'

Amelia laughed and held up her thumb and forefinger just a couple of millimetres apart. 'Maybe just a teeny-tiny bit.'

When they got outside there was no sign of Cam and Ben, and when Amelia checked, Ben's car was missing from the car park. 'Looks like the coast is clear,' she said to Hope with a grin. 'No chance of you rugby-tackling Ben by the ankles and begging him to move here permanently.'

Looking faintly embarrassed, Hope returned her smile. 'I did rather over-react, didn't I?'

'Not at all,' Amelia rushed to assure her. 'It's going to be a topsy-turvy few days – few months more likely, but you'll get there.'

'Ben said that too.'

'Well, then. There's hope for him yet.' They both laughed and Amelia felt the last bit of tension between them melt away. She'd all but made up her mind to take the cottage – and not only because she was fast running out of options. Hope needed her right now, as much if not more than Amelia needed her friend. Things would be tough for a while as they all adjusted to the reality of Ben being around – for as long as that turned out to be. Amelia crossed her fingers behind her back and sent up a silent prayer for good measure that he would stick it out. While they were dealing with that, Amelia could be a force for good, and steady the ship wherever and however they needed it. It would be better than worrying about the mess of her own life, that was for damn sure.

It was only a short drive to the farmhouse and Amelia stayed in Hope's Range Rover while her friend dashed inside to find the keys. The air was still cool, but Amelia pressed the button to let down her window anyway, enjoying the crisp edge that carried the promise of autumn with it. These in-between days were her favourite, before the overnight temperatures really began to drop, bringing misty mornings and eventually freezing fog as they moved into the heart of the winter. The estate and village lay in a natural valley so those damp mornings could last all day, leaving Amelia feeling as dull and dreary as the heavy skies.

When the back door opened again, it was Rhys who came out, dressed in a pair of blue overalls and boots. His sheepdog, Samson, was at his heels and the dog barked in recognition and ran over to rest his forepaws on the edge of the open window, a big doggy grin on his face. 'Hello, gorgeous boy,' Amelia said, giving him a big scratch behind the ear. She'd missed the easy affection of Rhys's dogs almost as much as she'd missed having him around.

'Do I get one of those?' Rhys asked as he leaned forwards beside Samson and grinned at her.

Playing along, Amelia reached up and ruffled his short hair. 'Good boy.'

'Get off, you nutter.' Rhys laughed as he pulled his head out of reach. 'You're going to check out the cottage, hey? Does that mean you're going to take Hope up on her offer to move up here?'

Amelia nodded. 'I think so.'

'Good.' Rhys said it like it had never been in any doubt, which was just typical of him. 'How's your mum? I've accelerated the timetable for the few repairs I need to do on the cottage and the decorator is booked in for Tuesday. I've told him white walls all the way through, because I know you'll want to put your own touches to the place, plus it'll make the whole job that bit quicker. You could move in next weekend if you don't mind the smell of paint. I might not get all the maintenance done in that time but they're only odd jobs so I can sort them over the next few weeks while you settle in.'

The concern in his tone was enough to dispel her momentary irritation at him. 'Hope told you about Eric trying to kick us out, I take it?'

'Yeah. She wanted my advice on how long it would take to get the cottage up to scratch in case you needed it.'

Amelia sighed. 'I wish she hadn't.'

Rhys frowned, all trace of his earlier humour gone. 'I'm not going to go around there and lump him one – even if he deserves it, the greedy bastard. You made it very clear to me that I was to mind my own business when it comes to you.'

Oh God, she'd really made a complete hash of everything. She thought they'd reached an understanding when he'd given her a lift to work the other day, but she could see now just how deeply she'd hurt him when she'd cut him off. 'I didn't mean it like that, I'm sorry. I'll keep saying that for however long it takes you to believe me.' Samson whined as though sensing her distress and she reached out to soothe him, soothing herself with the slow rhythmic stroking of her hand over his thick, wiry fur. 'I just don't want Ziggy finding out and trying to pay off even more of our debts, and you know he will the moment he finds out the real reason Hope offered me the cottage.'

'He's only trying to help.' *Just like we all are.* Rhys let the unspoken words hang in the air between them.

Amelia sighed, wishing she'd never said anything. 'I know, but this is a point of principle. I'm going to tell Eric to go and whistle. He was so insistent that the rental agreement is with Keith alone, thus giving him the right to terminate it, that he can chase him for the rent arrears; he'll not get a bloody penny more out of me!'

Rhys laughed, his expression brightening. 'Good for you! That's a bit more like the old Amelia I remember.' He leaned back down and lowered his voice. 'I won't say anything to Ziggy. I meant what I said when I promised not to interfere in your life any more.'

Amelia rested her hand on top of his. 'I'd really like to get my life to a point where no one needs to interfere in it.' A bit of peace and quiet, that's what she really wanted. She shook the yearning away. There was no chance of that any time in the near future so no point in pining for it.

'I have every faith in you.' He ducked back out and hooked his fingers gently through Samson's collar to tug him down from the window. 'Oh, looks like Ziggy's coming to have a word with you.' He made a quick motion over his lips like he was buttoning them up.

Amelia glanced over to see he was right, and a very concerned-looking Ziggy was following Hope towards them. 'Just what I need,' she mumbled under her breath.

Rhys stepped back, raising his voice a bit higher than normal. 'Hope has a list of the repairs I've noted down for the cottage; if you spot anything else while you're looking around, let me know and I'll get them sorted for you, okay?'

'Okay, thanks.' Amelia turned back in time to see Hope shoot her a slightly apologetic smile as she crossed in front of the car.

As she climbed in, Ziggy stopped next to Amelia's open window. 'I just wanted to check in with you and see how things are,' he said.

'Everything's fine,' Amelia replied, adding a quick smile to hide her impatience.

'I think it's a good idea, you know, for you and your mum to move onto the estate.' She knew they all meant well, but sometimes it was as if she was a gormless sheep, and if it wasn't one member of the Travers family, it was another behaving like Samson and trying to herd her in whatever direction they wanted.

'Well, nothing's been decided for definite,' she said in a tart voice, even though she knew she'd already pretty much decided.

'Perhaps we can have a chat about the rent after I've had a look because the figure Hope quoted me seems a bit low.'

Ziggy waved that off. 'The rents are fixed across all the cottages and we review them every three years. The last review was just before the start of the financial year so there's nothing to discuss.'

Amelia glanced over at Hope. 'I told you I wasn't doing you any favours,' her friend said, before she leaned across to speak to her uncle. 'We should probably get going.'

Ziggy nodded but he didn't move. 'How's your mum doing?'

There was such a deep concern in his expression that Amelia forgot her momentary exasperation with him. 'Not so great.'

Ziggy stared at her for a long, silent moment. 'Tell her she knows where I am.'

Amelia frowned as she watched him tuck his hands in his pockets and walk away. 'That was weird.'

Hope paused in the act of turning on the engine. 'What was weird?'

'That, just then, what he said about telling Mum she knows where he is.'

'Oh, that's just Ziggy being Ziggy.' She laughed. 'He's worse than me when it comes to trying to fix everything.' Hope started the car, did a quick three-point turn and started back towards the gate.

Amelia glanced over her shoulder to find Ziggy had stopped at the back door and was watching them. 'Yeah, I suppose you're right.'

10

'What do you think? Pretty great, huh?' Cameron asked Ben as he came back downstairs after checking out the first floor of the lodge that was to be his home for the weekend.

Tucked away in the woods and skilfully masked by some clever planting and discreet signage, the lodge wasn't anything like he'd been picturing when Hope had used the word. He'd assumed it would be a wooden chalet, something a step up from the mobile homes that were popular on campsites up and down the country. He paused at the bottom of the steps and took another look around at what looked like handmade furniture and the top-of-the-range appliances in the kitchen. This was on another level completely. 'It's fantastic.'

'Much nicer than my poky little flat near the university. Now you know why I'm happy to spend as much time as possible down here.' He grinned. 'Well, that's not the only reason, but you know what I mean.'

Ben couldn't help but return his smile. 'I know what you mean.' It was clear that Cam was completely gone for Hope and he was pleased she seemed to have found someone to share her life with. At least one of them had had some success on the romantic front.

Not that Ben had put much effort into it, if he was honest with himself. Oh, he'd had plenty of girlfriends over the years but the moment anything looked like it had the potential to turn serious, Ben had cooled things. It didn't take a psychologist to figure out his natural aversion towards relationships. Maybe if he could work things out with his mum, he'd be in a better headspace.

As he moved towards the kitchen, Cam hurried past him and opened the fridge. 'We've stocked you up, so there's no pressure to eat with the us or the rest of the family. I mean, I'm sure Rowena will be dying to feed you up, but that's just the way she is so don't read too much into it if she invites you to dinner.'

'A bit of a nurturer, is she?'

Cam laughed. 'She's a proper earth mother type. All kaftans and scarves and hugs and warmth. She's amazing.' His smile slipped. 'Not that Stevie isn't,' he said hurriedly. 'She's brilliant, too, just a bit quieter about things.' Cam winced. 'I should probably shut up now, shouldn't I?'

Feeling sorry for the poor guy, Ben eased the fridge door from his hand and pushed it closed. 'Please don't. I want to know what you think about everyone. It's hard to ask stuff of Hope because of course she's going to be biased about them, but you're a bit more of a neutral observer.'

'If you think I'm going to talk behind Hope's back, then I'm afraid you're going to be disappointed.' It was the first flair of anything close to anger Ben had seen from the other man and he made a note not to let his apparently easy-going manner fool him. Cameron wasn't a pushover.

Ben held up his hands. 'That's not what I meant. I just wanted to know your opinions because you're new to the family too, that's all.'

Cam leaned back against the opposite counter and folded his arms. 'I'm sorry, I shouldn't have jumped on you like that. You have to understand that Hope is my priority in all of this.'

'I wouldn't want it any other way. I'm just trying to get a bit of insight on the family dynamics, know what to look out for so I don't take something the wrong way. I'm walking on eggshells here. The last thing I want is to screw it up, or hurt someone unnecessarily. Least of all Hope.'

Cam nodded, looking somewhat mollified. 'They're a lot when you first meet them. Even with Barnie for back-up, I was kind of overwhelmed.'

'Barnie?'

'He's my best mate. We work together at the university and he was part of the team who came and helped out with the dig over the summer.'

Ben wanted to know more about the work Cameron was doing on the estate, but he also didn't want to get distracted. 'Overwhelmed in what way?'

The smile wreathing Cam's face was so full of affection that Ben felt something ease inside him. 'They just kind of suck you into their little world. The moment you sit down at the table, it's like you're one of them. I won't deny I was intimidated as hell to meet them. Worried I'd use the wrong fork, or drink out of the wrong glass or whatever, but they're not like that at all. My mum's a school dinner lady and my dad works as a security guard. Not that there's anything wrong with that,' Cam added quickly. 'I love my parents and they've worked bloody hard to give me chances they never had, but there's no pretending that Hope and I grew up in very different environments.'

'You expected them to be snobs?' Ben had wondered the same thing. His father had done very well for himself, but there wasn't anything close to blue blood in the veins of that side of his family.

Cam nodded. 'Maybe a bit, but they were just normal. Well, better than normal – they treated me as one of the family from the start. Even before Hope and I realised there was anything between us, so it's not even because of her. They're just really nice, really decent people. You ask anyone who works on the estate, and they'll all tell you the same thing. I can't think of a single person who doesn't appreciate the Travers family.' A frown marred his brow. 'Well, almost no one.'

Ben perked up at that juicy little titbit. 'That sounds like there's a story there.'

Cam straightened up. 'Not mine to tell. If you decide to stick around then I'm sure you'll find out soon enough. Come on, you wanted me to show you the walking routes.'

Ben had no choice other than to follow Cameron as he strode outside and down the back steps of the lodge, whistling to the dogs, who'd been lounging on the wide deck outside. With the brisk pace, they were away from the pair of lodges and into the woods before Ben was able to get abreast of him. 'If there's something bad I should know about, then I'd like you to be honest with me.'

Cam pulled up short. 'I'm sorry, I should have kept my mouth shut. It's not anything bad that the family have done, quite the opposite. Has Hope mentioned the problems they had over the summer?'

'She made an off-hand comment about trying to recoup some lost revenue, but I didn't like to pry and she didn't volunteer any other details.'

'I probably shouldn't say...' Cam ruffled an agitated hand through his hair. 'Sod it, you'll find out sooner or later. There were several acts of sabotage on the estate over the summer caused by a disgruntled employee that Rhys had had to sack for drinking on the job.'

'That sounds rough on everyone.' Ben wasn't sure why it was such a big deal, though. 'What is it that you're not telling me?'

Cam kicked at a stone lying on the path in front of him. 'It was Amelia's father. He's currently on remand awaiting trial for theft, arson and who the hell knows what else.'

'Bloody hell.' Whatever Ben had been expecting, it wasn't that. He thought about how spiky she'd been in the car with him earlier when he'd said he was worried about being the subject of gossip. 'That's got to be tough on her in a small community like this.'

'You're not kidding. Look, I don't want you telling Hope I've told you about this – and for God's sake don't let Amelia know because she'll never forgive me.'

Cam looked so concerned, Ben reached out and placed a hand on his shoulder. 'I won't say anything, I promise. I'm glad you've told me, though, because it means I won't accidentally say something stupid or hurtful around her.'

Cameron shot him a relieved glance. 'Cheers. I feel so bloody bad for her and I know Hope's been beside herself with worry about everything.'

'Is that why Hope's trying to get Amelia to come and live here? To show the community that she still trusts her?'

'I don't know. I mean I'm sure that's part of it, but that's just what the Travers do. They see a problem and they try and make things better. That's what I meant when I told you they're good people. Yes, they've got a title and all the trappings that go with it, but they take their responsibility for the estate and the people who live here seriously.'

'Still, it can't be easy for Amelia.' What kind of courage did it take to front up to not only the people who someone close to you had wronged, but an entire community who probably knew the ins and outs of everyone's lives? He hadn't lived at home for years, but he still knew more than he ever cared to about his father's friends and neighbours, and that was in a place that was probably three or four times the size of Stourton-in-the-Vale. He bet you couldn't blink here without someone knowing about it. It was one of the things he'd been most worried about when he'd agreed to come and visit.

Cam shrugged. 'Well, you'd have to ask her about that.' His eyes widened. 'No, don't breathe a word to her or Hope will have my guts.'

'I won't say anything, I promise.' Not unless Amelia gave him an opening, that is, and then all bets were off because there was more to this story than Cam was saying, he was sure of it.

Once Cam had shown him how the route markers worked for the different woodland trails, they headed back towards where they'd left Ben's car in a large, mostly empty car park that was used in high season for the estate's campsite. With the puppies safely ensconced once more in the hatchback's boot, Ben followed Cam's instructions and they began a leisurely tour of the estate. They paused next to a large fenced-off area by the river and Ben listened with interest as Cam gave him a brief rundown of what his archaeological investigations had turned up so far. It sounded very confusing, like an enormous jigsaw puzzle, only worse as there was no picture or plan to at least guide them on what to expect.

'Sounds like you still have a long way to go.'

Cam nodded. 'We've barely scratched the surface.' He laughed. 'Sorry, that's a terrible pun, but you get what I mean.'

'So, what's next?' Ben asked as he looked over the site. The compound next door was locked up tight and the field looked undisturbed apart from a few patches of brown in amongst the fading grass and the odd yellow flag flapping on short stakes. 'Will you be digging any more this year?'

'Depends on the weather. I've got a few of the kids who helped out over the summer who are keen to come down again for the weekend, so we might do a bit of survey work on what the family call the old chapel.' He pointed towards a large oak tree near the far end of the site and Ben was able to pick out a jumble of stones he'd not spotted earlier. 'Other than that,' Cam continued, 'it'll be doing what we can in the archives and scouring through county and national records for information. People think archaeology is all digging up priceless artefacts, but it's mostly grubbing around in the mud trying to make sense of random bits of stone or trying to fathom out someone's terrible handwriting on a blurry scan of an old microfiche of a crappy photocopy.' Which sounded like a nightmare to Ben, but Cam was grinning like he was talking about the best thing in the world.

He had that same natural enthusiasm Hope did when she talked about the estate, which Ben supposed was what happened when you were doing a job you loved. He thought again about the prospect of returning to the daily hassle of his Tube journey, the same overpriced sandwiches and takeaway coffees from Pret or Costa, checking the clock in the corner of his computer as he willed away the hours until home time. He found himself thinking about the workshops in the stable yard, about the giant metal still with all the pipes and dials on it he'd glimpsed through the window of the gin distillery, of the wistful way Amelia had talked about passing up a scholarship to art school. He thought too about sitting in the kitchen last night and how good it felt to be shaping clay once more, about what it would be like to have a proper space of his own where he could spend his days doing the one thing he'd always loved.

Once he sold his father's house, he'd have enough money to set himself up anywhere he liked – if he had the courage to stop dreaming about it and actually take the plunge. He was only thirty. That wasn't too late to start all over again, was it?

11

'Here we are,' Hope said as she pulled up in front of a neat row of Cotswold stone cottages and they climbed out. There were ten cottages in total, split into two terraces of five with a gravel parking area on the opposite side of the road that looked like a modern afterthought. A neat path ran from the road to the front door of each cottage, but there were no dividers between the properties and Amelia got the impression the front garden areas were treated as a communal space. The grass was all cut to the same length and a couple of benches sat beneath the splayed branches of a horse chestnut tree covered in fat, green conkers. What looked like a table and chair set from the bulky shapes beneath a dark plastic cover stood roughly in the centre of the green space in front of the furthest terrace.

The front doors were all a glossy black, the window frames white and the tiled roofs mottled with lichen, but as uniform as they looked, each cottage said something about the personality of the occupant. A set of delicate windchimes hung from the porch of one; a metal boot-scraper sat beside the door of another. An array of plant pots nestled along the windowsills of a third, packed full of colourful pansies in shades of red, yellow and orange. Some windows had nets obscuring the glass, the occupants guarding their privacy even in this quiet corner. 'It's this one,' Hope said, as she led her up the path of the cottage with the pretty pansy display. 'I think I told you Mrs Knowles had left her pots behind because it was too much hassle to cart them all the way to her sister's.'

'They're beautiful.' Amelia didn't have green fingers, but she could surely muster up enough skill to do her bit. She glanced towards the cottage on the left with the big boot scraper outside. A regimented row of miniature conifers marched beneath the windows, their tips each reaching the bottom edge of the windowsill. 'Didn't you say Denny lives there?' She recalled Hope mentioning his offer to keep the pots watered the previous evening.

'That's right,' Hope said, pausing with the key in the lock. 'And Carrie-Ann is on the other side.' Which made sense as she was the silversmith with a workshop at the stable yard and that was the one with the windchimes. Amelia had seen similar ones on display in her workshop. 'I should warn you that Mrs Knowles didn't just like floral things outside,' Hope added with a grin as she pushed open the front door.

'You weren't kidding!' Amelia laughed as they stepped inside the narrow hallway and were greeted with a riot of huge cabbage roses. 'Did she wallpaper everywhere?'

Hope nodded. 'The decorator is coming in to sort that out.'

Amelia smiled. 'I saw Rhys when I was waiting for you to grab the keys and he said as much. He said the plan was to take every-thing back to plain white walls.' She raised a hand to trace the outline of one of the roses on the wall. It seemed a shame as the paper was obviously good quality, but it wasn't really to her taste.

'It'll be a fresh start for you.' Hope put an arm around her shoulders, which wasn't easy in the narrow space, and gave her a squeeze. 'A blank canvas for you to fill in. Come on, I'll show you around.'

The door to the left led straight into the lounge, which was empty apart from a stone fireplace. 'You shouldn't need the fire as we installed central heating in all the cottages a few years ago, but we wanted to keep all the original architectural features.'

It was a bit smaller than their current place, although the jungle-print paper covered in tropical birds might have had something to do with it feeling a bit snug. Yes, white walls were definitely the way to go. Amelia couldn't help but smile as she thought of staid, strait-laced Mrs Knowles being a secret lover of bright and beautiful things. It just went to show you never knew what was beneath the surface veneer people showed to the outside world.

Amelia wasn't sure how much of their current furniture they'd be able to fit in. If she could afford it, she'd junk the lot and start again, leave everything behind and all the bad memories with it. Which was neither practical, nor realistic given her budget or the entire lack of one. She'd have to look into hiring a van, not just to move the things they were keeping, but to get rid of everything else. One thing that would be going to the dump was her father's armchair, along with the rest of his stuff. She didn't want a single thing of his crossing the threshold. Amelia sighed. It was something she'd avoided discussing with her mum so far, but they didn't have time to put the hard conversations off any longer.

'The kitchen's through here. It's compact, but there's also a little utility attached so you won't have to worry about squeezing a washing machine in.'

Amelia shrugged off her worries and gave Hope a smile. 'You should've been an estate agent.'

Hope laughed. 'I just want you to like it, that's all.'

'I love it already. I'll take it.' Just saying the words out loud was enough to lift an unbearable weight from her shoulders.

That stopped her friend in her tracks. 'But you've hardly seen any of it! Wait until you've seen upstairs at least. And what about your mum?'

'She'll come with me or she'll have to find an alternative arrangement.' The words felt harsh as she said them, but it was the plain truth. They couldn't afford to stay where they were and her mum didn't look like she was going to take charge of things anytime soon, beyond muttering the odd protestation about Amelia treating her like a child. 'It's the right thing for me, and like you said last night, it's time I put my own needs first for a change.'

Hope rushed over and hugged her tight. 'Oh, I'm so glad! I can't tell you how worried we've all been about you.' She dropped her arms and stepped back just as quickly. 'I won't crowd you, and I won't interfere.'

Hope looked so afraid that she might change her mind that Amelia couldn't help but laugh as she held out a hand to her. 'You probably will, a little bit.'

Taking her hand, Hope held her other one up with her finger and thumb a fraction apart just the way Amelia had teased her earlier. 'Only a teeny-tiny bit. Come on, let me show you upstairs! I think you'll love the room at the back; it's smaller but the view more than makes up for it.'

'Okay, but then you have to promise me that you'll go and find Ben and spend the rest of the day with him. I can drop the keys off later on my walk home.'

'There's two sets on the ring so you can hang onto one. I'm sure your mum will want to see it, and you'll need to take some measurements and stuff.'

Amelia opened her bag and pulled out a measuring tape and a notebook. 'I'm going to do that after you've shown me around, if that's all right?'

Hope grinned. 'I should've known you'd be two steps ahead of me. Come on.'

Hope wasn't kidding about the view. Each of the cottages had a small back garden so there would be a private space to escape to if she wanted it. It was in shadow at the moment, but she could tell it would be a lovely sun trap in the evenings. Each garden had a rotary washing line, and bedding and clothing danced in the breeze from half a dozen of them, adding a splash of colour. The thick, dense canopy of the woods backed onto the gardens, the leaves beginning to turn, and Amelia knew there would always be something different to see as the seasons turned. In the far distance, Stourton Hall stood like a miniature model on the top of the hill, its honey-coloured walls glowing in a shaft of sunlight.

Yes, this was a view Amelia could get used to. This was a little spot she could make her own. Moving here would get her mum out of the village, safe behind the walls of the estate where no one could hassle them. Hope had promised to try and find Daisy some more hours so she would have something to occupy her time – and the money wouldn't go amiss. If they both put their minds to it and worked hard, they could climb out of this awful bloody hole Keith had stuck them both in.

And then... Well, she didn't have the energy to think about then; all she could do was focus on the here and now and the future would have to take care of itself. Her eyes strayed once more to the shaft of sunlight shining down on the Hall and something unfamiliar stirred inside her. She felt good, she realised, for the first time in a long time.

12

They were just about finished with their tour of the estate when Cam's mobile phone rang. It was Hope calling to say she'd finished with Amelia and wanting to know how they were getting on. 'She wants to know the best place to meet up with us,' Cam said.

Not able to get the wild idea of the stable workshops out of his head, Ben suggested the café. 'Although I have no idea how to get back there from here,' he added with a laugh.

'It's a bit of a rabbit warren until you get used to it, hang on.' Cam relayed the suggestion to Hope, who said she would drop the keys off with Ziggy and have a quick catch-up with him so would be at the café in about fifteen minutes, which gave Ben just enough time to do what he'd been putting off.

'Can we go via the hotel, or is that too far out of the way?' he asked Cam after he hung up.

The other man did well to hide his surprise as, though they'd seen the Hall from the distance at several points on their drive around, Ben hadn't mentioned it and Cam had clearly picked up on his wish to avoid it. 'We've got time. If you turn left at the next crossroads, we'll be back on the main road that leads from the entrance gate to the hotel.'

As soon as they reached the junction, Ben recognised the avenue of trees stretching back to the right and felt like he was finally getting his bearings. 'If we crossed straight over, that would take us back to the stable yard.'

'Yeah, but like I said, we've got time to pop down to the hotel if that's what you want.' Cam's voice was calm, his tone conversational as though it was no big deal. 'I can get out here and walk if you want to go on your own.'

Ben wasn't sure what he wanted, but something was tugging at him and he knew that the longer he avoided the inevitable, the harder it was going to be. 'If you don't mind?'

Cam smiled. 'Not at all. I need to get those two out of your boot before they chew their way out.' He shot a thumb over his shoulder to indicate the puppies. To be fair, they'd been very well-behaved and the car was old enough that Ben didn't care about the toothmarks in the plastic trim.

'I won't be long.'

Cam popped his belt and slid out of the car. 'Take your time,' he said before shutting the door and moving around to let the suddenly excited puppies out the back. Ben waited until the three were clear on the opposite side of the road and Cam had given him a quick wave goodbye before he sucked in a deep breath and turned left onto the main driveway.

The avenue of trees ended and the estate opened up before him like someone had unfurled a beautiful patchwork blanket of every shade of green and brown. In the centre of that blanket, the Hall rose tall and proud on a hill so perfectly balanced in the setting Ben wondered if it was a manmade contrivance.

The Hall was even more impressive up close. Ben steered around the fountain that served as a mini roundabout and parked at the foot of the wide staircase. He turned off the engine, but couldn't bring himself to get out. His eyes roamed every which way, taking in the blunt majesty of the thick square stone blocks, the elegant scrollwork along the balustrades and above the portico. The windows gave the building an open, airy feeling and he was curious as to the size of the rooms inside. There'd been some photos on the website, but he'd only flicked through them once and couldn't recall anything beyond a general impression of stylish period furniture and pastel shades on the walls. It seemed impossible to think that his ancestors had once lived here. Had classed this as their family home. His eyes strayed to the narrow windows tucked under the eaves and he wondered how many servants it had taken to keep a place like this running without the benefit of modern conveniences.

One side of the front door stood open in welcome to visitors and he was contemplating whether he could nip up and take a quick peek inside when a woman stepped out onto the top step. She raised a hand to shade her eyes from the morning sun as she stared down at him. Her hair was shorter than in the faded photo he had at home, but he would know her anywhere. Without thinking, without breathing, he shoved open his door and started up the stairs.

'Is there something I can help you wi...'

The question died on her lips as he drew to a halt a couple of steps below her and smiled. 'Hello, Mum.' It felt right to say it, because whatever else had happened, that's who she was.

'Ben? Oh my God, *Ben!*' They moved in unison, almost bumping into each other as they tried to take up space on the same step. Stevie gave an awkward laugh as they shuffled sideways and then her arms came around him and Ben was enveloped in a scent so elusive and yet so familiar it was like being caught up in a dream. She was crying now. Great racking sobs that soaked the front of his T-shirt in seconds and his hands were moving automatically over her back, soothing her in the way he'd imagined she must have done for him when he was a baby. He strained for those memories, but apart from the whisper of perfume there was a hollow, empty space. The pain of it made him flinch and Stevie was pulling away from him before he could stop her, her hands raised to wipe the tears from her eyes.

'I'm sorry, I should've asked before I hugged you. It's just been so long and there were times I never thought I'd get to see you again, especially after the letter.'

'It's all right, Mum.' Ben held out his hand to her and had to close his eyes briefly as she took it. 'I didn't write that letter. I mean, I never instructed the solicitor to write it. It was all Dad's doing and I knew nothing about it until last week.'

Stevie nodded. 'Hope told me, but even when she said you were coming here today, I didn't quite let myself believe it. I'm sorry, darling. I'm so sorry for everything.' Her free hand came up to cover her lips. 'I shouldn't call you that, should I? I shouldn't presume and I promise I'll try to give you as much space as you need.'

She would've pulled her hand away if Ben hadn't tightened his grip. 'It's okay,' he said again, then laughed. 'I mean it's not, not really, but I want it to be one day.'

Tears spilled down her cheeks once more. 'That's all I need to know, and I'll do whatever it takes to get us there. I'll answer whatever questions you have.'

Ben pulled a handkerchief out of his pocket and handed it to her. 'The only question I have for the moment is whether you'd like to come and have lunch with Hope and me over at the café?'

It took a few minutes before they were ready to leave. Stevie rushed back inside to sort out her make-up and arrange for some cover. Ben waited at the top of the steps, pacing the length of them as he tried to still his racing heart. Was he doing the right thing? He felt out of control again, just like he had with Hope earlier. He knew there were mountains to climb and yet he wanted to be over that, to move past everything and look ahead.

Only ahead.

He almost convinced himself that was what he was going to do. Almost made up his mind to decide he didn't care about all the old hurts and to let them go. He had control over his life; he could make a choice about whether or not he let the past overshadow his future.

Be the shark. Keep swimming or die.

It had been one of his father's favourite sayings whenever Ben had struggled with a test, or had a bad game on the rugby pitch. Be the shark or be a minnow and get swallowed up by one of the other predators in the ocean. And Ben had put a brave face on and given his father a high five and agreed that no, he didn't want to be a minnow, which had been true.

But he'd never been a shark, either.

Surely there had to be something between the two. Predator or prey couldn't be the only options in life. He was still turning the question over in his mind when Stevie reappeared, looking so flawless and composed Ben wasn't sure if she had a will of iron or just a very, very good concealer in her make-up bag. Maybe a bit of both.

'Ready?' He gestured for her to go ahead of him down the steps. With a nod, she adjusted the strap of her handbag on her shoulder then headed down towards his car.

They both did their best to try and ignore the slightly awkward silence as he drove them towards the stable yard. Asking her to lunch had seemed like the right thing to do. He needed to spend as much time as possible with both Stevie and Hope while he was here, because he wasn't sure when he'd be able to get back again. Even if he chose to explore what being part of life here on the estate was like, he still had loads to sort out at home and at work.

'It's here on the left,' Stevie said, breaking the silence as they approached the crossroads.

'Thanks.' The silence fell again. 'So, umm, you run the hotel, then?' he asked, groping for an easy topic to cover the rest of the short journey.

'Yes. With Rowena. You'll meet her later if you come over for dinner. She's Rhys's mother.'

'Hope sketched me a little family tree and left it in the stuff she gave me at Da— umm, at the funeral.'

'Don't feel like you can't mention him around me. Regardless of what happened between Benjamin and me, he will always be the man who raised you.' Stevie's hand touched his arm, reminiscent of the way Hope had done earlier, and he found himself wondering what other similarities there would be between them. Loads, probably. How many times had he caught himself mirroring things his father did?

He pulled into the car park at The Old Stable Yard, noting how much it had filled up since that morning. People wandered back and forth between the buildings and Ben could see a small queue had formed outside one of the workshops. Switching off the engine, he half-turned in his seat to face Stevie. 'I just don't want to get into all of that, not this weekend, anyway.'

She hesitated for a long moment before lifting a hand to softly cup his cheek. 'As long as you were happy, that's all I need to know.'

'I was.' At least he thought he had been for the most part, even with his father's tendency to be domineering. It was so hard to be sure of anything any more. The revelations since his father's death had totally knocked him off his axis.

'That's one good thing, at least.' Her hand dropped from his face and Stevie began to unbuckle her seat belt.

'Were you happy, too?' Ben found himself asking. 'I mean, after you left us and everything? Things were better for you?'

She glanced up at him, eyes shining with unshed tears. 'I tried my hardest to be. I had to, for Hope's sake as well as for my own sanity. I had to tell myself I'd done... not the right thing, perhaps, but the best thing under the circumstances. But I need you to know that there wasn't a day that went by when I didn't think about you, or that I didn't miss you.'

'I had a picture of you by my bedside. I've still got it, actually.' He didn't know why he'd mentioned it, only that he wanted her to know that he hadn't forgotten about her either. Remembering the clay rose sitting on the back seat, he retrieved it and handed to her.

Stevie traced the delicate petals with one finger. 'Did you make this?'

Feeling suddenly shy, Ben nodded. 'I couldn't sleep last night, and I found some of my old gear in the garage. It's just a hobby, but, well, I thought you might like it.' It couldn't make up for all the things they'd missed out on, but it was a start.

'It's beautiful. Thank you.' She looked like she might cry again and, honestly, Ben didn't think he'd be much behind her if she started. He reached for the handle and opened his door. 'Come on, let's not keep Hope waiting any longer.'

* * *

Lunch went really well, better than Ben might have expected given the heightened emotions still hanging over them all. Cam did a great job of filling in any awkward silences and had them all laughing over a text Barnie had sent him, entitled 'SOS'. He'd been dating one of the hotel spa staff since meeting her over the summer and it looked like things were starting to get serious between them. Meena's birthday was coming up and Barnie was having a flap over what to get her. 'I've never seen him like this about someone before,' Cam said after texting a list of helpful suggestions Hope and Stevie had come up with on the fly.

'He should commission Ben to make her something,' Stevie said, picking up the little clay rose. She'd been playing with it all through lunch, as though she couldn't leave it alone.

Ben's cheeks heated. 'Oh, come on now. Like I said, it's just a hobby. Last night was the first time in months I've touched a piece of clay. I'm really rusty.' He wanted to berate himself as soon as the words were out because it was the voice of his father speaking, the voice he'd let dominate him for far too long. 'I mean, it's always been a hobby until now, but I'm thinking that maybe it's time for a change in career.' Saying it out loud made him feel a bit dizzy, but if he was really going to do it then he needed to start owning it.

'A new career sounds exciting,' his mother said, with an encouraging smile. 'I'm sure you'll make a success of it if this is an example of your work.' No scoffing about pottery being a waste of time, no questions about how he would make ends meet. Just acceptance and support. Was that what it had been like for Hope all these years?

Jealousy roiled in his veins, taking him off guard with the strength and suddenness of it. Why did she get to be the one raised by the easy-going parent? Why had he been left behind to deal with his father's domineering ways? Why hadn't his mother done more to get custody or at least maintain some form of contact? His father had only been allowed to lie all these years about her being dead because she'd stayed away.

Something must've shown on his face because Stevie shot him a frown of concern. 'What is it?'

Ben shook his head as he tried to rein in the ugly wave inside. 'Nothing, it's just a lot of stuff to think about, you know?'

'I can only imagine how difficult things have been for you. If it hadn't been for Hope, I would've tried harder, but I couldn't risk your father finding out about her because I knew he'd move heaven and earth to take her away from me.' She reached across the table towards him, her fingers halting when Ben shifted his hand into his lap. Silence settled over the table and Ben knew it was his fault, but he couldn't trust himself to speak again in case some of that poisonous resentment spilled out. He knew Stevie was trying to make him understand the dilemma she'd been in, but all he could hear was that she'd chosen Hope over him.

'This doesn't look like the work of a hobbyist,' Hope said, picking up the rose from the table and twirling it slowly as though intent on examining it from every angle. 'This is really good. Do you decorate your pieces as well?'

Ben nodded, grateful for distraction. He knew he couldn't keep ignoring the conflicting feelings inside him, but now wasn't the time to address them. It was already clear that hugs and tears weren't going to be enough to cancel out the past, no matter how much he might wish that they could. Best to stick to lighter subjects for now. 'Yeah, I'm not bad with a paintbrush but pottery is my first love.'

'Would you make me something?' Hope asked. 'Not now, but when you have a bit more time?'

'If you really want me to, it would be my pleasure.' She was his little sister after all and he owed her a lifetime of missed birthday and Christmas presents.

Hope smiled as she handed the rose back to their mother. 'I really want you to.'

'And if you are taking commissions, Barnie needs all the Brownie points he can get,' Cam added with a grin.

'I'll think about it,' Ben said, not sure what else to say. Those idle daydreams he'd had earlier when walking around the stable yard were suddenly starting to feel very real. And quite scary.

Stevie made a big show of looking at her watch, the smile she gave him at odds with the crease between her brows. 'I really must be getting back. I left Rowena dealing with everything and she'll be starving, poor thing.'

Ben couldn't be sure if she really meant it, or if his earlier rejection had made her uncomfortable. He couldn't bring himself to apologise – he would be lying if he told her everything was fine – but he could accept what she was saying on face value and let them all escape this first meeting unscathed. 'I forgot when I invited you that Hope had mentioned you being short-staffed this weekend. Shall I go and grab her a sandwich for you to take back?'

His mother's stiff smile warmed to something more natural. 'That's very thoughtful of you. Maybe chicken or tuna salad, if they've got it?'

'Leave it with me.' There was a chicken salad sandwich in the pre-made display in the fridge, so Ben chose that and a bottle of sparkling water just in case. Reaching the front of the queue, he set them down. 'These and I'll pay the bill for our table as well, please.' It felt like the least he could do when he'd been the one to bring things to a halt so quickly.

The woman behind the counter gave him a curious glance. 'I've already put it on the estate account, but I can cross that out if you'd prefer.'

Ben nodded. 'My treat. Speaking of which...' He eyed the very tempting contents of the cake display. A little peace offering wouldn't go amiss, something to show his mother that he was trying his best. 'I'm going to rely on your insider knowledge and ask for two slices of whatever Stevie and Rowena's favourites are.'

The woman grinned at him. 'That would be the Victoria

sponge and a chocolate brownie. I'll put them in takeaway boxes, yes?'

'Thanks. Oh, and whatever you think Cam and Hope would like as well. Can you put those in a separate bag?'

By the time he'd paid for everything, the others were waiting for him by the exit. They stepped out into the fresh air to find the number of people had swelled even further as they made the most of the sunshine. All of the occupied workshops were open and Ben itched to have another look around. If he was really going to take the plunge, then it would be useful research to see how the different traders had set themselves up. He hadn't thought about the need for a retail space as well as a working studio, but it was definitely something to add to the mix. It would depend of course on how much money he had to spend, and where he decided to settle. He'd have more cash to play with if he gave up the London flat, but was he prepared to let that go? The wisest choice would probably be to keep it as a back-up in case he couldn't make a go of things.

Realising the others were watching him, Ben offered Stevie one of the bags he was holding. 'Rowena's lunch and a little treat in there for the two of you for later.'

She took the bag as though he was handing her the crown jewels. 'That's so lovely of you, thank you. Will you be coming over to the farmhouse later for supper? No pressure if you'd rather not,' she added hurriedly.

'I'll let Hope know later if that's all right. I've got a few things to think about.'

'Of course. This is all on your timetable, Ben. Please don't feel you have to pretend things are okay, if they're not. You have every right to be angry with me.'

'I'm trying not to be, but it isn't easy.'

Stevie nodded. 'I'm grateful you've given me this much of a

chance.' She pressed a finger to the corner of one eye as though trying to stop a tear, then stiffened her spine. 'Right. I must get back and relieve Rowena.'

'Will you be all right having a wander around here for a bit while I drop Mum off?' Hope asked. 'I'm headed that way as Cam needs to go back to the lodge and work this afternoon. I've got a couple of calls I need to make, but I shouldn't be too long.'

Ben was grateful once again at the easy way she smoothed the tension. 'I'll be fine on my own,' he assured her. 'I'll have a quick nosy around here, then I was thinking I might take advantage of the weather and go for a run this afternoon, do a bit more exploring if that's all right?'

'Whatever suits you is fine with me. Will you text me later and we can make plans for this evening? We can have a drink on the deck if you decide supper with everyone is too much to deal with.'

'I did warn Ben that you're a lot to handle when the whole clan gets together.' Cam gave him a grin as he put his arm around Hope's shoulders.

'We're not that bad!' Hope protested before turning to Ben with a laugh. 'Well, maybe we are a bit!'

'You're making it sound almost too tempting to refuse. Let me have a run and clear my head and I'll see how I feel after that.' He handed her the other bag he'd been holding. 'There's a little afternoon treat in there for you and Cam, by the way.'

'Oh, that's very sweet. You didn't have to!'

'I know. I wanted to.' When he leaned in to hug her this time, it already felt like something they'd done a thousand times.

He exchanged an awkward look with Stevie, wishing he felt the same natural ease with her that he did with Hope. 'No hug for me; I don't want to have to fix my make-up again.' Her smile said she could sense his conflict and wouldn't push him.

'Me neither,' Cam said. 'Just in case you were thinking about it.

Come on, Stevie.' He offered her his arm in a gallant gesture and Ben liked the way his mother leaned into Cam's shoulder as they walked away.

'Are you sure you'll be okay on your own?' Hope had her car keys out but hadn't made any move to follow the others.

'I'll be fine.' Perhaps if he repeated that often enough it would be true.

13

Cutting through the milling groups of visitors, Ben decided to bypass the silversmith's as she was working on something at a bench in the open doorway of her workshop and the crowd watching was already three or four deep. He opted instead for the leatherworker's next door. The rich smell of leather and polish settled over him as he stepped inside. It was larger than he'd been expecting with a shop-cum-display area in the front and a spacious work area behind. A large rack of tools hung above a work bench where a man was seated, bent over a saddle. An open door beside the bench suggested there was a further area, perhaps for storage. Ben took a few minutes to admire the belts, wallets and purses that made up the majority of the stock on display. There was a smaller section that seemed to be dedicated to items for animals from dog and cat collars to reins and all kinds of other bits and bobs of riding kit his limited knowledge didn't have names for.

'Anything I can help you with?' The man at the bench had looked up from the saddle and was regarding him with a friendly, open expression.

'Just being nosy, if that's all right? I'm here visiting some, um, friends for the weekend and it's my first time on the estate.'

'Help yourself.' The man gestured that Ben was welcome to look around and turned his attention back to the saddle. Ben continued to explore, his eyes drawn to the impressive tool kit on the wall. 'Live in the village, do they, your friends, I mean?' the man asked, his eyes still on his work.

'What? Oh, not exactly.' Ben gave an awkward laugh, wishing he'd not volunteered any information about himself. 'I'm visiting Hope and Cameron.' Which was enough of the truth that it didn't feel like he was being deceitful.

The man looked up with a smile. 'They're great, aren't they? I keep pestering Cam to let me have a go up at the dig site. It was too busy over the summer to justify shutting the shop for a day, but I'm fascinated to see what they do.' He set down the tool in his hand and offered it to Ben. 'I'm Jason, by the way.'

'Ben. And, yeah, I know what you mean. Cam showed me the site earlier and I have to admit I was a bit disappointed there wasn't more to see. He did say he's trying to organise a survey weekend in a few weeks, so he might have room for a volunteer or two.'

Jason grinned from ear to ear, his enthusiasm plain. 'That sounds great. I'll have to pin him down for a date. Hopefully it's not one of the event weekends coming up.' He pointed to a poster pinned on the wall advertising a pumpkin carving event as part of the Halloween weekend activities.

'Are you running that?'

Jason nodded. 'Yeah, it's something Carrie-Ann and I cooked up together. The village shop is getting us in a job lot of pumpkins and we're going to set up a fake patch in the field behind the café so the kids can go and choose their own pumpkin. If the weather's with us then we can set some tables up in the yard; if not then we'll use our workshops, plus Sandra's agreed we can use the café if there's enough people on the day.'

'Sounds like it should be a lot of fun.'

'It's going to be a good weekend. Hope's planning a couple of spooky walks through the woods as well. Carrie-Ann wants to go, but I've told her I'm only doing the kiddies trail because I'm a complete wuss.' He laughed, clearly not the least bit embarrassed to admit his fears.

Ben smiled, thinking how much he liked this man. 'I had a girlfriend once who was a complete horror movie junkie. She begged me to go with her to this Frightfest cinema weekend and I was foolish enough to agree.' Ben grimaced. She'd been a fantastic girl, but that weekend had proven to them both that their interests were not compatible.

Jason pulled a face. 'I couldn't even watch *Shaun of the Dead* without getting nightmares. I dated someone who was obsessed with those escape rooms. The first two or three were a laugh, but she had us driving up and down the country trying different ones.'

They shared a smile of mutual sympathy. 'So, can I have a look at what you're doing?' Ben asked, pointing to the saddle.

'I'm just about done, but sure.' Jason shifted his stool to the side so Ben had room to approach. 'The stitching on one of the stirrup leathers had come loose so I replaced them both. I've done my best to stain the leather to match the rest of the saddle, but it's impossible to recreate the individual patina each one gets through use.'

Ben could see what Jason meant, but only because he was standing right over the saddle. From even a few feet away, the repair work would be unnoticeable. 'It looks fantastic. And you stitched this yourself?'

Jason nodded. 'I've got a heavy-duty sewing machine in the back. I can show you, if you're really interested?'

'Sure, that would be great.'

Jason led the way through the rear door and Ben stopped in surprise at the size of the space they entered. 'Wow.' Rather than the poky little storage room he'd imagined, the area was at least half the size of the shop. To the left, a wooden staircase led to what must be a second storey.

'It's like the TARDIS,' Jason said. 'That leads to what was originally the old hayloft. I use it for the other part of my business. There's a big riding community around here,' he continued as they began to climb. 'Once word got around about me, I was inundated with customers who wanted a local service. One of the main requests I kept getting was about rug repairs and cleaning, which wasn't something I'd really thought about.'

As they reached the second floor, Ben was ushered into what could only be described as an industrial laundry. A pair of huge washing machines stood on one side, a couple of large laundry bags stuffed full of rugs sitting next to them. A matching pair of dryers sat on the other side next to a long bench with a stack of neatly folded clean rugs sitting on it. 'Quite the set-up you've got here.'

Jason laid a hand on top of one of the machines. 'I made some enquiries and leased a couple of machines to see whether it would work out, and honestly I couldn't have anticipated the response. Within a few months it was bringing in nearly half my revenue so I had a chat with Ziggy and he agreed an interest-free loan so I could buy my own equipment rather than keep shelling out on the rental costs. I'll have the last instalments paid off by the end of the year,' he concluded, shooting Ben a proud smile.

'That's fantastic. You get a lot of support from the Travers family, I take it?'

Jason nodded as he led the way back downstairs. 'They literally changed my life. I was a nightmare when I was kid. Too much energy, but no focus. I mucked around in school and started to get

into trouble. I got assigned a social worker who found me a place-
ment here on the estate. I was working for Zap at the farm every
weekend and during the holidays. I loved it because there was
always something different going on and I was out in the fresh air,
not cooped up in a classroom or hanging around on the streets
bored out of my head. That's how I got to know Rhys. He was only
a couple of years older than me, but he had all these plans about
how he was going to take over running the place within five years
so his old man could focus on the distillery. That was just a hobby
of Zap's at the time, but you could tell it was a proper passion of
his. I used to sit there and listen to the two of them talking about
their vision for the place and I was jealous because I wanted that
too. Not to run a farm or make gin, but I wanted *something* I could
get my teeth into.'

Ben could empathise with the man, because he knew what it
was to be bored and frustrated. If his father hadn't been there to
keep him on the right path – well, not the right path, but the path
that had been dictated to him – things could've gone differently for
him as well.

Jason's expression turned shamefaced. 'I got so frustrated with
Rhys boasting about this ideal future he had mapped out and we
ended up having a fight. I thought I was done for when I got called
in to speak to Zap and Ziggy. I assumed they were going to report
what had happened to my social worker, but instead they told me
about this bursary scheme that they run. They told me if I got my
head on straight and managed to finish school with pass grades
then they would fund an apprenticeship.'

Jason shook his head, his eyes slightly unfocused, and Ben
could tell he was picturing himself back in that room. 'All I had to
decide on was what I wanted to do. As if I had any idea about that!'
He laughed. 'They let me experiment over the next few months. I
had a go at shadowing Ziggy, but he was always stuck in his office

dealing with one thing or another. They put me in the hotel to see if maybe the hospitality industry was something I might want to get into, but I couldn't be doing with all the people around. The thing I liked most about the farm was being able to work on my own, apart from the animals, especially the horses. I say horses, but really they were a couple of lazy old ponies that belonged to Hope.

'She was a bit of a pony club fanatic back in her younger days,' Jason added, with a grin. 'But I think she grew out of it, so they were left to their own devices until I came along and started giving them a bit of attention. And then Roger came over one day to collect a pile of what I thought was broken tack waiting for someone to chuck it away. He brought it back a few days later, looking like new and I couldn't believe it. We got chatting and he invited me over to his livery yard, and, well, that was that.' Jason paused and looked at his watch. 'Bloody hell, look at the time. The client's coming to pick up that saddle in ten minutes so I'm going to have to get cracking.' He held out a hand for Ben to go ahead of him back into the shop area. 'Sorry for bending your ear like that!'

Ben held out his hand and they shook. 'Not at all, it was fascinating. Great meeting you, Jason, and thanks so much for your time. It was really informative.'

'Maybe we'll catch up again sometime?' Jason asked as he resumed his seat on the stool.

'Yeah. I'm hoping to make these visits a regular occurrence so maybe we can have a pint down the pub, or something?'

'That sounds like a very good idea. Hey, Ben, I forgot to ask – what is it that you do?'

Ben hesitated for a long moment before he gave Jason a shy smile. 'I'm a potter.'

14

Amelia's good mood lasted the rest of the morning as she explored the cottage inside and out, filling the pages of her notebook not only with measurements but little pencil sketches of anything that caught her eye. She'd taken loads of pictures on her phone as well, but photos never captured something like shaping it with a pencil did. She took her time on the walk back, letting her feet take her where they would as she cut through the woods behind the row of cottages. She knew she would eventually find her way onto one of the woodland walks and she'd be on familiar ground from there. And so she simply walked. The woods were wilder here, unlike the carefully curated walking trails. That wasn't to say they weren't maintained. She came across a handful of felled trees that had been cut and stacked in neat piles for later collection, and another that was leaning at a haphazard angle, the trunk marked with a splash of white paint to show it had been checked by someone.

After about half an hour of aimless wandering, Amelia came across a break in the trees and stepped onto a wide, grassy path. She spotted a discreet red marker sign with a little arrow pointing forwards and turned in that direction. It was the longest of the three mapped routes and she wasn't sure how far along the trail she was. Not that it mattered; she was happy to follow it and daydream about how the little cottage would look with gleaming white walls and her own things scattered around. She and her mum might not be able to change the furniture, but with what they would be saving on rent they could manage a trip to one of the big discount outlet shops and pick up a few throws and cushions, which would be enough to freshen things up.

Ten minutes later, she reached a large clearing with several different paths branching off from it and Amelia knew where she was. If she followed the green route to the right, it would bring her back to the car park used by the estate campsite and she would be able to cut across the parkland directly towards the main gate. She'd just turned in that direction when she heard her name being called. Startled, she turned to see Ben jogging towards her, dressed in black running shorts and red T-shirt that was dark with sweat across the chest. He caught her up and smiled as he bent over at the waist. His breath came out in gasps, the air cool enough to turn it to mist. The damp shirt clung to the contours of his back and she couldn't help but notice the way the ends of his hair turned curly when they were wet, or how muscular his legs were in those shorts. As if life wasn't complicated enough! Amelia forced herself to look away before he caught her staring. 'I thought you'd be with Hope.'

Ben straightened up. 'We had lunch with Mum and then Hope had some work stuff she needed to sort out. I'm catching up with her and Cam later for a drink.' He sounded cheerful enough but there was a tightness around his eyes that spoke of a hidden tension.

'How was it, meeting you mum again?' As soon as she said it, she worried he would think the question intrusive. 'I'm sorry, I shouldn't have asked you that.'

He gave her a lopsided smile. 'It's okay, I don't mind. My head's a bit all over the place if I'm honest. There's a bit of me that feels like I remember her, but I can't work out if that's wishful thinking or not.'

'You must've been very young when she left, so that's understandable. Even if you did remember her, it's going to take time.' She laughed. 'Listen to me talking like I'm any kind of an expert on healthy family dynamics!'

'I'm trying not to get ahead of myself, but it's hard.' He looked away then back at her. 'If I tell you something, will you promise not to talk to Hope about it?'

Amelia frowned. 'I don't like keeping secrets.'

He propped his hands on his hips and scuffed a foot through the handful of fallen leaves on the ground. In a few weeks, the ground would be blanketed in them as the trees prepared for their winter dormancy. 'I know it's not fair to ask, but there isn't anyone else I can talk to.'

He sounded so forlorn that she found herself taking a step closer. 'I'm listening.'

Ben swallowed. 'When we were having lunch earlier, I was overcome with jealousy that Mum basically chose her over me.' He stared down at where his trainer was digging at the ground. 'I didn't like it, didn't like that I was capable of feeling something so ugly, and yet I can't help myself.'

Amelia swallowed a sigh of relief, grateful it wasn't something awful that she would struggle to hide from Hope. 'That sounds like a perfectly natural reaction to me. I've been jealous of her myself a time or two when I thought she had it easy compared to my own situation. I think you need to give yourself permission to feel whatever emotions come up while you try and process what has to be an enormous change in your life.'

When he looked up at her, some of the tightness had eased from his face. 'It's the anger that's the worst. It catches me off guard and it's not something I'm used to dealing with.' He huffed out a slow breath, then managed a smile. 'I feel better just for admitting it, so thank you for that.'

'I don't feel like I really did anything, but you're welcome, I guess.'

He shook his shoulders like he was trying to shake off the last of the tension. 'Anyway, enough about me. How was your morning? Hope said you were pleased with the cottage. Is that where you've just come from?' He looked past her like he expected to see a building hiding in the trees behind them.

It was an abrupt shift in conversation, but she could tell he didn't want to talk about his situation any more, so she went with it. 'Yes. The estate cottages are on the other side of the woods, and I knew if I cut through I'd pick up one of the woodland trails and find my way back from there.'

He stretched his arms over his head, making the hem of his T-shirt ride up to display a couple of inches of very toned, very distracting muscle. Amelia tried not to stare, but goodness, he was making it hard for her not to notice how in shape he was. 'You're very fit.' The words were out before she could stop them and all Amelia could do was close her eyes and wish she was invisible. 'I can't believe I just said that. Carry on with your run and we can pretend we never met.' It was a struggle not to raise her hands to the heat she could feel rising on her cheeks. It didn't help her blushes when Ben started to laugh. 'Go away,' she wailed, which only made him laugh even harder.

'If I swear I never heard anything beyond you describing where the cottage is, will you open your eyes?'

Amelia cracked one lid open to find Ben grinning at her.

'You were telling me about the cottage?' he prompted, a hint of laughter still in his voice.

She opened her other eye, resigned to the fact that her powers of invisibility had let her down again. 'It's a bit smaller than what we have now, but it'll be fine for Mum and me.'

'It's just the two of you?'

There was something in the way he asked it, all hint of his earlier laughter gone, that made Amelia's hackles rise. 'Well, it didn't take long for the gossip to reach you, did it? I can't believe Hope told you!'

Ben held his hands up. 'She never said a word, I swear.'

Amelia narrowed her eyes at him. 'But someone's been talking out of turn.'

'Look, it was Cam, okay? He didn't mean to tell me; it just sort of came out when we were talking. He made an innocuous remark but Hope had mentioned in passing about losing some revenue over the summer and I kind of put the threads together and forced him to tell me. Would you have preferred if I carried on pretending that I didn't know?'

Amelia glared at him for a moment longer before she let go of her anger. 'No, that would've been even worse. I've had enough lies to last me a lifetime.' Besides, whatever his current misgivings, he was a part of the Travers family so was bound to find out sooner or later. She gave a resigned shrug. 'Now you know why I said earlier that *you* wouldn't have to worry about being the subject of gossip.'

She expected him to laugh, or at least give her credit for trying to lighten the mood once more, but his expression remained grave. 'Not around here, maybe, but I'll be going home to plenty of it. You're not the only one with a dodgy father.'

'I thought your dad died recently?'

Ben rested his hands back on his hips and blew out a long breath. 'He did. What you probably don't know is that he played the grieving widower for years and garnered a great deal of support and local sympathy for it. I can't imagine the neighbours are going to be too impressed when they find out he lied to them all this time.'

There was a lot of information in those few short sentences and Amelia struggled to process it. She knew Hope hadn't known about Ben until a few months ago, but she hadn't grasped that he'd been in the same boat. 'He told you Stevie was dead?' Her heart ached for him. What an awful thing to do to a child. 'Do you need to tell them? About your family, here, I mean? It's not like it's anyone else's business.'

He shrugged. 'You're not the only one who's sick and tired of all the lies. Our family solicitor colluded with Dad for years about it. He's been named as the executor of my father's will and to make matters worse we're practically next-door neighbours.'

Amelia covered her mouth with one hand. 'But that's awful!'

'No kidding. I'm trying to get rid of him but it'll be hard to do that without word spreading when everyone knows everyone, or at least that's how it feels sometimes.' He scuffed the ground with his foot. 'You might as well know the whole sorry tale now I've started. Dad persuaded the solicitor to write a letter, claiming to be acting on my behalf, telling Stevie I didn't want anything to do with her or any of the family. That's why they never told Hope about me. Stevie thought she was honouring my wishes all this time.' He shook his head. 'Pretty fucked up, right?'

It was almost impossible to believe what she was hearing. What kind of a monster would do that? *What kind of monster would set fire to a field next to a campsite full of families and kids?* 'Almost as effed up as having your father try to destroy your best friend's family and their livelihood.'

Ben's lips quirked in a lopsided smile. 'What a pair we are, eh?' A shiver ran through him, and she realised he'd been standing there all this time in nothing but a sweat-dampened T-shirt.

'You must be freezing! Do you want my jumper?' She'd taken it off when looking around the cottage and tied it around her waist. It was one size and though Ben was several inches taller than her, he wasn't so broad through the shoulders that it wouldn't fit.

He shook his head. 'Won't you need it? I'll be all right once I get moving again.'

Amelia took one exasperated glance at the goosebumps on his arms and untied the sleeves before thrusting it at him. 'I'm not the one who looks in danger of catching hypothermia.' A bit of an exaggeration, perhaps, but looking at him shivering was starting to make her feel cold.

'You don't take no for an answer, do you?' Ben shook his head, but he was smiling as he tugged the jumper over his head. The fit was pretty good, apart from the sleeves, which ended several inches short of his wrists. He held his arms out with a laugh before shoving the short sleeves up to his elbows. 'At least it's black.'

'Next time I'll lend you the one with a big sad kitty on the front of it.' When he raised a sceptical eyebrow, she grinned. 'What? I don't strike you as the animal jumper type?' She wasn't really. Hope had bought it for her years ago as a joke after they'd spotted it in a shop window and had been horrified by the sheer awfulness of it.

'If it had a spiky little hedgehog on it, maybe.' Ben's grin was too wicked for Amelia to feel offended.

'You might have a point.' She groaned as she said it, the pun not registering until the words were out. 'Lots of points.'

They walked in companionable silence for a few minutes before Ben spoke. 'So when do you think you'll be able to move into the cottage?'

She glanced up at him, but he was staring up into the branches of one of the huge oak trees that spoke of the age of the woods. 'Rhys reckons as soon as this coming weekend, but I'm not sure I'll be able to get everything arranged by then.'

'I have to go back to work on Monday, but I might be down again, depending on how the rest of this weekend goes. If I am, and you need an extra pair of hands with the furniture and whatever, I'll be happy to help.'

'Oh, you don't need to do that! Won't you want to spend time with Hope and the others?'

Glancing away from the tree, he shot her a grin. 'And where exactly do you think they're going to be that weekend?'

Amelia had to laugh. 'Good point.' There was simply no way the Travers would expect her and her mum to manage on their own. 'You'll be doing a lot of travelling back and forth, I guess, while you try and sort things out.'

Ben nodded. 'Either here or down to my dad's. I might have a chat with my boss, Matthew, next week about whether I can switch to remote working for a few weeks. If I can only spend odd days here, I'll never get to know everyone properly. Besides, 90 per cent of what I do needs a laptop and a decent internet connection so it makes no difference whether I'm sitting in the office or at the kitchen table. The other 10 per cent is spent sitting in meetings I don't need to be in, and I could Zoom in if they insist I have to be there.'

'Is the office environment one of the reasons why you don't enjoy your job?' she asked, recalling how he'd sympathised with her own work woes in the car earlier.

He shook his head. 'Nah, it's fine. I just don't want to be there, full stop. I'm thinking about chucking it all in and giving the pottery thing a go. It's been weighing on my mind for a while and I had a long chat with Jason over at the stable yard earlier and he really inspired me. It'll take me time to settle my dad's affairs and I'll need to hunt around for somewhere to establish myself, of course. But it feels like the right thing to do.' He shrugged. 'If I don't do it now, I feel like I'll still be sitting at that desk in ten years' time, staring out over a grey London skyline and wondering what the hell I'm doing with my life.'

Well, she certainly knew that feeling and she hoped Ben would be able to make a go of it. If he was going to be a regular fixture on the estate, perhaps she could use his journey as motivation to make the positive changes she wanted to for herself. 'It would certainly make things easier if you don't have to keep dashing up and down the motorway and now's the perfect time to see Juniper Meadows in all its glory. Autumn here is always spectacular,' Amelia said. One of the things she was most looking forward to was being able to follow the changes of the season on her morning walk from the new cottage to the bus stop. It would mean getting up an hour earlier, sure, but what a way to start the day.

Ben nodded. 'Like I said, I'll have to see how the rest of the weekend goes before I commit to anything else. Plus there's the small matter of finding somewhere to stay while I'm down here. I don't feel ready to muck in with everyone at the farmhouse, you know? I'll have to talk to Hope about it, see if I can use the lodge for a few weeks.'

'The lodges are actually part of Rhys's project to develop some glamping sites around the estate, but I'm sure he hasn't got plans for them for the rest of the season.'

'See! There's so much about this place that I don't know.' He shrugged. 'Anyway, this is all academic at the moment as I haven't even met the rest of the family yet. I'm supposed to go over for dinner later...'

'Maybe it'll be easier than you think.'

He laughed. 'It can't be any worse than what I've been building it up to be in my head!' His expression grew serious. 'I didn't think things through; I just picked up the phone and now I'm here and it's all a bit too real.'

Amelia wasn't sure what she could say to help ease his doubts. 'All you can do is be yourself and be honest about your feelings.'

'Oh well, now you've said that it's going to be fine.' He was laughing, thank goodness.

'Advice is always so much easier to give than receive,' she said, with a sheepish grin.

'I do feel better for talking to you, though, so that's something.' He shivered again, even with her jumper on.

'I need to get back home and talk to Mum about the cottage, and you need a hot shower!'

'Now that's a bit of advice I can get on board with.' They shared a smile, then began to walk briskly.

When they reached the end of the trail, they both paused. 'I'm this way.' Amelia gestured towards the path that would take her back to the main road. 'It was lovely to meet you, and I really hope things go well for the rest of the weekend.' She hesitated, then gave him a cheeky grin. 'I have a vested interest after all because you've promised to help with our removals next weekend!'

'I think "promised" is a bit strong,' Ben protested with a laugh.

'No, no, I definitely heard you promise.' Still grinning, she turned away and headed for home.

15

She retained that smile the rest of the way home, until she walked into the kitchen and found her mother sitting at the table, still in her dressing gown with a cup of cold tea in front of her. From the curdled look of it, it might have been the same one Amelia had made for her before leaving the house – she glanced at the clock on the wall in reflex – nearly six hours earlier. Daisy blinked and gave her a distracted smile. 'Hello, love. Back so soon?'

'It's after two, Mum.' Amelia tried to keep a note of chiding out of her voice. It was Saturday, after all, so it wasn't as if Daisy had anything much to do that day.

'Oh! I hadn't realised it was that late.' Daisy reached for her mug and took a mouthful before Amelia could stop her. She pulled a face and stood up with a laugh that didn't sound altogether steady. 'I'll make a fresh one, shall I? And how about a bit of lunch? There's still some of that nice ham so I can make us some sandwiches.' She stood up and wobbled a bit and Amelia rushed over to steady her. 'I'm fine,' Daisy said in a tone sharp enough to make her take a step back.

'You don't look fine.'

'It's just a headache; I'll be okay once I've had something to eat.'

Amelia wasn't convinced, but she also didn't want them to fall out, so she bit her tongue and turned her attention to making lunch. She rustled up a couple of sandwiches using the ham Daisy had mentioned, took a banana for each of them from the fruit bowl and carried everything over to the table. She put one plate deliberately in front of her mother, giving the edge a little nudge as she took the opposite chair.

Between bites of her sandwich, Amelia described the cottage and showed her mum the photos she'd taken and the sketches she'd made. 'I think you'll really like it there. It's such a quiet spot and with the woods right behind we'll be able to go on lots of walks together.'

'That sounds nice.' The words sounded genuine enough but there was still a bleakness around Daisy's eyes and the sandwich Amelia had made for her remained untouched.

'Don't let your tea go cold,' Amelia said, trying to keep her voice light. She managed to hold back the word 'again'. If her mum carried on neglecting herself much longer, she might have to try and speak to the doctor. The thought of it filled her with dread because there was no way of getting through to Dr Tate without speaking to Nell on reception first and she made Bill Walker look like the soul of discretion. She always demanded to know the reason anyone asked for an appointment and wouldn't book them in without it. Amelia could still remember the way Nell had given her a wide berth in the village store a few years ago only to find out Rhys had lost it when he'd phoned up to make an appointment about a recurring sore throat and had told Nell he had a nasty dose of the clap, so fed up was he of her sticking her nose in.

She supposed she could say she needed to speak to the doctor about a repeat prescription or something. Then again, that would only set more tongues wagging as the only thing she'd ever taken regularly was the contraceptive pill and she'd come off that last year because – unless what Kelly Smart had told both her and a horrified Hope back in primary school was true and you could get pregnant from sitting on a toilet seat if a boy had sat on it before you – Amelia hadn't seen any point in continuing with it. She'd just have to fake a stomach bug or something.

Daisy dutifully picked up her mug and took a sip, even managed to nibble on the corner of the sandwich, and Amelia decided it was enough to be going on with. There were other things they needed to discuss. 'So, anyway, Rhys reckons we can start moving stuff in next weekend, as soon as the decorator's finished. We don't have to do it all in one go and I'm sure they'll let me borrow one of the Range Rovers to make a few trips so we'd only need a van for the big stuff like the beds and the sofa.'

She hesitated and then pressed on. 'We need to decide what to do with Keith's stuff.' Her mum always frowned when Amelia used his first name but she refused to say the word 'Dad' out loud.

Daisy's brow creased in bafflement. 'We'll have to box it up and store it for him.'

Amelia pressed her lips together and took a deep breath. 'There's not going to be enough room for all our things as it is. I'll help you clear it out and we can put what's decent in the recycling bank when we go to the dump with the rest.'

Daisy's eyes widened. 'You can't mean that. What will he do when he gets out? He'll need his clothes at the very least.'

Amelia shook her head, unwilling to believe her mother was this naïve. 'Look at what he's been charged with! It wasn't just a one-off act he did on the spur of the moment. He waged a campaign against our friends and did his best to ruin them. He's not going to get six months and a slap on the wrist. He'll go down for years when they find him guilty.'

'He wasn't thinking straight; you know what he gets like when he's on a bender.' Daisy was shredding the sandwich into little pieces, her eyes staring off into the distance.

'He poured petrol on a field and set fire to it, right next to the campsite on the estate. People could've been killed!' She couldn't believe she was having to make this point again. Reaching out, she pushed the plate to one side and took hold of her mum's hand. 'Keith has no one to blame but himself. We have to forget about him and concentrate on helping ourselves.'

'I can't.' It came out as more of a sob than actual words.

Amelia wanted to shout and rail, to grab her mother and shake her until she stopped with all this nonsense. After everything Keith had put her through – put them both through – how on earth could Daisy still try and defend him? 'What is it with you and him?' An awful thought occurred to her then and she stared at her mother in disbelief. 'You can't possibly still love him!'

The vacant look in her mother's eyes sharpened and Amelia felt like she was finally fully present for the first time in weeks. 'Love him?' Daisy gave a bitter laugh. 'I've *never* loved him.' Pulling her hand free, she sat back and folded her arms across her chest. 'There. Now you know the truth of it. I never loved Keith. Never liked him much, even. I was just angry and upset and he was there. Things got out of hand and I wound up pregnant with you and before I knew it we were both trapped.'

Amelia had long suspected the circumstances of her parents' hasty marriage, but she'd assumed they'd at least genuinely cared about each other at some point. 'Why didn't you tell me any of this before?'

Daisy reached a hand across the table towards her. 'I never wanted you to be caught up in our mess. I tried my best to make a go of it, at least for the first few years, but deep down he always sensed the truth of it. He knew I could never truly love him, because I was already in love with someone else when we got together. Knowing that poisoned his mind as much as the alcohol did.' She pulled her hand back and wrapped it around her mug. 'So you see, I'm as much to blame for all of this as he is.'

Amelia couldn't believe what she was hearing. She knew things had been rough between her parents for a long time, but it hadn't all been bad. If she set aside the later years, she had memories of birthday celebrations, of the excitement of waking up on Christmas morning and finding a stocking at the end of her bed. Of Keith spending hours putting together a dolls' house in the middle of the sitting room floor. If she went in there now and pulled out one of the drawers of the sideboard, there'd be photo albums full of such moments. 'You really never loved him? Not even for a little while?'

Daisy shrugged. 'I did care for him, especially when you were first born.' A sad smile played at the corners of her lips. 'He doted on you. He'd be up in the night when you cried, even when he had work the next day. And he tried so hard to make ends meet. I wanted to get a job and do my bit, but he begged me not to. He'd been a latchkey kid, you see, and he didn't want you coming home to an empty house. So I gave in, and we got by. And, honestly, I'm grateful for those special years I got to spend with you. Once you started at school, I did part-time hours but without much work experience and five years at home, there wasn't a lot I could do. I thought about going to night school, but your father was drinking by then and I couldn't trust him to take care of you.'

'You must've felt so trapped.' Amelia had often been frustrated at her mother seeming to put up with anything from Keith, but she'd only ever viewed their relationship through the eyes of a child. 'Couldn't you ask anyone for help? What about Nan?' Her grandmother had died when Amelia was fourteen, but she had been around before then.

Daisy sighed. 'Appearances mattered more to my mother than anything else. She was the one who pushed for the marriage and even then she made us do it in the registry office because she wouldn't have the shame of me standing pregnant in church. I'd made my bed and I was going to have to lie in it.'

'She was very set in her ways,' Amelia agreed. They'd paid her a visit every Sunday morning for an hour after Nan got back from church. 'I still can't stand lemon barley water,' she said, grinning at the memory of having a glass of the horrible stuff plonked in front of her.

'And if you didn't drink it, I'd never hear the end of it!' Daisy's smile faded. 'She was hard to love, sometimes.'

Amelia squeezed her hand. 'Not a problem I've ever had.' For all their ups and downs, Amelia had never once felt anything other than loved by Daisy. Keith too, though his self-destructive tendencies had broken that bond between them in the end. 'So you really felt like you had nowhere to turn?'

'The only place I could get regular work and the kind of hours that suited me was up at Juniper Meadows and that just made everything worse. Your father hated me going there, and believe me, if I could have avoided the place, I would have. I had no choice, because at the end of the day we needed the money.'

'But wh—?' The question died on Amelia's lips as the final puzzle piece clicked into place.

Tell your mum she knows where I am.

'Oh my God,' she whispered as she stared at her mum in disbelief. 'It's Ziggy. You're in love with Ziggy.'

Daisy pulled her hand away and rose abruptly. 'I was, a long time ago.'

'But how? I mean, what happened between the two of you?'

Daisy gathered their plates and mugs and looked for a moment as if she would leave the table without responding. With a sigh, she set everything back down. 'It's ironic, really. The thing your father always worried about was that he wasn't good enough for me, but it was me that was never good enough. Not for him, because he deserved more than I was able to give him. And certainly not for the heir of Stourton Hall.'

16

After his hot shower and his chat with Amelia, Ben really was starting to feel a little better. He sent Hope a text saying he'd join her and Cam for a drink and asking her to let the rest of the family know he wanted to join them for supper. If there was going to be any chance of lancing the poison in the wound of his mother's betrayal, he needed to keep spending time with her. Avoidance had been Ben's preferred tactic for as long as he could remember, but where had it got him other than stuck in a rut and living the life his father had mapped out for him? Not wanting to show up empty-handed, he'd made a quick visit to the shop in the village and been pleasantly surprised at the decent selection of produce. Clearly there were some advantages to being in the heart of the London weekender belt.

Armed with a selection of cheeses and a couple of good bottles of red wine, Ben walked the short distance between the two lodges. Rounding the side of the building, he found Hope and Cam both seated on the deck, with an open bottle of white wine, three glasses and a selection of snacks in small earthenware dishes. His sister jumped up with a smile and met Ben at the top of the steps with a hug. 'Hello. We thought we'd sit outside while we still can. You don't mind, do you?'

'Not at all.' He'd layered a padded waistcoat over his sweater and collared shirt, knowing they'd be walking to and from the farmhouse. 'Might as well make the most of it. Can I leave this here?' He set down the bag with the cheese and wine and Hope immediately peeked into the top of it.

'Oh, that's thoughtful, but you didn't need to bring anything.'

Ben shrugged. 'I don't like turning up empty-handed and, besides, it's just a small token of appreciation for the welcome I've received.'

'You're always welcome. This is your home.' When he didn't respond, Hope scrunched her nose in a rueful expression. 'I need to stop saying that, don't I?'

'I appreciate the sentiment,' Ben said, 'but I think we'd all benefit from a little bit of expectation management. You don't know me any more than I know any of you and we need to keep in mind that things might not work out, no matter how hard we might wish them to.'

She nodded. 'Point taken. I'll try not to be so pushy.'

'You're not pushy, my love,' Cam said with a smile, 'You just like everything to be the way you think it should be.'

Hope rolled her eyes. 'That's boyfriend speak for "pushy".'

'It's good to have a vision, I suppose,' Ben said, doing his best to hold his face poker-still.

'Exactly!' Cam agreed. 'And I for one will welcome you as our supreme leader once you achieve world domination.' Ben couldn't hold in a snort of laughter.

'I hate you both,' Hope said, but she was laughing as hard as both of them as she collapsed back into her chair. The constant worried buzz that had filled Ben's head all afternoon was drowned out for a minute and he let his shoulders relax as he settled into his own chair and stretched his legs out.

He accepted a glass of wine from Cam with a nod of thanks, then glanced around. 'Where are the dogs?'

'They're in disgrace,' Hope replied, pointing to the closed patio doors.

Ben couldn't hold back a smile as his eyes met two of the saddest sad-puppy expressions he'd ever seen in his life. 'Oh dear, what did they do?'

'Two words,' Cam said. 'And the first one is "fox".'

Ben wrinkled his nose with a laugh. 'Our spaniel was an absolute nightmare for rolling in unmentionable things. Imagine how much fun it was trying to wash everything off those floppy, curly-furred ears.'

'Don't.' Hope shuddered. 'I seem to be bathing these two every other day at the moment.' She glanced over her shoulder and her expression softened. 'I won't leave them in there for much longer. I'd just like them to stay clean until we head over to the farmhouse.' She turned back to Ben. 'You're sure you're okay with seeing everyone? Because it's not too late to change your mind and we can have a quiet meal just the three of us.'

It was tempting for a second, but that was just his usual tactic of seizing the path of least resistance. 'I won't say I'm not feeling a bit stressed about it, but I want to meet the rest of the family.'

'Was it hard seeing Mum this morning?'

Ben nodded. 'When she hugged me, it was like a missing jigsaw piece slotting into place, but then when I saw the two of you together it made realise how enormous the puzzle is that we're trying to build and I'm not sure I'm up to the task.' He took a sip of his wine, then decided if he was ever going to be open and honest, now was the time to start. 'I got really angry and I didn't like it. Jealous too, a bit.'

'Of me?'

His cheeks suffused with heat and Ben had to duck his head to avoid the sympathy and understanding in Hope's gaze as he nodded. 'Yeah.' He forced himself to look back up. 'The rational bit of my brain understands that none of this is your fault, but you've had her all these years...'

'I'm angry with her too, angry with all of them except Rhys, who was kept as much in the dark as I was. We never knew about you until a couple of months ago.'

Ben sighed. 'I keep forgetting that I'm not the only...' He groped for the right word, not wanting to call himself a victim because that implied a sense of suffering he simply hadn't experienced. Compared to a hell of a lot of people, Ben had had a wonderful childhood with a parent who doted on him, even if he'd been over-bearing in some ways.

'Innocent bystander,' Cam offered quietly.

Yes. That sounded right because though he still didn't know the ins and outs of everything, his parents' marriage sounded like a terrible car crash. 'The person I'm most angry with is Dad for dying before he ever explained any of this to me.' He thought again about that bloody awful letter Stevie had been sent. 'Though perhaps I need to accept that he never had any intention of telling me the truth.'

'Maybe there were things he couldn't talk to you about because he found it hard to admit them, even to himself.' Hope rubbed a hand over her face, suddenly looking exhausted. 'I wasn't sure if I should tell you this or not, but there was another baby. Before me, I mean.'

The revelation left him stunned. 'What happened?'

'I don't know the exact details but there was some sort of alter-cation between them and Mum... well, she lost the baby.'

Altercation. There was something in the way she said the word that told Ben she knew more than she was letting on. Had his father hurt Stevie? It didn't seem possible. He could count on the fingers of one hand the number of times his dad had raised his voice, and on those few occasions he lost his temper, he would shut himself away in his study. He thought again about the messy jumble hidden away in his father's desk drawers, the contrast to the obsessive neatness of the rest of the room. Did that desire for control he'd exerted over both their lives hide something terrible? Ben felt the axis on which his entire life had turned wobble once more.

When Hope spoke again, her voice was barely more than a whisper. 'Finding out she was pregnant with me...'

He tried to put himself in Stevie's shoes for a moment, to understand how scared and confused she must've been to make such an earth-shattering decision. 'She felt like she had no choice,' Ben concluded.

'But there are other choices that came later, and it's those I struggle with the most.' Hope sighed. 'I can forgive Mum's decision not to tell me about you when I was too young to understand, but if I'd never gone searching in the first place then there's a parallel existence where you and I live out our entire lives never knowing about each other.'

The truth of it struck him like a hammer blow. If Hope had left things alone, Ben would be quietly mourning the father he thought he knew, not wrestling with this new image of a cruel and vindictive stranger who had used his son as an unwitting tool to punish the woman who'd had the temerity to leave him. 'But you did go searching and whatever happens from now on in, I won't ever regret learning about you.' Even if he and Stevie never found peace with the past, Hope was his sister, and he would do whatever it took for them to remain in each other's lives.

When they arrived at the farmhouse, the back door was open, spilling noise and a warm, welcoming light out into the darkness of the yard. Below the hum of conversation, a radio was playing, something classical with soaring strings. Ben ground to a halt, his brain flooded with a thousand and one images of his father standing at the oven, conducting with a wooden spoon as he made them dinner. Anger and despair crashed over him like a wave. Why couldn't his father have been a bastard to him, rather than leaving him with a lifetime of these simple, shared moments that instead of being a comfort were now making Ben question everything he thought he knew?

'Are you okay?' Hope rested a hand on his arm. 'It's not too late to change your mind.'

Ben shook his head, touched at her never-ending reserve of understanding and kindness. 'Dad loved Classic FM. It was always on in whatever room he was in.' He sank down on a bench near the back door. 'That's who he was to me. Sunday roasts after hours standing on a freezing touchline cheering me on. Front row at speech day, pizza and the pictures as a treat when I came home with a good school report. Teaching me to ride a bike, not teaching me to drive a car because we couldn't get the damn thing out of the drive without having a massive argument.' Ben found himself smiling at that, despite himself.

Hope came and sat beside him, Cam taking the space at the other end of the bench, but keeping his attention on the puppies, who both immediately tried to climb into his lap. 'I'm glad you have those memories, Ben. It makes the years we missed out on together that much easier to bear.'

'I just don't know how to reconcile my memories with what you've told me about him.' And it wasn't something he was going to resolve any time soon, he suspected. He pushed himself to his feet and held out a hand to help Hope up. 'Let's put all that away for the rest of the evening, though, before we get completely maudlin.'

'Good idea.' She nodded towards the door. 'You ready for this?'

Ben shook his head. 'Not really, but let's do it anyway.'

Cam brought the puppies over and took up position in front of both of them. 'Once more unto the breach and all that,' he said, grinning at Ben over his shoulder.

The image of them going into battle made Ben laugh and he was still smiling as he walked through the back door. He made it all of two steps before a female voice cried, 'Oh, he's here, our darling boy is here at last!' and he was enveloped in a cocoon of silky material, the scent of a warm, almost spicy perfume that reminded him of a holiday he'd once had in Morocco and what could only be described as love.

As the short woman who'd rushed to embrace him leaned back to beam up at him through a sparkle of tears on her lashes, Ben couldn't help smiling as he said, 'You must be my aunt Rowena.'

Reaching up, she cupped his cheek. 'Call me Ro, because anything else makes me feel a million years old. Here, let me look at you. My, you're a handsome one.' Still cupping his cheek, she turned to speak to Stevie, who was standing on the other side of the kitchen table. 'You didn't tell me how handsome he was!'

'Let the poor lad breathe, Ro,' a man with shaggy silver-brown hair said with a shake of his head. He was sitting at one end of the kitchen table, a scruffy terrier of some kind sprawled across his lap. A man who was his double apart from his hair being cut short stood at the kitchen counter, a striped butcher's apron tied on over a casual shirt and jeans. He raised a large knife in greeting and Ben could see a neat stack of already chopped vegetables piled up next to him.

Rowena stepped back, a slightly abashed expression on her face. 'I was just saying hello.'

'Don't mind Mum,' Rhys said, coming forwards to shake Ben's hand. 'She's a natural-born hugger. It's good to see you again.'

'You too.' Feeling a bit sorry for Rowena, Ben turned to her. 'Thank you for making me feel so welcome.'

'Ro gives the best hugs,' Cam said as he stepped forwards and put an arm around the small woman and Ben was impressed again at the way he stepped in to smooth things over.

Ben held up the bag he was carrying. 'Where shall I put this?'

'I'll take that, shall I?' It was his mum who spoke, holding her hands out across the table. Deciding they could do better than that, Ben walked around to join her, standing close enough that their shoulders brushed as he opened the bag and began setting out the things he'd brought in front of her. 'I didn't want to come empty-handed.'

Stevie picked up a large lump of blue cheese and showed it to the still-seated man. 'Your favourite, Zap.'

Zap's face creased into a wide smile. 'Well done, that man! You can definitely come again.'

Ben grinned, setting the wine on the table next. 'I was impressed with the selection in the shop, I must say. These aren't necessarily for today; I just wanted to say thank you for letting me gatecrash the weekend.'

The man with the shorter hair, who, by Ben's process of elimination must be his other uncle, Ziggy, abandoned his chopping board to come and examine the wine. 'Very nice – perhaps I should pop these away in my office for safekeeping.' He winked at Ben, his sly smile changing to a look of disappointment when Stevie leaned across from the other side to rescue the two bottles from his clutches.

'Nice try. There's a bottle opener in that drawer behind you, darling,' she said to Ben, gesturing with her head to show the one she meant. 'Let's get the corks out so they can breathe, shall we?'

Ben opened the drawer without thinking about it, only realising afterwards how naturally he'd responded to his mother's instructions. He didn't have time to get bogged down in over-analysing it, though, as the action moved on around him. Everyone was teasing Ziggy over his attempt to snaffle the wine while he protested that of course he'd only been joking as he took the opener from Ben and pulled the corks with practised ease.

Hope opened the fridge and surveyed the rammed shelves with a laughing groan. 'I see Waitrose profits will be up again. Where on earth are we going to put the cheese?'

'There's plenty of space in the bottom,' their mother said, giving Ben an I-don't-know-what-she's-making-a-fuss-about look before bustling over. With Stevie and Hope busy trying to reorganise the packed contents of the fridge, Ben found himself in a little conveyor belt as Rhys started pulling mats, silverware and plates out of various cupboards and handing stuff to him. Ben worked his way around the table, laying places until he reached the chair where Zap was sitting. 'Here, I'll get out of your way,' his uncle said, standing up with the terrier in his arms. 'Hercule needs to go out anyway.' Ben expected him to move away but the older man looked at him for a long moment before leaning over to brush a quick kiss on Ben's cheek. 'It's so good to have you home, son. You've been sorely missed.'

Feeling suddenly choked, Ben couldn't do anything other than nod as he watched his uncle set the terrier on the floor and usher him towards the open door.

Dinner was a chatty, fun-filled affair and though Ben didn't feel quite comfortable enough to join in with the banter around the table, he didn't miss the way each and every one of them made an effort to include him. The conversation mostly revolved around what had been going on around the estate and the plans for the forthcoming Halloween weekend. He was happy to sit back and try to get his head around who did what around the place and offered a polite opinion whenever a question was addressed towards him. He'd been ushered to a chair near the top of the table between Rhys and Hope and he didn't miss the fact his mother took a seat on the opposite diagonal so she was close to the fridge and could get up and down to fetch things. He wondered if it was a deliberate effort on her part not to sit too close to him, and hoped his awkwardness with her at lunchtime hadn't made her feel like she couldn't approach him. Whenever he looked over, she was watching him and smiling, at least, so perhaps she was trying to give him space.

When she got up to start clearing the table, Ben got up and helped her, ferrying the plates to the dishwasher so she could load them in, or putting the serving dishes on the counter to be hand-washed later. The conversation behind them had increased in volume after the second bottle of wine and Ben was glad of an excuse to get up for a minute. 'Noisy lot, aren't they?' his mother said, sharing a conspiratorial smile with him as he handed her the last of the dirty plates.

'It'll take a bit of getting used to,' he admitted.

'But you're okay?'

She looked so worried, Ben found himself reaching out to touch her shoulder in reassurance. 'I'm okay. I'm glad I came even if it's been a lot to deal with. I have to head back to London tomorrow as I need to get back to work, but I was thinking I might ask if I can switch to a more flexible arrangement, maybe even work from home so I can spend a bit more time here getting to know everyone.'

Stevie straightened up and pressed one hand to her chest. 'I'd like that, very much, if you're sure that's what you want? I don't want you to feel under any pressure.'

He shook his head as he smiled. 'I don't, I promise. I'm just not sure where I can stay, though, because I'll need somewhere quiet to work during the day.'

'Well, you could always stay here because Hope's old room is free, but you'd struggle to work as there's only a dressing table to sit at.' She gave him a look full of understanding. 'Plus, you'd probably feel more comfortable with your own space for a while yet.'

He was struck again by how sensitive and aware of his feelings she was, how she didn't try and steer him towards what she might prefer. 'It might be a bit easier all round. I was wondering if Rhys might let me rent the lodge for a bit – if it's not booked for other guests, that is.'

'What's that?' His cousin turned in his chair, obviously having caught his name being mentioned.

'Ben's going to try and spend a bit more time here, but he needs somewhere he can work as well so he wants to use the spare lodge,' Stevie replied before Ben could open his mouth.

'I'll pay rent for it, of course,' Ben added quickly.

'You bloody well will not,' Rhys said, looking frankly horrified at the suggestion. 'I've no plans for the place until at least the spring so it's yours to use as you wish for the foreseeable.'

'You're moving into the lodge?' Rowena asked, her whole face lighting up at the prospect.

'Oh, that's wonderful news,' Zap interjected. 'You'll have to come over and I'll give you a tour of the distillery. A tasting tour, of course.' He added the last with a wink.

Ben held up his hands. 'I said I'm *hoping* to spend a bit more time here. There's lots of things I need to sort out first so it's just an idea I was floating.'

'I've got an artists' retreat coming up in a couple of weekends' time,' Rowena said, ignoring his protestations. 'Your mum showed me that beautiful rose you gave her and I'm always in need of an extra pair of hands. What do you reckon?'

'I haven't had much time to spend on my art lately,' Ben protested. 'I'm not sure I'd be any use to you.'

'Oh nonsense, talent like yours doesn't just vanish overnight, and besides it'll be the perfect excuse to get your eye back in.'

'But what about the Halloween event? I was thinking I might pitch in and lend a hand with that.' Everything seemed to be moving very fast all of a sudden. There was no way he was ready to spend a weekend trying to teach other people art when he'd barely had a brush or a pencil in his hand for months. It was that familiar nagging sense of self-doubt, he realised. The voice of his father whispering in his ear that art was just a hobby, not something to be taken seriously. If he couldn't face a couple of days helping out with a few drawing classes, then how on earth did he think he was going to make a go of opening his own pottery studio?

'That's the weekend after so you'll be able to do both.' Rowena beamed at him as though none of this was any problem at all.

Rhys stood up and clapped a hand on his shoulder, a sympathetic smile on his face. 'Looks like you'll be spending a lot more time here, eh?'

'Looks like it.' Though he still had a lot of reservations about the future, there was no denying they were determined to treat him like one of the family. He turned and smiled at his aunt. 'It would be my pleasure to help out.'

17

Ben did his best to slip quietly into the office on Monday morning, but his efforts were foiled almost the moment he stepped out of the lift onto his floor and was engulfed in a hug from Carly. Smart as a whip and brim-full of enthusiasm and ideas, she'd joined the company on a graduate scheme two years previously. The way she was going, he expected her to be running the entire operation one day. 'Oh, Ben, I was so sorry to hear about your dad. How is everything?' She stepped back, looking unusually flustered. 'Stupid question, forget I said it. What do you need? Can I get you a coffee?'

'Thank you. Pretty grim but I'm getting there. I'm fine. I've already got one, thanks.' He held up the takeaway cup with the extra-large, extra-shot cappuccino he'd picked up from the coffee shop on the corner.

'Well, you let me know if you need anything, okay?'

He really needed her to go away and let him get to his desk, but she was being kind and Ben had never thought putting someone down was clever, no matter what sort of mood he was in. 'I promise I will,' he assured her instead and breathed a sigh of relief when she moved back towards her desk. It was short-lived as he had to run the gauntlet of everyone else who sat between the office entrance and his cubicle tucked away in the back corner. There were hugs and handshakes and heartfelt condolences and it was all Ben could do not to say, 'Turns out my dad was a bastard who hurt my mum so badly she ran away and, oh, by the way, I've got a sister and a whole load of relatives I knew nothing about a fortnight ago', but again he just smiled and thanked everyone.

When he finally made it to his desk, he dropped into his chair with a sigh and closed his eyes. 'It's not home time just yet,' a familiar voice said.

Ben opened his eyes to see Matthew, one of his best mates, who was also technically his boss, grinning at him from over the other side of the partition that separated their desks. 'If you say anything nice to me, I'm going to get up and walk out and not come back.'

'Like that, is it?' Matthew's face had taken on a serious expression but when Ben simply nodded in reply, the corners of Matthew's mouth ticked up once again. 'Luckily there's no chance of that from me. There's about a hundred emails waiting for you so stop moping about and get some bloody work done.'

Ben laughed, because it was a taste of normality and something he was sorely in need of right then. 'I knew you wouldn't be able to cope without me here to cover your arse.'

Matthew nodded. 'Damn right. I didn't become a manager to actually have to do stuff, you know.' He was one of the hardest-working people Ben knew – well, until he'd met his new family, because none of them seemed to understand the meaning of downtime.

His overflowing inbox turned out to be a blessing as Ben was able to get his head down and lose himself in work for a couple of hours. He hadn't slept at all well; his flat, always a haven before, had seemed stark and cold in comparison to the cosy warmth of the little lodge tucked away in the woods back at Juniper Meadows. By lunchtime the extra shot in his morning coffee had worn off and he was yawning every couple of minutes. Matthew stood up and pulled his jacket from the back of his chair. 'Lunch,' he said, in a voice that brooked no argument. 'My treat.'

Ten minutes later, they were ensconced in a booth in the old-fashioned boozer they'd found down a side street when they'd both first joined the company as young, and in Matthew's case hungry, graduates. It was a million miles from the shiny wine bars and cut-and-paste coffee chains. There were three beers on tap and not a fruity cider or a trendy IPA to be seen. The wine choices ran to white or red or a mix of the two for anyone who made the mistake of asking for a rosé. But the food was great, and they could always find a seat. Matthew took a sip from his pint of Diet Coke. 'So how was it, then, the funeral and all the other bollocks?' They'd been friends long enough for Matthew to know things had sometimes been difficult between Ben and his dad.

'About as awful as you'd expect, until my sister showed up.' Ben reached for his own Coke to hide his smile as he waited for that to register.

'Hang on, I didn't know you had a sister!'

Ben lifted one shoulder in a casual shrug. 'Me neither.'

They barely registered the arrival of their lunch as the madness of the past couple of weeks poured out of Ben in a torrent of words. Matthew interrupted occasionally, mainly to swear or express his disbelief, usually a combination of both. When Ben finally sat back, his friend could only shake his head. 'And he really never breathed a word of this to you?'

'Nope. I swear to God that as far as I was concerned, my mum died when I was a kid.'

'Bastard! How could he have done that to you? And that trick with the solicitor's letter? I'm sorry, mate, but he must've been

twisted in the head to come up with something like that.'
Matthew's lips curled as though he'd tasted something nasty.
'Sorry, I know he was your dad, but that's a next level of fucking
cruel.'

'You don't have to apologise because it's not something I haven't
already thought about him myself.' Ben picked up his glass and
swallowed what was left of his drink. 'I can't get my head around it
because for all his faults, the man who raised me doesn't seem
capable of doing something like that.'

'But he did.'

Ben propped his head in his hands and stared down at the
scarred surface of the table. 'I know, I know. And the worst thing
about all this is that I'm never going to find out why he did it. I lay
in bed last night and that's all that was going round and round in
my head. Why did he do it? Why did he carry on living this awful
lie for so many years?'

'Perhaps he was afraid of losing you. After your mum left it's
like he changed his whole life to put you at the centre of it. He
never remarried, or even had a serious relationship that you've
ever mentioned to me.'

Ben shook his head. 'The solicitor said something horrible
about him shagging half the ladies in the village, but honestly I
never knew anything about that, and I don't want to know.'

'You can't trust a word he said, anyway,' Matthew pointed out.
'He doesn't exactly come out of this smelling of roses. You should
report him for what he's done.'

'Yeah, you're right.' Ben sighed. 'But that'll mean dragging
everything out for God knows how long. I'm tempted to keep my
mouth shut and just let him get on with the probate so I can be
done with it all.'

Matthew's expression remained belligerent for a moment

before he gave a resigned nod. 'That's probably for the best; it just gives me the arse that he might get away with it.'

Ben couldn't help laughing, although it took him by surprise that he could find anything about the awful situation amusing. 'You sound even more angry with him than I am.'

'I'm your mate, what do you expect?' Matthew pointed to his empty glass. 'Another one?'

'Shouldn't we be getting back?' Ben was happy to sit there all afternoon, but he felt like he should at least show willing after taking nearly a week and a half off.

Matthew reached for his phone and a few seconds later Ben's phone vibrated. He looked at the notification and shook his head as he read it.

Strategy Meeting 1–2 p.m.

His friend picked up both their glasses with a nonchalant shrug. 'Perks of being the boss. And besides, it's true because we need to work out what the hell you're going to do next.'

* * *

Late the following evening, Ben was back in Juniper Meadows. He'd called in to his flat after work and loaded his car with everything he thought he might need for the next few weeks, along with his work laptop and a headset the IT department had sorted out for him to make calling into the office easier than trying to use the speakerphone on his mobile all the time. Matthew had agreed to Ben's request, saying a few people had floated the idea of working remotely, so Ben could be a guinea pig and help Matthew persuade their big boss to move with the times a bit. He had even offered Ben the chance to take some more leave if he wanted to. Although he had a couple of weeks left of his annual allowance, Ben wanted to hang onto it as he'd have to go back to his dad's and sort things out there at some point. He'd also spoken to his friend about his desire for a career change, which seemed only fair given how supportive and loyal Matthew had always been to him. Instead of trying to talk him out of it, Matthew had told him he should go for it. 'It's not like your heart's been in this job for a long time,' he'd said, and Ben couldn't disagree with him on that. In the end they agreed Ben would work until the end of the year to give Matthew time to recruit a replacement.

It didn't take long for Ben to settle into his new routine. He got up every morning and went for a run, showered and had breakfast and was still at his laptop well before eight. No endless commute on the Tube, dodging people on crowded pavements, or kamikaze cyclists and grumpy drivers jumping the lights at the pedestrian crossings. No queuing for coffee and overpriced sandwiches.

The view was a damn sight better, too.

The little garden behind the lodge was a haven for wildlife and there were always birds hopping around on the deck. He'd noticed the empty bird feeder on the wall and after a rummage around in the cupboards he'd found a bag of mixed seed and filled it up. After that he was inundated. He'd even caught a squirrel out there one afternoon trying to work out how to break into the feeder. Perhaps he should take a trip to the DIY store before the weather got too much colder. They were bound to have something he could hang up for the squirrels to stop them stealing from the birds.

With only a couple more weeks to go before the Halloween weekend, the family were in full swing with preparations. There wasn't much he could do around his work commitments, but he did a couple of extra hours on Thursday evening and caught up with everything outstanding in his inbox. With Matthew's blessing and the understanding he'd drop everything if anything important came up, Ben blanked a couple of hours out in his diary on Friday morning and headed over to the distillery, where Zap was planning to brew a couple of limited edition batches of gin to sell at the Halloween event. Arriving at the distillery, he found one of the big double doors open. Ben took a step inside, knocking as he did so.

'Just a minute!' His uncle's call was followed by the patter of claws and Hercule trotted over to greet Ben. Crouching down, Ben gave the little dog a scratch, which soon ended up with him sitting cross-legged on the floor with the terrier stretched across his lap, a blissful expression on his face. 'I see you've found another human cushion for yourself, Hercule,' Zap said with a laugh as he appeared from somewhere in the back of the large room, carrying a large plastic jar full of some kind of brown powder.

Ben scrambled to his feet, much to Hercule's disgust, and hurried over. 'Can I give you a hand with that?'

Zap set the jar on a long steel counter, then turned to face Ben. 'Let's get a proper look at you, then. With the ladies fussing over you at dinner, I hardly got a chance to say much more than hello.' He leaned forwards and gave Ben a one-armed hug, pressing a quick kiss on his cheek before stepping back. 'It really is great to have you here with us.'

He'd said as much on Saturday evening and Ben felt that same glow building from the inside out at the sincerity of his uncle's words. 'It's good to be here. I know it's going to take time to get used to such a big change, but I'm really glad Hope reached out to me.'

'As are we all, though it's a shame it's taken this many years. We should've done more. *I* should've done more.' His uncle's expression clouded. 'It was so hard for Stevie when she first came home, especially as Ro and I had Rhys romping around the place as a constant reminder of what she'd lost. There were times when I wasn't sure she'd cope with having to leave you behind; if it hadn't been for her wanting to hide the pregnancy from your father, I don't think the devil himself could've stopped her from getting you back.' Shaking his head, he forced a smile. 'Enough of that. Let's make some gin!'

It was frustrating to get another glimpse into the past only to feel like the door was being shut on him again, but Ben held his tongue. It was a conversation he needed to have with Stevie, when the time was right for both of them. Not wanting to put a damper on the day, he borrowed a bit of his uncle's enthusiasm and clapped his hands together. 'Let's do this!' he said.

'I was so pleased when you offered to show me how you do things here,' Ben continued as he followed Zap into the storeroom, where there were racks of clearly labelled ingredients. Ben didn't know what he'd expected, but the vast array of different items surprised him. Along with tightly sealed tubs of herbs and spices, there were boxes labelled as everything from rose petals to favourite childhood sweets.

'Grab those, will you?' Zap tapped a box labelled with the name of a popular brand of toffees and when Ben did as he was told, Zap added a box of dried apple slices on top. 'And pop them out on the counter. I'll sort out the last couple of things we need and be with you in a sec.'

Ben set the toffees and the apples next to the jar Zap had placed there earlier, which turned out to be powdered cinnamon. 'What are we making?' he asked when his uncle joined him.

'Toffee apple liqueur. We'll weigh everything out and add the ingredients to Mary over there.' He gestured towards the left-hand of the two huge copper stills. 'I've already charged the still with the required base alcohol and purified water, so once everything goes in we'll close her up and leave it to macerate for twenty-four hours.'

'Twenty-four hours?' Ben tried to keep the disappointment out of his voice. 'I had hoped to witness some of the process.' Amelia was supposed to be moving tomorrow morning and he hadn't forgotten his promise to help out.

Zap smiled and patted his arm. 'Don't worry. I filled Edward up yesterday so he's ready to go.'

Ben grinned back. 'Edward and Mary?'

His uncle nodded. 'Named for the first baron and his wife. Right, let's get cracking.' It didn't take long for Zap to weigh out each of the ingredients. He started with the usual infusion of herbs and spices that made up the special blend that was Juniper Meadows' signature gin. 'Each distillery has a unique recipe,' his uncle explained. 'And we guard them fiercely.'

'I won't breathe a word to anyone.' Ben crossed his fingers over his heart the way he had when he'd made a solemn promise as a child and his uncle laughed.

With everything weighed and measured, they carried the mix over to Mary and added it to the clear liquid that filled about a third of the still. 'You don't fill it right up?'

Zap shook his head. 'Consider the still as a bit like an oversized kettle. We force pressurised steam into it, which turns the infused alcohol into vapour. Come on, I'll show you.' He led Ben over to Edward. 'The vapour travels through here and into the condenser, where it is cooled and turned back into liquid.' Zap pointed to the different parts of the still. 'We decant the highly concentrated alcohol here in three parts. The heads and tails – the first and last parts of the concentrate – are discarded and it's only the hearts we use as that's the smoothest part of the blend. We store that for around seven days to let it settle and really let the oils and flavourings infuse and then we cut it with the requisite amount of distilled water to reduce the alcohol content to the correct percentage, which for us is around 42 or 43 per cent.'

'And you bottle it on site?'

Zap nodded. 'We've got a fancy contraption next door to help with that, but it's still a lot of work.'

'Will you give me a shout when you're bottling this up? Because I'd be happy to help out.'

His uncle smiled. 'I normally get Hope to help me, but I know she won't mind.'

'Won't mind what?'

They turned to find Hope watching them from a few feet away. 'Ben here was just volunteering to take your place at the next bottling session, assuming you don't have any objections.'

Hope laughed. 'Good God, no!' She turned to Ben. 'You can take my place permanently if you like. The bloody labelling machine hates me. Speaking of which, have you signed off the proofs for the design for these batches?'

Zap raised his hand to his head in a mock salute. 'Signed and waiting on your desk, ma'am. The post is up there, as well.'

'That makes a change.'

Zap turned to Ben, his hands held out in a why-me gesture. 'You lose a couple of invoices once and you never hear the end of it.'

Ben took an exaggerated step back. 'Don't try and drag me into this!' They all laughed and Ben got that funny feeling inside, because this is what families did: they joked around and teased each other.

'Well, I'll be upstairs trying to find a new contractor for the portable toilets we ordered,' Hope said. 'Don't let anyone tell you I don't lead a life full of glamour. I'll see you guys later.' Though she'd smiled as she said it, there was no missing how tired she looked.

On a whim, Ben called after her. 'Hey, if you're free tonight, why don't you pop round for dinner?'

'That would be lovely, but I'm not sure what time I'll be

finished. Plus I'm expecting Cam at some point, but that'll depend on the traffic.'

'Doesn't matter. I'm going to work late this afternoon to make up for skiving off this morning. There's chicken in the freezer so I'll make a casserole of some description and chuck it in the oven on low and we can eat it whenever. I'll pop out to the village shop on my way back from here and grab us some nice, crusty bread to mop it up with.'

'Sounds perfect! I'll text you later when I've got more of an idea of how my day's going.' There was a definite bounce in her step as she climbed the stairs.

When he turned back to Zap, it was to find his uncle beaming at him. 'You're a good lad, looking out for your sister like that. Come on, let's make some gin.'

18

The weekend of the move was upon them before either Amelia or Daisy knew where they were. Though she'd done her best to winkle more information from her mother about what had gone on between her and Ziggy, Daisy had refused to discuss it further. Still having to slog into work on the bus every day, and with every evening spent sorting and packing, Amelia had neither the time nor the energy to pursue it. She'd been worried about how Daisy would feel about living on the estate, and as they sat in the kitchen enjoying a final cup of tea before they packed the kettle away, she tried one last time.

'We don't have to stay at the cottage for long, Mum. I know it won't be easy for you to be living so near to Ziggy so I'll do my best to find us something else if you'd rather?'

Daisy set down her tea with a patient smile. 'Ziggy and I have spent the past twenty-five years being politely distant to one another and we'll carry on doing so for the next twenty-five. If there are any issues with the cottage, I'm sure you and Hope can deal with them well enough.'

'Of course we will. I just don't want you to feel uncomfortable.'

'It was all a long time ago, darling. The water is well and truly under the bridge, all the way downstream and out into the sea.'

Maybe for Daisy, but when it came to Ziggy, Hope wasn't so sure. The doorbell rang, startling them both even though they'd been expecting it. 'That'll be Rhys now.' He was collecting the van they'd hired – something Amelia had argued with him over until he'd asked her how she was going to get to the hire place with her car still off the road and she'd had to give in. At least the car was out of the village hall car park and safely tucked away in the car park opposite the cottages. Amelia had been convinced she was going to get stopped by the police for the whole of the three minutes it'd taken her to drive from the village hall and through the main gate of the estate, but she'd made it without seeing another vehicle, never mind one with a big blue flashing light on the roof.

Only it wasn't Rhys, it was Eric. 'Hello!' he said, giving her a broad smile. 'A little mouse told me you were on the move. I must say I was surprised I hadn't heard anything from you in reply to my letter.'

'What were you expecting, exactly? A thank you card and a box of chocolates?'

That wiped the smile off his face. 'Well, no, of course not, but I thought you'd at least do me the courtesy of letting me you know you'd made other arrangements. Plus, there's the matter of the outstanding rent.'

'You'll have to take that up with the leaseholder and, as you made clear in your letter, that isn't me. If you google "HMP Bullingdon", you'll be able to find the address and you can write to Keith there.'

'You can't be serious!' Eric sputtered, his face turning an alarming shade of purple.

At that very moment, a plain white box van pulled up and

Rhys, Ben and Ziggy climbed out. *Oh, just perfect.* Ignoring them for a minute, Amelia looked Eric dead in the eyes. 'You'll have to excuse us. We've got a lot to be getting on with.'

Before Eric could answer, Rhys reached the top of the path and Amelia didn't miss the way he stepped into Eric's personal space. 'Come to give us a hand with some boxes have you, Eric? Never had you down as the helpful type; still, there's a first time for everything, I suppose.' Amelia had to bite her lip to stifle a giggle at the blatant rudeness.

Eric puffed himself up like a disgruntled hen. 'Amelia and I have some urgent business to attend to. You'll have to wait.'

'No you won't – come on in.' Amelia stepped aside to let Rhys and then a bemused-looking Ben in through the front door. 'As I've already told you, Eric, you need to write to Keith and take it up with him.'

Ziggy hesitated on the doorstep, looking between the two of them. 'Is there a problem?'

'No!'

'Yes!'

Ignoring Eric, Amelia smiled at Ziggy. 'Mum's waiting for you in the kitchen.' It was awful to use what she knew against him, but she'd be damned if she was going to let him start interfering.

Ziggy raised an eyebrow, the only movement in his otherwise immobile expression. 'I'd better go and see her, then.'

As soon as he'd stepped inside, Amelia grabbed the edge of the door and shoved it closed. 'Goodbye, Eric!' she shouted as she clicked on the deadbolt, then slid the security chain across for good measure. He probably had a spare set of keys and she wouldn't put it past him to try and barge in behind her. The harsh *ring, ring* of the doorbell followed her into the kitchen. 'Must be faulty,' she said, sitting down at the table and calmly picking up her tea. The others stared at her with a mixture of surprise, amusement, and in her mother's case, worry. *God, please make him stop soon.*

As if by some miracle, the ringing did stop but Amelia didn't have more than a second to enjoy the blessed silence before the letterbox rattled and Eric yelled through it. 'If you think you're going to get away with this, you're in for a shock! You're a bloody thief, Amelia Riley! Like father, like daughter!'

For a second, Amelia thought she might be sick and then she didn't have time to worry about her roiling stomach because she had to launch herself out of her chair and make a grab for a furious Rhys, who was storming towards the front door. 'Leave it!' she begged him. 'You promised me you wouldn't interfere.'

The anger in his eyes blazed so fiercely, it was all she could do to hold her ground in the face of it. 'And you ask too much of me, sometimes. You aren't seriously going to let him get away with saying crap like that about you?'

She didn't know how she managed it, but she dredged a smile up from somewhere. 'It's just words, Rhys.'

Ziggy came up behind them and placed a hand on Rhys's shoulder. His eyes were hard as flint, but his voice was mild as he said, 'Best thing we can do now is get Amelia and Daisy out of here as quickly as possible. Come on.'

To Amelia's relief, Rhys glared for a moment longer before nodding. 'Where do we start?'

'Front room, please. Mum has taped a label to the things we want to take with us.'

Ben came to join them. Amelia didn't want to look at him, worried what she'd see on his face. People who got to know her circumstances generally fell into three categories: polite concern, judgemental disappointment and pity. The first two she could cope with, but the last never failed to make her feel ashamed, even when she knew none of what had happened was her fault.

They'd got off on such a good footing; trust bloody Eric to ruin everything with his terrible timing. When she finally met his gaze, Ben was smiling at her. His left eye twitched, just the ghost of a wink, but it was enough to buoy her deflated spirits. 'Why don't I help Rhys with the heavy stuff and you start bringing boxes down from upstairs?' Ben suggested, and she was grateful to him all over again because it was clear that Rhys was still fuming and she was happy to stay out of his way until he'd had a chance to calm down.

'That's a great idea. Shall we stack everything against the wall in the kitchen? That way you'll have more room to work.'

An hour later, Ben tapped on the door of the front room and poked his head around it. 'Rhys and Ziggy are doing a run up to the cottage to unload the van so I'm at a loose end for a bit. Do you need a hand?'

'Oh, yes please.' Amelia pointed to a cabinet underneath the TV. 'Can you grab those DVDs and box them up? They're for the charity shop, assuming they still take stuff like that.'

'Sure.'

They worked in silence for a few minutes, Amelia wrapping the ornaments her mum wanted to keep in newspaper to protect them while Ben methodically cleared the cabinet. 'You got what you wanted sorted out at work, did you?' she asked him.

'Hmm?' Ben made a distracted noise, and she glanced over to see he was reading the back of one of the DVD boxes. He gave her a sheepish grin. 'Sorry, I was miles away. This used to be one of my favourites, though I haven't seen it in years.' He held up the box to show the cover of an Arnold Schwarzenegger action film.

'I'd say you can borrow it, but you probably don't have a DVD player any more.'

He shook his head. 'There's one at Dad's still, but I wasn't planning on keeping it.' He pulled a face. 'I'm not looking forward to the day when I have to go through all his stuff and work out what to get rid of.'

It was bad enough when she had her mum to help split the task; she couldn't imagine what it would've been like having to face this on her own. 'Well, it won't be for a while yet and when it is time then perhaps I can return the favour and help you.'

Ben glanced down then back to give her a shy smile. 'That'd be really good, thanks. It wouldn't feel right to ask Hope to help me...'

'Just tell me when and I'll be there.' It felt like the least she could do given how willingly he'd thrown himself into helping her when he surely had better things he could be doing. It felt like a safe promise to make him because it would be months before she could pay off the money she owed to Ziggy, surely enough time for all the legal stuff Ben would have to deal with to go through. She couldn't deny there was a part of her that was curious to see where he'd grown up, as well. It wouldn't do any harm to get to know a bit more about him. 'So, you got everything sorted out at work?' She repeated her earlier question.

'Yes. I've agreed to stay on until the end of the year so they can find a replacement for me and I can work at home in return for giving an extended notice period.'

'You're serious, then, about that change in career?'

Ben nodded. 'I feel like if I don't get on with it there's a risk I'll fall back into what's familiar just because that's easier than trying and maybe failing. Rowena's asked me to help out next weekend at an art retreat she's running at the hotel. It's been ages since I've done something, so I'm a bit nervous, but I'm excited about it too.'

'Sounds like fun.'

'And I thought it would be a good way to get to know how they run things up there. I'm trying to get to grips with what everyone does on the estate. I had a session with Zap yesterday in the distillery, helping him make some themed gins for the Halloween weekend and I know Hope's got all sorts of activities planned for up at the stable yard so I'm going to try and find something I can do to help out then as well, even if it's just lugging tables around and tidying up afterwards.' He gave her another one of those embarrassed grins. 'I'm rattling on too much, aren't I? I know there's still a lot of stuff to be worked out but I'm trying to make the most of this opportunity I've been given to get to know another side of my family; perhaps it'll help me discover another side of myself too.'

He sounded so wistful, Amelia wanted to reach out and take his hand and tell him it was going to be okay. 'I think you're being incredibly brave and I'm sure that whatever you want to join in with, the whole family will be delighted. I'll be around over the Halloween weekend as well. I've told Hope I'm available for whatever they need.'

'Maybe we could do something together? When I was chatting with Jason the other day, he mentioned they're doing pumpkin carving at the stable yard and though I've only ever worked with clay, I'm sure I'd get the hang of it with a few practice goes.'

'I bet they'd be grateful for anyone with artistic experience,' she said without thinking.

'I hadn't really thought about that, but that's a great point. You could help out there too – weren't you telling me you almost took a scholarship to go to art school?'

Amelia shook her head. 'I am not to be trusted with a knife in my hand. Besides, Hope was talking about needing stewards for the spooky trails so I'm sure that's more what she's got in mind for me.'

'But that won't be until the evening. If you don't want to do the carving, then what about something else? What's your specialty?'

She couldn't remember the last time she'd talked about her art before meeting Ben, and here they were having their second conversation about it in as many weeks. What was it about him that brought the urge out in her? Perhaps she sensed a kindred spirit. 'Well, I wouldn't call it a specialty, but painting and drawing is much more my thing than sculpting anything.'

Ben clicked his fingers. 'Face painting! With all the kids who are bound to be coming for the pumpkin carving, you'd have a captive audience. They'll be queuing around the block to be turned into witches or zombies or whatever.'

His enthusiasm was infectious. 'I've never done anything like that, though.'

'So you'll practise! I'll be your volunteer. And if you're free next weekend, you can come and hold my hand at Rowena's art retreat! It'd be good for both of us.'

Amelia held up her hands, trying to slow Ben down a little before he swept her along on his tide of enthusiasm. It wasn't easy because doing something positive felt like exactly what she needed right now. 'Slow down a minute – you're going too fast for me to think.'

'What's to think about?' He sounded faintly exasperated. 'What would you rather be doing? Painting or unpacking boxes?'

'Well, when you put it like that...' Was she really going to let him talk her into this? It seemed so.

'Great! I'll let Hope know what we're planning.' He jumped up and dashed from the room, leaving Amelia to stare after him open-mouthed. He might not have been raised at Juniper Meadows, but Ben was a bloody Travers to the tips of his fingers and the ends of his toes.

19

By Sunday evening, the cottage in the village was empty and everything transferred to their new home on the estate. Daisy had cleaned each room as they emptied it so there was no reason for them to return. Closing the door for the last time, Amelia shoved the keys into a padded envelope addressed to Eric and walked to the end of the road to drop them in the postbox. With that done, she climbed into Hope's waiting car and slumped in relief against the seat. Instead of saying anything, her friend gave her thigh a comforting pat, then put the car in gear and drove them the few hundred yards to the estate.

As the noise beneath the wheels changed from the quiet hum of tarmac to the crunch of gravel, Amelia blew out a breath and opened her eyes. It was done.

'What's this Ben said about you wanting to run a face-painting stall at Halloween? Hope asked as she steered them along the sweeping driveway of the estate.

Amelia was almost too tired to lift her head, so she rolled it to the right to see Hope had half an eye on her and half on the road as she crept along at the designated low speed. 'Oh, we were just chatting yesterday, and he said he wants to help with the pumpkin carving and the next thing I know he's decided I should do face painting even though I don't know the first thing about it. He wants me to help out with Rowena's art retreat next weekend as well.'

'Seems like he's keen to spend time with you.' Hope's voice was bland, but there was no missing the mischievous smile curling her lips.

Amelia bolted up in her seat. 'Whatever you are thinking, you can stop it right this minute!'

'Who's thinking anything? I just think it's nice that you and Ben are making friends, that's all.'

'*Hope!*' Amelia did her best to sound stern but it was hard to ignore the little spark her friend's speculation had ignited inside her. He had shown up to help with the move when there was no reason for it, and he had made plans for them to spend the following two weekends together. 'He did say I could practise my face-painting skills on him.' She wondered if that meant he wanted to practise other things with her. The thought of it made her face heat and she turned away to stare out at the setting sun before Hope could catch her blushing.

'Did he indeed?'

Amelia closed her eyes and pretended she couldn't hear her friend chuckling.

Hope drove into the spacious yard behind the farmhouse and parked the Range Rover in the space next to three other identical vehicles, turned off the engine and they climbed out. Amelia waited for her to say something more about Ben, but Hope was all innocence as she led the way across the yard. The back door was open, light and laughter spilling out into the yard and, drawn by the sound of their arrival, Sooty and Sweep were already racing to greet them.

Laughing, Hope finally managed to control the excited puppies enough to usher them back inside. She made a shooing motion towards Amelia. 'You next.'

Stepping into the kitchen when all the family were present was always like stepping into the arms of a warm hug. Half a dozen different conversations stopped for a chorus of greetings as if they'd been gone for days, rather than the half an hour it had taken to do the final walk-through. Zap reached them first. 'Here, you'll need this,' he said, thrusting a goldfish-bowl sized glass into her hand. 'And let me take that,' he added, tugging at the shoulder of her coat to help Amelia out of it.

'Thank you.' She raised the rather daunting glass to her nose and took an experimental sniff. She caught a hint of ginger, something warm and spicy and something else she couldn't quite put her finger on. Taking a sip, she grinned as she recognised the taste. 'Pumpkin spice!'

'Clever girl!' Zap brushed a kiss on her cheek, grinning with delight. 'It's one of the two limited editions I've made for next weekend. What do you think?'

Amelia took another sip and nodded in approval. 'It's really good, thank you.'

'Another satisfied customer,' Zap declared in triumph.

She smiled up at him. 'I hear you had a new assistant helping out.'

Zap laughed. 'And so I did.' He nodded over at Ben, who grinned and waved from where he was leaning back against the kitchen counter, chatting to Cam. 'He's a natural. I'm going to try and recruit him,' Zap leaned down and added in a conspiratorial whisper.

'Good luck,' she whispered back. It was so wonderful to see the way the Travers family had embraced their newest member, though maybe her inner glow had something to do with the gin and tonic. Zap always was a generous pourer. Yes, it must be that.

Amelia flicked another quick glance across the room to see Ben was still watching her with a smile that did all sorts of funny things to her insides. Bloody Hope putting stupid ideas in her head! Amelia took a gulp of her drink and almost choked as the heat of the gin hit her throat. She set it down carefully before she knocked the whole lot back and did something foolish. Making a point of not looking at Ben, she addressed the room in general. 'What can I help with?'

'Nothing at all,' Rowena said, bustling around from her usual station by the oven to give her a hug. 'You look worn to a frazzle, darling, but at least you are in and your mum said the beds are made and you've got the kitchen mostly unpacked, which is a good start.'

Amelia hugged her back. She'd always been close to Rhys's mum and she'd missed her gentle kindness in the years since they'd called it quits. 'It'll take us a while to get properly straight, but we'll get there.'

Rowena stepped back to cup her cheek. 'And a little bird tells me you might be getting into your painting again? I can't tell you how happy I was to hear it! Are you going to come and join us next weekend? It would be so much help if you could!'

I haven't touched a paintbrush in months,' Amelia said, feeling the need to warn her.

'It'll be a breeze for someone with your skills, and of course I'll pay you for your time. It's a beginner's group and they always need a lot of extra attention.'

'I think it sounds like a great idea,' Daisy said, giving Amelia an encouraging smile. 'It'd be nice for you to do something with your art. It's been too long.'

It really had been. 'If you're sure you won't mind if I'm a bit rusty?'

Rowena waved it off as if the idea was of no consequence.

'You'll be back in the swing of things in no time. And besides, you won't be on your own because Ben's going to help out too. I can't tell you what a balm it is to my soul to have other creatives around me again.' Her smile was so infectious, it was impossible not to join in.

* * *

'It's such a nice night,' Ben said as they picked their way a little unsteadily across the yard behind Hope and Cam, who were walking ahead with the puppies. Stevie had only had tonic water, so she'd given Daisy a lift home earlier. Amelia had thought about going with them, but honestly, she needed the fresh air if she didn't want to be riding the bus to work in the morning with a hangover, especially after Zap had broken out the toffee apple liqueur after dinner. The man was a menace – a lovely, kind-hearted one, but a menace nonetheless.

Amelia paused to look up at the sparkle of stars tossed across the velvet blanket of the dark sky. 'It's so pretty.' Her head began to spin slightly and she quickly straightened her neck. 'Bloody toffee-apple liqueur,' she muttered.

Ben laughed. 'It was a bit potent, wasn't it? Hopefully the fresh air will sort us out.' They carried on walking. 'So you're going ahead with the face painting, then?'

'Looks like it, thanks to a certain someone volunteering me.'

Ben stopped in his tracks. 'Are you mad at me about that? I just thought it would be something fun.'

Amelia sighed. 'Don't mind me, I'm just feeling a bit nervous about the whole thing, plus we've got next weekend with Rowena as well. I haven't even thought about where I'm going to get the stuff I need from.'

'That's why God invented Amazon Prime.' Ben pulled his

phone out and started tapping on the screen. 'There's loads to choose from – here, have a look.' He handed the phone to her. 'Pick a couple to try and we can have a practice run later this week!'

The choice was dizzying, or maybe that was the booze. On a whim, Amelia clicked on a couple of different kits that had decent star ratings and added them to the basket, together with a stencil set of Halloween designs.

Ben took his phone back and fiddled around again before tucking it away with a triumphant smile. 'Sorted. They'll be here tomorrow. Why don't you come round for supper and I'll be your guinea pig? If it's a disaster then it's not too late to cancel. It's not like it's on the promotional material or anything.'

'You don't have to do that,' she protested, though it would be a lot easier than trying to practise on herself with a mirror. *Seems like he's keen to spend time with you.* The reminder of Hope's earlier observation sent a warmth that definitely wasn't the gin spreading through her.

Ben held open the gate for her to step through. 'It's the least I can do seeing as I'm the one that volunteered you for it in the first place. It'll be a laugh if nothing else, and what else were you planning to do on a cold October Monday night?'

'Soak in the bath for an hour and be in bed by eight.' She was already stiff and aching from humping and dumping boxes all weekend; she couldn't imagine what he must be feeling like after lifting all the furniture he and Rhys had shifted between them. A sudden wave of disappointment settled over her. The bathrooms in the cottages had been refitted a couple of years previously and the tiny bathtubs had been replaced by showers. 'Oh, I don't have a bath any more.' A hot shower would help, but it wouldn't be the same.

Ben leaned closer and whispered against her ear. 'I've got a bath. And a hot tub.'

She didn't know if it was the surprise heat of his breath against her cheek or the unfamiliar nearness, or just the promise of being able to soak up to her chin in hot water, but that might have been the sexiest thing anyone had ever said to her. 'Dinner and a bath? Are you trying to seduce me, Mr Lawson?'

'If I was trying to do that, I'd have offered to have you in bed by eight as well.' He was silent for a long moment, then added, 'And I'm too much of a gentleman to do that on the first date.'

Good God, what on earth was she supposed to say to that? *First date*? 'I'm not sure me painting a giant bat on your face constitutes a date, even with dinner included.'

'You forgot about the bath.'

Amelia laughed. 'Behave yourself – I am not using your bath!' She'd seen the upstairs area in those lodges and they were definitely set up for romance with a huge copper tub and a king-size bed.

'I notice you didn't say no to the hot tub.'

She drew to a halt and faced him. She could barely make him out in the dark, the torch he was holding illuminating only their feet and ankles. 'You shouldn't flirt with me.'

'Why?'

Where was she supposed to start with that one? 'Because we barely know each other, for one thing.'

'Surely spending more time together would be the perfect remedy for that?'

She hesitated. 'Well, yes, I suppose that's true. But there's other things you don't know about.'

'Like what?'

He sounded amused, which should have annoyed her but strangely only made her want to forget all about the reasons why this was a terrible idea. He was fun and funny, and she knew they'd probably have a great time together, but there were two very big stumbling blocks between them and he deserved to know about them. 'I used to go out with Rhys.'

'Ah, that makes sense of a lot of things.' The humour was gone, his tone more reflective now.

'Like what?'

'It's hard not to miss how protective he is around you. I know you and Hope have been friends for a long time, but I couldn't piece together how he fits into the equation.' He moved away, taking the little circle of light from the torch with him, leaving her feeling suddenly much colder. 'I wouldn't want to get in the middle of something if you two are going to work things out, so I'm glad you told me.'

She found herself stepping towards him. 'No. It's not like that. We were very close once but we've both moved beyond that. I love Rhys, I'll always love him but we haven't been *in* love for a very long time.'

'So supper with me shouldn't be a problem, then.' He moved this time, close enough that their toes were almost touching.

That shouldn't have been enough to set her pulse racing but there was something about the intimacy of that little circle of light in the pitch dark. It was all she could do not to shuffle close, to stand toe to toe, to lean in and press other parts of her body to other parts of his. But as fun and as charming and, yes, as damn sexy as he was, what would be the point in starting something that would have to finish? 'I'm leaving.' Regret swept over her at what might have been, but it was only fair for him to know the truth before things got out of hand between them.

'What do you mean?' The torch flashed up from the floor to her face and Amelia yelped, raising her hand to try and shield her eyes from its suddenly blinding light. 'Shit, sorry.' The light vanished, leaving her completely disorientated as tiny spots continued to dance before her eyes. A hand clasped her shoulder, steadying her. 'God, I'm really sorry. Are you okay?'

Amelia blinked a few times and the spots faded. 'Yes, I think so. You just startled me.' She looked around and could make out the faint bobbing circle of Hope and Cam's torch some distance ahead. 'Come on, we're getting left behind.'

'Here.' Warmth engulfed her fingers as he took her hand. 'Just until you're steady,' he said, as though to forestall any objection.

And she should object, she should pull her hand away and take the torch from him and tell him she was capable of finding the rest of her way home by herself. If he hurried, he could catch up with Hope and Cam so she wouldn't be stranding him in the dark. She didn't do any of those things. She remained silent and followed alongside as he started back along the path. 'Your fingers are cold,' he said, rubbing his thumb over them. 'Don't you have any gloves?'

'They'll be in a box somewhere. I'll probably find them sometime next year, which is about when I think I'll be able to face unpacking everything.'

He laughed. 'I still haven't got half the stuff I brought with me out of my car so I can't say anything to that.'

'How long will you be staying here?'

'I don't know; I'll have to see how everything goes. I'll have to spend some of my time over at my dad's until I get all that sorted out. And I'll be back up to the office, no doubt, for a few meetings.'

'You've got a place in London as well?' Imagine having a choice of places to live. Amelia tried not to get jealous about other people's circumstances, but being friends with the Travers family didn't always make it easy. Here she was relying on their kindness – and yes, charity, though she knew Hope hated her thinking of it that way – and Ben had two homes, three if you counted the estate.

'Yeah. I'm going to hang onto it, just in case.'

In case things didn't work out here at Juniper Meadows, she guessed. It was still very early days but she didn't think Ben needed to worry about anything there. He'd slipped seamlessly into the Travers family like he'd always been a part of it. And she supposed for the older members that was true because they'd always known he existed and was out there in the world somewhere. What must that have been like for them, especially Stevie, knowing she had a child and having been led to believe they wanted nothing to do with her? 'If I had a flat in London, I'd be up there every weekend,' Amelia mused. 'There's so many museums and galleries to explore, it would take me months.'

Ben squeezed her fingers. 'You'd be welcome to use it any time.'

She laughed, not bitter, just realistic. 'I wouldn't be able to afford the train fare.' Her laughter faded. 'I wasn't joking about leaving, you know. It won't be tomorrow, but my future lies elsewhere – I've decided that much at least. Once I've paid Ziggy back all the money I owe him and the trial is over and I know Mum is safe and settled, then I'll be on my way. I've already wasted too much of my life stuck here.'

'It's so strange to hear you talk like that when Juniper Meadows feels like such a warm and welcoming place to live.'

'You chose to come here. You've been given choices all your life. Mine were taken from me before I had a chance to make any.' She didn't mean for the words to come out quite so harshly, but she didn't need him judging her when he had no idea what she'd been through.

'You could've left home, taken one of the bursaries you talked about and gone to art school.'

Amelia pulled her hand from his. 'And leave my mum to deal with everything on her own? What about you? You could've pushed back when your dad forced you to sideline your pottery for other stuff.'

'You're right. And I had less excuses than you for not doing it.' His voice was bleak.

It was her turn to reach out. Fumbling in the dark, she found the soft wool of the sleeve of his coat and slid her hand down until her fingers curled around his. 'As far as you knew, your dad was the only family you had. Wanting to please him, wanting to keep the peace was only natural in the circumstances.'

'I hadn't really thought about it like that.' He gripped her hand a little tighter. 'You're right. I always tried to be as easy on him as I could, because I thought he'd been through too much already. We both had. But that was all a lie.'

He sounded so sad, so lost, her heart felt like it might break. 'I know I'm probably the last person who should say this, but try not to let what you know now poison all your memories.'

'Is that what's happened with you and your dad?'

Amelia sighed. 'I've been angry with him for so long. I'm still angry with him and I know it'll only get worse when the trial comes around. It's changed me. He's changed me, and not for the better. I'm more negative about everything, including other people. I expect them to let me down and I'm quicker to lash out. And I don't like that about myself.' It was one of the reasons she wanted to get away. If she could just go somewhere where no one knew her, maybe she could change too.

'Can you tell me what happened with that bloke on Saturday? The one who shouted abuse at you through the letterbox?'

She cringed inside at the memory. 'Eric? He's the owner of our old house. I found out recently that even though I was giving him pretty much every penny I was earning, Keith hadn't paid the rent for over six months. I tried to renegotiate with Eric and asked him to transfer the lease into my name and he kept saying it was okay, you know? That I wasn't to worry and we'd find a solution.'

'But you didn't?' Ben prompted.

'Oh no, he found a solution, all right.' Amelia couldn't keep the bitterness out of her voice. 'He sent a letter saying he'd found a buyer for the property and we had thirty days to not only pay him the full amount owed in back rent but also to match the offer to buy the house. As if I'm going to be able to get a mortgage when I haven't got a penny saved for a deposit, never mind match the asking price! I was so angry with him that I told him he could get stuffed. If he wanted his money back, he'd have to write to Keith in prison and sort it out with him.'

Ben squeezed her hand. 'I'd have probably done that and more in your shoes. That's a shitty way for him to behave even without taking into consideration everything you and your mum have been going through. No wonder you were angry with him.'

Amelia sighed again. 'It was a stupid thing to do. All I've done is create more unnecessary drama. I just couldn't face going cap in hand to Ziggy again. I already owe him so much because Dad took out all these loans and credit cards and hid it from us. We only found out when the demand letters started dropping through the letterbox after he'd been arrested.'

She paused and then decided he might as well hear the whole of it. 'He gambled it away. All those thankless hours spent doing a job I never liked just to try and keep a roof over our heads and he was playing these stupid online games and losing a fortune. He had accounts with half a dozen different bookmakers. I thought it must be horse racing, or football he was betting on, but when I looked on his iPad it was those Vegas-style slot machines.' She had to close her eyes against the sudden sting of tears. 'What a bloody waste.'

Ben's thumb ran over her knuckles in a soothing gesture. 'I'm so sorry. I had no idea things have been so awful for you.'

'It's been pretty rough.' Amelia sucked in a deep breath and forced herself to straighten her shoulders. 'But I can't keep dwelling on the unfairness of it because that only makes me feel worse. I'll give it a few days to settle down and then I'll contact Eric and try and sort things out with him. Even though I'm mad at him for not letting us know earlier that the rent wasn't being paid, none of this is really his fault.'

'Well, let me know if there's anything I can do to help.'

Amelia laughed. 'If you have a spare twenty grand knocking about, that would make life a damn sight easier.' Ben was silent to the point she was worried he might have thought she was being serious. 'Oh God, Ben, that was a joke! I don't want your money. Please, forget I ever said anything.' She couldn't imagine anything worse than him thinking she was sharing her sob story so that he would take pity on her.

Before he could answer Amelia was distracted by a flashing movement up ahead. 'Everything all right back there?' Hope called out. She and Cam had reached the campsite car park and were silhouetted against the night by the dull illumination of one of the low-level lights lining the edge of the car park and the road beyond. As she saw the torch move again as though Hope was seeking them out, Amelia became acutely aware that she and Ben were still holding hands and tugged free of his grip.

Putting on a burst of speed, she walked quickly towards where they waited. 'Everything's fine, we just got chatting and hadn't realised we were dawdling along. I know where I am from here; you guys go on and I'll be fine.' Amelia pulled out her phone and quickly flipped on the torch mode.

'Wait, I'll walk with you,' Ben said, having caught up with them.

Amelia took a step away, not wanting to be alone with him again in case he brought back up the topic of loaning her money. 'I'll be fine! I'm going to follow the road anyway so it's not like I'll be tramping through the woods on my own.'

'If you're sure.' He didn't sound convinced.

'I'll be fine,' she repeated.

'Text me when you get in,' Hope said, stepping in to give her a hug.

'Text both of us,' Ben added as he pulled his phone out of his pocket. 'I'll need your number anyway so we can finalise arrangements for tomorrow.'

'What's happening tomorrow?' Amelia didn't miss the interest in Hope's voice as she asked the question.

'Oh, nothing really – I'm a bit nervous about the face painting thing because I haven't tried it before so Ben's agreed to let me experiment on him.' Not wanting to give Hope any suspicions about anything – because there wasn't anything to be suspicious about – Amelia added, 'You're welcome to join us if you've got nothing better to do. You too, Cam.'

Cam laughed. 'Thankfully I'm hitting the road at silly o'clock in the morning to get back to the university before my first tutorial starts.'

'I'll pass too,' Hope said. 'I want to go over the plans for the Halloween weekend, just to make sure everything's in place.'

Cam pulled her close and kissed her temple. 'You've already checked them a hundred times. Stop fretting; it'll go like clockwork.'

Hope curled an arm around his waist. 'I promise I will... after tomorrow.'

'Well, if you change your mind just message me,' Ben said. 'I'm making dinner and there'll be more than enough for you.'

Hope smiled up at him. 'Honestly, that's really lovely of you but I'd rather just enjoy the quiet without any interruptions.'

Having given Ben her number, Amelia waved them all goodbye. The effects of the gin had thankfully faded and now she was on the road and could see where she was going, she set a brisk pace. The temperature had really dropped the past couple of nights, and given how clear the sky was, she wouldn't be surprised if she was crunching over frosty fields on her walk to the bus in the morning. She shoved her hands in her pockets, wondering how long it would take them to unearth the box with all the outdoor accessories in it from the hallway cupboard.

Her mum had not only left the outside light on, but when she got upstairs there was a flask beside her bed with a note stuck to it:

I thought you might need a hot drink after your walk home xxx

Smiling at the thoughtfulness of the gesture, Amelia unscrewed the lid and took a sniff. Hot chocolate. Perfect. She scrambled out of her clothes and into her pyjamas, then dived under her quilt and pulled it up over her chest. The heating had long since gone off and the little bedroom was chilly. She poured herself a hot chocolate and sent a quick text to Hope, letting her know she was home. She hesitated over Ben's number for a minute before tapping out a quick message:

I'm home

A reply popped up a few seconds later:

Thnx for letting me know. Don't forget your swimming costume tomorrow

He'd added a grinning emoji at the end. Amelia had forgotten all about his offer to use the hot tub. She glanced over at the stack of boxes piled against the opposite wall. She'd packed a case with enough clothes to see her through the next few days so hadn't planned on tackling the rest of her unpacking. Oh well, at least she had the perfect excuse for refusing when she saw him tomorrow.

But where's the fun in that?

Before she could question the thought too deeply, Amelia set her alarm half an hour earlier. If she couldn't find her costume before work, then that was fate's way of telling her it wasn't meant to be. If she did find it, however? Well, Ben knew all her dark and shameful secrets already. He even knew she was planning to leave and hadn't seemed put off by it. So where was the harm in making the most of each other's company while they could?

20

Ben was lost deep in a spreadsheet early the next afternoon, muttering curses under his breath. He'd run a weekly actuals report on Friday morning before he'd bunked off to spend time with Zap in the distillery. Thinking he was being helpful, Eoin, a junior member of his team, had used the data to update some of the forecasted figures. Unfortunately, he'd overwritten a load of the formulas in the process. Eoin hadn't realised there was a problem until he'd spent most of the morning doing it. He'd then managed to compound his error by backing up to the cloud server and overwriting the master copy, leaving Ben no option but to go through and try to fix it. Poor Eoin had practically been in tears when he'd called Ben to confess. 'I thought I was helping,' he'd said for the tenth time in about two minutes, and not having the heart to be cross with him, Ben had lied about it being an easy fix.

He'd set his internal messenger status to Do Not Disturb and put his phone on silent, knowing that any interruptions would only make things more difficult. He'd shoved on his headphones, found a playlist on Spotify that claimed to be soothing and relaxing and was now working his way through the spreadsheet line by line.

Thump, thump, thump.

What was that? Irritated at being disturbed, Ben glanced up and burst out laughing to see Hope's face all squashed up against the glass of his patio door. He yanked off his headphones and tossed them on the table, getting up to unlock the door. 'Sorry, I was miles away!'

'That's all right. I can't stop; I just came back because I finally found time to walk the dogs and realised I'd forgotten one of the leads so I had to nip home and grab it. I tried to call you but your phone went directly to voicemail. I sent you a text too.' Hope raised her hand to show him a couple of Amazon parcels. 'This arrived for you.'

'Ah, thanks, those will be the face paints I ordered for Amelia last night.' He'd added a couple of extra items after getting home, but had been hopeful, more than expectant, that it would arrive so quickly. 'The powers of Prime delivery reach all the way out here,' he said with a grin. 'That could prove dangerous.'

Hope laughed. 'The Amazon man and I are on first-name terms. He drops everything off at the distillery and I message people to collect from there. I should be on commission.'

'Well, thank you for the special delivery service. I appreciate it. Hey, are you sure you don't want to join us for dinner tonight?' His flirting with Amelia the previous night had been fun and there was no denying his attraction to her. He'd been pretty sure she'd been flirting with him too, but again that might have been a bit of gin-induced overconfidence. If Hope was there when she arrived, it might make things a bit smoother all around if Ben discovered he'd misread some of the signals between them. And if he hadn't, there was still no rush for anything to happen between them, regardless of how much he was finding himself drawn to her.

For all Amelia's protestations about wanting to get out of there, if the figure she'd quoted had been anything close to what she owed to pay off her father's debts then it was going to take her months, if not a couple of years to be able to get that kind of money together. He didn't know how much she earned, and frankly it was none of his business, but it couldn't be that much if she was so worried about trying to make ends meet. He hadn't missed her comment about not being able to afford the train fare when he'd said she could use the flat in London anytime she wanted.

'It's sweet of you to offer,' Hope replied, pulling his attention back to the current situation. 'But I'm still going to pass. I know Halloween is still a couple of weeks away, but I really want things to go well so I can't help obsessing over every little detail.'

He didn't like how stressed-out she looked, but he also didn't feel like he knew her well enough to judge if this was her usual working style or if there really was a problem. Cam had been pretty chilled out when he'd teased her about it, so Ben decided he would trust the other man's judgement and let Hope deal with it in her own way. 'Okay, well, if you change your mind or you want me to pop round with a plate later, send me a text.' When she raised her eyebrows at him, he grinned. 'I promise to read that one!'

'I could get used to you living next door.' The smile they shared warmed Ben to his toes because he could see himself getting used to it as well. 'Send me some photos of Amelia's handiwork, okay? Now shut this door before you let all your heat out.' She stepped back and he slid the glass closed, laughing when she pressed her lips to the window and blew out her cheeks.

'You're a brat,' he called, raising his voice so she would hear him. She poked out her tongue, looking thoroughly pleased with herself, then bounced down the steps of the deck two at a time. Yeah, she was fine.

Still chuckling to himself over Hope's antics, Ben returned to his laptop and glared at the spreadsheet for having the audacity not to have fixed itself while he and Hope were chatting. With a resigned sigh, he popped his headphones back on and got down to work.

By the time he finally fixed the last formula, Ben was as stiff as a board. Two days of lugging furniture and boxes followed by one spent hunched over his laptop was not a good combination and his shoulders were all but screaming in protest. Opening the patio doors once more, Ben decided to check the hot tub. Even if Amelia decided to pass on the offer, he might treat himself to a soak after she'd gone home. He flipped back the cover and tested the temperature. It felt so good even just against the skin of his hand, he was tempted to strip to his pants and jump in there and then. He checked his watch and was disappointed to see there wasn't time. He still hadn't made a start on dinner.

Twenty minutes later, he was sliding a dish full of diced chicken, tons of veg and a cheat's packet of casserole mix he'd picked up from the village shop when he'd gone out to grab some fresh bread at lunchtime. He'd picked up some potatoes and was halfway through peeling them when his phone pinged to say he had a message. It was from Amelia.

I've just got home. Give me 30 minutes and I'll be with you.

He wiped his hands dry on a tea towel and replied.

No rush, dinner's only just gone in the oven.

Ooh what are we having?

Chicken casserole. Mash or sauté potatoes?

Mash, please.

Amelia added three yummy-face emojis, which made him grin.

When she knocked, Ben had cleared his laptop off the table and set the face-painting sets out ready. 'It's open,' he called as he walked towards the door.

Amelia slid it open and stepped inside before he reached it, pulling the patio doors closed with a firm click. 'Brr. It's freezing out there already.' Her nose and the tips of her ears were red with cold and she set down the bag she was carrying to chafe her hands together.

'No luck finding your gloves?' he teased, feeling rather happy about it because his impulse purchase wouldn't go to waste after all.

She shook her head. 'I didn't even have time to look yet; I was too busy hunting for this.' Reaching into the bag, she pulled out a plain black racing-style swimsuit and waved it like a flag.

'You didn't have to bring that with you,' Ben said, suddenly worried she might have felt under pressure from him the previous evening.

Amelia widened her eyes as though shocked. 'Naked hot-tubbing is definitely not a first-date activity! Or even a second, or third.' She tapped her chin as though she was considering it. 'I think I'd need at least six or seven dates before I could even consider it.'

Ben could feel his grin stretching wider with every word. 'But you would consider it?' He tucked his hands in his pockets before he could be tempted to seize her by the waist and kiss the cheeky little smile off her lips. He couldn't stop himself from stepping closer, though.

She glanced up at him through thick lashes. 'I might.'

His heart began to thud so hard he was surprised it wasn't

bouncing away under his shirt like it did to the Looney Tunes cartoon characters he'd watched as a kid. 'Are you flirting with me, Miss Riley?'

'Is it a problem with you if I am?'

'No, not at all. It's a very pleasant change of heart.'

'I don't want you getting the wrong idea, though.' She placed a hand on his chest. 'I meant what I said, last night. I'm getting out of here as soon as everything else is sorted out. Nothing is going to change my mind about that.'

Ben leaned down until their lips were just inches apart. 'I can live with that.' He wasn't sure which of them closed the gap, but at the first velvety touch of her mouth on his, he wondered if perhaps he was making a terrible mistake. When her lips parted and her tongue darted out in a teasing touch, Ben realised he was already too far captivated by her to care.

* * *

'Show me,' he demanded for about the fifth time in as many minutes.

'Keep still,' Amelia admonished, tapping the end of his nose with the paintbrush she was holding. 'I'm nearly done.'

'You said that five minutes ago.' He didn't really care what the design she'd been painstakingly painting looked like; he just wanted her to finish so they could go back to the kissing bit of their evening.

'Umm hmm.' She wasn't really listening to him. He could tell by the slightly off-focus look in her eye. Just as he thought his patience might finally fail, she leaned back in her chair with a nod. 'That'll do.'

Ben reached for the mirror he'd fetched earlier from the bathroom, tilting the stand until he could see his reflection clearly. The upper part of his face was covered with a bold black bat design, the jagged tips of the wings flaring out across his cheeks. She'd used silver highlights to detail the ribs. 'That's incredible.'

The smile she gave him was a little shy. 'You think so?'

He nodded. 'I think it's brilliant. And I think the kids will love it.' He turned back to his reflection, touching his cheek to trace the outline of the bat. 'It wouldn't take much to adapt the design to be a butterfly, either.'

'I was thinking the same thing. I'd just need to round out the edges and add a smaller part below on each cheek for the bottom half of the wings.' She pointed at the palette. 'It didn't use as much paint as I expected, either. I reckon I can get away with what you've bought already plus one of the bigger ones I saw online when I was browsing at lunchtime. I might throw in a couple of pots of specialist glitter paint. I don't want to spend a fortune and end up not making any money. Plus the stencil set should speed things up on the day.' She reached for her bag and pulled out her purse. 'You'll have to tell me what I owe you for everything.'

It was on the tip of his tongue to tell her a few quid didn't matter, because to him it really didn't. *But it might do to her.* 'Thirty will more than cover it.'

'Are you sure?' She scrunched her eyes at him like she thought perhaps he was making it up.

'I'll get my phone and show you the receipt if you like.' She pulled two notes out and handed them to him and he shoved them in his pocket. 'Do you want me to go and wash this off and you can try something else?' Though he did really want to get back to the kissing, he'd promised he would be a model for her tonight, and he really wanted her to go into the event with as much confidence as possible.

'Why don't we have dinner first and we can see how well the paints stand up to you eating and drinking? If it all runs in five minutes, I'll end up with complaints and have to try something else.'

The bat design survived the meal and Ben was more than a little relieved when the promises on the packaging were true and the dark paint came off with hot water and soap. He resumed his seat at the table. 'What next?'

'I want to try these sponges, see what the coverage is like as it'll be a lot quicker to do the base than with a brush.'

Ten minutes later and Ben's face was a ghostly white, his eyes ringed in deep black shadows, his lips bright red with a trickle of what was supposed to be blood trailing down from one corner. 'I make a pretty decent vampire, don't you think?'

Hope laughed and tugged the mirror towards herself. 'Let me try a couple of these stencils.' She held one shaped like a pumpkin against her cheek and loaded a brush with orange paint. By the time she'd finished, she'd added a ghost, a jagged lightning bolt and an ugly-looking scar across her forehead.

'Look towards me.' Ben held up his camera and took a photo. He leaned closer and took proper close-ups of each of the individual stencilled images then sent the whole lot together with him as both a bat and a vampire to Hope as promised.

You are having far too much fun! Brilliant. Tell Amelia she's going to be a big hit x

He showed Amelia the reply, then set his phone down on the table. Reaching over, he pulled her chair close until their hips were all but touching. 'As I've been so patient, I think I deserve a reward.' He bent down and claimed a kiss, a second and then a third.

Before he could deepen their embrace, Amelia murmured against his lips. 'Didn't you promise me a soak in the hot tub?'

Grinning, Ben sat up. 'I did. How rude of me to forget. Why don't you go upstairs and get changed and I'll set it up?'

By the time he'd removed the cover and got the jets going, Amelia was back. She'd put a baggy T-shirt over her swimming costume and tied her blonde hair into a messy knot high on her head. Her face was scrubbed clean of the face paints, which was just as well because the steam in the hot tub would probably play havoc with them. 'Help yourself to a drink if you want one,' Ben told her. 'I'll be right back.'

Taking his cue from her, Ben washed his face before changing into a T-shirt and a pair of running shorts that also worked as swimwear. He collected two thick towels from the cupboard, grabbing the pair of luxurious dressing gowns that had come with the lodge and were hanging on the back of the bathroom door. He carried everything out and dropped it on one of the patio chairs and was immediately struck by how cold it was.

'Get in before you freeze!' Amelia was already in the tub, the bubbles reaching almost to her chin, one wet arm rested along the side of the tub holding a plastic wine glass. A second glass waited for him in a drinks holder on the opposite side.

Ben hurried up the little set of wooden stairs and stepped into the water, almost closing his eyes at the blissful heat. 'That's amazing.' He sighed, sinking down until he was chest-deep. There was a shelf to sit on and as he eased his way around it, he found a spot that dipped deeper and he settled onto the lower level. 'This is the life.'

Amelia grinned and raised her glass in a toast. 'Cheers. I only poured us half a glass after last night.'

Ben reached for his drink and returned the toast before taking a sip, savouring the contrast of the ice-cold wine in his mouth to the heat surrounding the rest of him. 'Lovely.'

Amelia tipped her head back against the edge, closing her eyes as a smile crossed her lips. 'I could get used to this.'

'So could I.' He wasn't talking about the hot tub. She was so beautiful, the delicate line of her throat exposed, the shadows of the evening highlighting the sharpness of her cheekbones. She was still a little thinner than he thought was completely healthy, but the worst of the dark rings beneath her eyes had faded and there was a bright sheen to her hair and eyes that had been missing before. He extended his foot beneath the water until he found the silky softness of her calf and stroked a caress along its length.

Her eyes opened and her smile warmed. 'Are you misbehaving?'

Ben laughed then groaned as one of the heavy jets behind him hit a tight spot on his hip. 'I'm never moving again.' He closed his eyes and let the water work its magic on his aching muscles as he and Amelia played footsie with each other.

They stayed in the water a few minutes longer than the recommended maximum time, both reluctant to move. 'I should be getting home,' Amelia said, making no effort to move.

'I'll walk back with you... just give me one more minute.' They looked at each other and laughed. He tried to muster the will required to get out. 'Come on, we'll be a pair of boiled lobsters if we don't get out soon.' It wasn't too much of an exaggeration as her cheeks were more than a little flushed and when Ben touched his own face he could feel the heat there.

'But it'll be cold,' Amelia protested, though she did at least sit up a bit straighter.

'I'll go first.' Ben forced himself to move, gasping as the chilly air turned his T-shirt to a clinging, ice-cold wrap in seconds. 'Bloody hell!' He hurried down the steps, wrestling the clammy top off. Grabbing one of the towels, he wrapped it tightly around his already shivering body until he was covered from chest to knees. He snatched up a robe and pulled that on over the top, belting it tightly at the waist. Only then did he pick up the second towel and hold it open. 'Come on, your turn.'

Amelia pulled a face but waded out of the tub. 'Oh my God!' she exclaimed, dancing down the stairs towards him and all but throwing herself into his arms.

He wrapped the towel around her, pulling it quickly away again. 'T-shirt off,' he instructed and she tugged it over her head and dropped it on the floor at their feet. Enveloping her once more in the towel, Ben rubbed his hands with vigour rather than any thoughts of seduction as he dried her off. 'Tuck that around you.' While she did that, he picked up the second robe and held it out so she could shove her arms in the sleeves and let him tie it tight. 'Quickly, let's get inside.'

'Remind me to bring something for my feet next time,' Amelia said as they scampered on tiptoes across the freezing boards of the decking and back into the cosy warmth of the lodge. 'Do you mind if I have a quick shower?' she asked.

Ben made himself busy while he waited his turn. He loaded the dishwasher, braved the cold of the deck – with his trainers on this time – to retrieve their plastic glasses and wet T-shirts, which he wrung out in the sink before hanging them on a radiator to dry. Anything to distract himself from the thought of a naked Amelia just a few feet above him. The dull hum of the shower shut off and then he was tortured with images of him holding a towel out for her as he had on the deck. In his mind's eye he was much more thorough, drying every inch of her soft skin until it glowed.

'It's all yours.'

Ben nearly jumped out of his skin. He'd been so lost in his fantasy, he hadn't heard her pad down the stairs in her bare feet. She'd undone her hair, letting it fall to her shoulders in a neat, pale curtain and he wanted to reach out and trail his hand through the soft silkiness. But that would mean turning away from the counter and he wasn't certain the towel and robe would be sufficient in hiding the evidence of his fertile imagination. 'Thanks. I'll just rinse these out.' He picked up the plastic glasses and turned on the tap. When he glanced around, she was busy packing her things up so Ben was able to make a dash for the stairs.

Five minutes later he was dressed and back under some semblance of self-control. He came downstairs to find Amelia standing a bit awkwardly by the table. 'I hope you don't think I'm being rude by wanting to head home.'

Ben hid his slight disappointment behind a smile and a joke. 'Don't worry, I know you only want me for my hot tub.'

As he hoped, her expression lifted and she grinned. 'Not just for your hot tub.'

Closing the space between them, he bent his head to brush a very gentle kiss over her lips. 'I've had a really nice evening.'

Amelia curled her arms around his waist and leaned against his chest. 'It's been great, but it was a really busy weekend and I'm almost dead on my feet now.'

He kissed the top of her head. 'It's fine, honestly.' And it was, because, regardless of the images his brain had been tormenting him with, he wasn't ready to push for more. 'I like spending time with you.'

Leaning back, she smiled up at him. 'That's good, because I like spending time with you.' It was too much temptation not to bend his head and kiss her again, but he kept things light and easy, even when she seemed to melt against him.

He stole one final kiss, then took her gently by the shoulders and set her away from him. 'You're making it very difficult for me to behave like a gentleman.'

'Sorry.' The saucy smile she gave him said she wasn't in the least bit sorry, that she might even be enjoying torturing him just a little bit.

'Get your coat on and behave.' He fetched his own coat from the cupboard and shoved his feet in his trainers while she pulled on her boots and buttoned up her red jacket. The colour reminded him of his impulse purchase the night before and he looked around until he spotted the Amazon box on a side table. 'Hey, I got you something.'

She stared at the box he placed in her hands. 'What's this?'

'Open it.'

She ripped off the tape and pulled out something red and fluffy, holding it up with a laugh. 'You bought me a hat?'

'Put it on,' he instructed, taking the box and removing the other item. 'I got you these as well.'

'Oh, you shouldn't have.' Her smile told him something different as she pulled on a matching pair of mittens. 'They've got fingers inside as well.'

'Here, I'll show you.' Ben unhooked the hood of the left mitten and folded it back, securing it with the Velcro tab, leaving her wearing a fingerless glove. 'You'll still be able to paint in them.'

'They're brilliant.' She tugged the other one on, secured the mitten part back and waggled her fingers at him, eyes bright with laughter. 'Genius! When on earth did you find time to buy them?'

'I ordered them last night. I remembered what you said about your gloves being stuck in a box somewhere.' He shrugged, feeling embarrassed but pleased at her delight. 'I thought these would do until you'd got unpacked.'

'I love them.' Amelia stretched up on tiptoe and kissed him. 'It was so thoughtful of you.'

21

The following Saturday morning didn't so much dawn as creep slowly out from under a blanket of thick, damp mist. Amelia showered quickly, having washed her hair the night before, and dressed in a comfortable old pair of jeans she wouldn't worry about if she got paint on and an aquamarine-coloured long-sleeve top her mum had once told her really made her blue eyes shine. She layered a black cardigan over the top and tucked her feet into her most comfortable training shoes. Rowena had been at pains to stress casual comfort as they'd be on their feet for a lot of the day. Butterflies were a constant companion in her tummy as she did her best to get through a small bowl of cornflakes, though she wasn't sure if it was the prospect of painting or of seeing Ben again that was the root cause of her nervousness. They hadn't seen each other since Monday evening; between work and helping her mum with the unpacking, Amelia simply hadn't had time to think about making other arrangements. Plus she knew they'd be spending most of the weekend together and she didn't want to come across as too keen. They'd messaged back and forth and she'd spent way too many hours lying in bed replaying those heated kisses when she should've been sleeping.

Having washed her things up in the sink, Amelia re-boiled the kettle, then took a cup of tea upstairs and knocked softly on Daisy's bedroom door. 'I'm awake, love,' her mum called out. 'You can come in.'

She was sitting up in bed, an open book splayed on the covers beside her. 'I'm off in a minute,' Amelia said as she carried the tea over and set it down on the bedside cabinet.

'How are you feeling about today?' Daisy asked after smiling in thanks for the drink.

'A bit nervous. I don't want people to think I'm a fraud. They've paid good money for this weekend.'

'You have a wonderful talent, love, and didn't Rowena say this was a beginner's retreat? I don't think you'll have anything to worry about, and she's not expecting you to teach them, just offer a bit of encouragement and maybe pass on a few tips and tricks if someone needs help.'

Amelia felt her shoulders relax and her spine straighten. It was amazing what a little pep talk from her mum could do. 'Thanks. I needed that.'

Daisy smiled as she reached for her tea. 'I could tell from the look on your face as soon as you walked through the door. The last time you looked that nervous was before your GCSEs! Go on now, you'll be fine.'

'Yes, Mum!' Amelia gave her a little salute and bounced down the stairs on much lighter feet. It wasn't just the pep talk that had cheered her up; it was like moving into the cottage had given her mother a new lease of life. Amelia wasn't foolish enough to think that all their problems were going to be solved in one fell swoop, but it was beginning to feel like the fresh start they both needed. She tugged on her coat, adding the matching hat and gloves Ben had given her, and stepped outside. A misty veil hung in the air and fine droplets clung to the sleeves and shoulders of her coat before she'd made it to the end of the road. She hoped it would lift at some point as the light was very flat for anyone wanting to paint the landscape.

The cold air was a good incentive to move briskly and she soon reached the main driveway, which she could follow all the way to the Hall. It'd be a bit longer than cutting across the fields, but her feet would be soaked from the wet grass. A bright flash of yellow shone through the mist and she smiled as a figure turned and she spotted Ben peering out from under the fake-fur brim lining the hood of his jacket. 'Hello! I thought we were meeting up at the Hall.'

'I figured you'd stick to the road so I thought I'd wait for you here.'

'Were you worried I was going to chicken out?'

He laughed and held out his hand. 'Come here.' She took his hand and let him tug her close. He bent his head and kissed her, the edges of his wide hood offering a semblance of privacy, although there was no sign of anyone else around. The morning was so quiet and still, it was easy to believe they were the only two people in existence, especially when he opened his mouth against hers and she forgot about anything other than the taste of him. When they came up for air, he sent her a wicked grin that had her toes curling and her insides heating. 'I've been thinking about doing that again ever since you left on Monday night.'

'You might have crossed my mind a time or two,' she admitted with a grin. 'Or three or four.'

Ben laughed. 'Come on, let's get going before I haul you back to the lodge and show you all the things that have been crossing *my* mind this week.'

It was an intoxicating thought, and she couldn't remember the last time she'd felt so desirous of another person and had that same desire returned. Her relationship with Rhys had ended in a long, slow fizzle a million miles away from their early youthful passions. The only person who'd asked her out since they'd broken up was one of the sales reps at work, and though he'd always been nice enough, she hadn't felt anything like the excitement being close to Ben inspired and it hadn't seemed worth the risk of making things awkward around the office.

She almost forgot they were holding hands until they approached the wide circle of driveway around the fountain in front of the Hall. The front door was open, and an older couple were making their way down the steps. When she would've pulled her hand free, Ben's fingers tightened just a little and she relaxed when she realised it wasn't anyone they knew. Not that there was anything wrong with the pair of them holding hands – she just didn't need to give people something else to gossip about.

The couple smiled as they approached. 'Looks like we aren't the first ones out for a walk this morning,' the man said, clearly taking them for other guests.

'It's a good way to work up an appetite.' Ben squeezed her hand again as he turned to look at her with a wicked gleam in his eye.

It was all Amelia could do to keep her face straight when the woman started chattering about how much she was looking forward to tucking into a full English when they got back. 'If you can't be naughty now and again, honestly, where's the fun in life?' she added.

Amelia bit her lip, not daring to look at Ben as she said, 'I quite agree.'

With a quick wave, the couple were on their way and Ben all but dragged Amelia up the stairs and inside the front door before they collapsed against each other in a fit of giggles. 'I'm all for being naughty now and again,' Ben murmured against her ear, turning her giggles to gasps as he nipped the delicate lobe between his teeth.

'Stop it,' she whispered, though she couldn't resist arching against him for a moment.

'It's not too late to go back to the lodge, you know. Or I can see if there's a room here.'

It was tempting and ridiculous in equal measures. 'I can't wait to see you march up to the reception desk and say, "Hello, Mum, have you got a spare room as I want to take my girlfriend to bed, please."'

Ben's eyes shot wide and his head whipped around as though he really expected to see Stevie standing there rather than a junior member of staff. He turned back to her with a scowl. 'Jeez, don't scare me like that!'

She shot him an unrepentant grin as she tugged off her hat and began to unzip her coat. 'Well, behave yourself then. Come on, let's go and find Rowena and see what she needs us to do first.'

Not easily cowed even by the thought of his mother catching them fooling around, Ben followed her across the grand entrance hall that now served as the hotel lobby. 'All right, I'll be on my best behaviour for the rest of the day.' She pretended not to notice the way he'd emphasised the word 'day'.

They asked at the reception desk and were sent through to the orangery, which overlooked the formal gardens at the rear of the Hall. It was a light, airy space even on this gloomy morning, filled with potted plants and cosy seating nooks where one could gaze out of the windows and watch the world go by or curl up with a book. Rowena was wrestling with an easel and Ben hurried over to take it from her. 'Bloody things drive me bananas,' Rowena said, shaking her head. Her wild auburn curls were held back with a purple and gold scarf and big gold hoops hung from her ears.

'Hello, darling,' she said, sweeping Amelia into a bangle-jangling hug. 'How are you?'

'A bit nervous, if I'm honest,' Amelia admitted.

'Oh, there's really no need to be! I had dinner with everyone last night and they're all lovely.' She released Amelia, then turned to give Ben a hug and a kiss on the cheek. 'It's a bit of an eclectic mix. There's a few who are definitely here to learn but I've got half a dozen ladies on a hen weekend who are as interested in the spa as they are in painting and I think they're just looking to have some fun.' She pointed to an area at the other end of the orangery where she'd set up a group of easels in a circle on their own. 'I thought I'd separate them and maybe you could look after them for me, Amelia, as they might find Ben a bit of a distraction.' She winked up at her nephew. 'I don't want them mistaking you for a strip-pergram.'

Don't think about Magic Mike, *don't think about* Magic Mike... but it was too late and Amelia's brain was already filled with images of hot men with glistening abs and low-slung jeans barely clinging to their hips. She made the mistake of catching Ben's eye and then all she could think about was the glimpse of naked torso she'd seen when he'd stripped his T-shirt off after they'd been in the hot tub. He might not possess the exaggerated six-pack body of the actors in the film, but his lean runner's build was far sexier in her opinion. She knew if she raised her hand to her cheek she'd feel the blush burning there. Thankfully Rowena had already bustled towards a table piled high with sketch pads, paint palettes and brushes. Ben leaned close. 'I can't wait to find out later what put that look upon your face,' he murmured before gliding over towards his aunt and leaving Amelia to try and collect herself as best she could.

By nine o'clock they had the room set up to Rowena's liking and the first of the guests drifted in. Rowena greeted them like they were already the best of friends and Amelia could see the way they responded positively to her natural warmth. Though they'd likely just come from breakfast, there was tea and coffee available, and Amelia kept herself busy fetching whatever was wanted while Rowena settled the guests in one of the seating areas made up of a group of white cane sofas with overstuffed cushions that looked like plump marshmallows.

A group of six women walked in, all clutching mimosas. Five were wearing white T-shirts that declared them to be 'Bella's Besties' in sparkling gold letters. The other wore a flamingo-pink T-shirt and a tiara and her T-shirt simply said 'Bella' on the front in the same glittering font. They were older than Amelia had expected, maybe early or mid-forties, and she started to relax a bit. When Rowena had mentioned a hen party, Amelia had visions of one of those rowdy gangs of young women she'd seen on those documentaries set in airports or that followed the police on Saturday nights.

Amelia went to meet them, offering her hand to Bella. 'Hello, I'm Amelia, and you must be the bride-to-be! Congratulations, I was so excited when Rowena told me we were going to be helping you celebrate this weekend.' It was only the whitest of lies and she wanted to make them feel welcome as well as start off on a confident footing, even if she wasn't feeling it. She nodded at the half-empty glass Bella was holding. 'I'm pleased to see you've started off the day in the right spirit.'

'Hello! Isn't this place amazing?' Bella waved her hand to encompass the beautiful room around them. 'I couldn't believe my bedroom when I saw it last night. It has a proper four-poster and everything. I sent Will some photos and he was gutted because he's in an Airbnb place in Spain with his mates and it's chucked it down since they arrived yesterday.'

'Perhaps you can talk him into a return visit here for your first anniversary,' Amelia suggested, thinking it wouldn't do any harm to do a bit of marketing.

'Oh, that's a fab idea!' Bella hooked her arm through Amelia's like she was her new best friend. 'So, what have you got in store for us today?'

Amelia led them over to the group of easels at the other end of the long room. 'This is where we're going to be working this morning so feel free to make the space your own.' She gestured to a seating area next to them. 'You can put your things there if you like and there's a menu on the table showing you what drinks and snacks are available. It's all included so don't be shy, and if you have any special requests that aren't on the menu just let me know and I'll do my best to arrange it.' Rowena had taken her through the spiel before they started, and her emphasis had been on maximum guest satisfaction.

'Can we have some more bubbles?' one of the other women asked.

'Gill!' exclaimed another. 'We'll be blotto by lunchtime at this rate.'

'Nonsense,' Gill replied. 'It'll help the creative juices to flow.'

'Perhaps I should add a jug of orange juice as well,' Amelia suggested. 'Just so those creative juices don't flow completely off the page.' The women laughed and Amelia left them to settle on the chairs while she nipped out to the bar to order the drinks.

'Everything all right?' Rowena called to her on her return.

'All good. I think we're in for a lively morning, though.'

Rowena chuckled. 'I'll get everyone else going, then pop over and see how you are getting on in a bit. Shout if you need me in the meantime.'

'Will do.' Amelia returned to her ladies, only to find one of them had gone AWOL already. *Keep calm.* 'Right, shall we get started?' she said to the others. The five women followed her to where the easels were set up and gathered in a loose circle around her. 'I want to tailor this weekend to whatever will be most enjoyable for you,' she said. 'Have any of you done any sketching or painting before?'

'Not since school,' Gill said, and the others nodded in agreement. 'Bella loves those artist-of-the-year shows; that's why we thought this would be fun for her.'

'So if I treat you all as beginners then everyone will be happy with that?' They nodded again. 'Let's start off easy, then, with some charcoal sketching, shall we?' The view through the window was still a bit damp and uninspiring so Amelia cast her eye around the orangery and settled on a huge potted palm tree. She chose half a dozen other plants that were perched on stands nearby and arranged them around the base of the pot so their trailing vines and pretty flowers added contrast and texture.

Amelia had just finished rearranging the easels into a line facing her impromptu display when the missing woman showed up. She was a little out of breath and was clutching something in her hand. 'This is for you,' she said with a grin as she thrust the bundle at Amelia.

She shook it out and laughed when she saw it was a spare 'Bella's Besties' T-shirt. 'What do you think?' Amelia asked as she pulled it on over her own top.

'Perfect,' Bella replied as the others gave her a little round of applause. 'Now you're officially one of the gang!'

Amelia picked up one of the pieces of charcoal and took a long calming breath to settle herself. 'Right, if you want to gather around me, I'll show you a few tips and techniques and then you can have a go yourselves, okay?' She took a moment to study the display she'd set up, then turned the charcoal in her hand and stroked a broad, confident line up the centre of the blank sheet of paper in front of her. She mirrored the sweep of the line, broad at the bottom, tapering in the middle and widening out again at the top. 'This will be the trunk of the palm.' She added a few other lines. 'And this is the pot. I know we can't see all of it, but by adding it in I've got a framework to set out the other plants, which will help me keep the proportions.' A handful of other marks and she had the suggestion of the trailing vines on the page.

'It's like magic,' one of the women said in a hushed voice.

'Just a lot of practice,' Amelia assured her over one shoulder. 'We're going for the feeling of what we're seeing. Art is as much about what something makes you feel as it is about recreating a faithful image of what's in front of you.'

'Oh, I like that,' Bella said.

'Another mimosa and all I'll be feeling is merry,' said Gill, and her friends giggled.

Amelia added in the first curling fronds of the palm, keeping it simple with a main strand and lots of quick feathered lines falling on each side. 'Right,' she said, setting down the charcoal on the edge of the easel and picking up a cloth to wipe her fingers. 'That should give you enough of an idea to get started. Don't worry about making a mistake because charcoals are very forgiving.' Using the edge of the cloth, she smudged over the lines of one of the fronds to soften them. 'See how easy it is to change?'

The six women set themselves up and Amelia stepped back to give them a little bit of space without feeling like she was looming over their shoulders. There were nervous giggles, a few whispered exchanges and eventually Gill picked up her charcoal and began to draw. Once she started, the others followed suit and Amelia gave a silent sigh of relief. It was tempting to intervene when she saw a mistake, but she decided to let them settle in a bit before offering any advice. Swooping in too early to point out an error, even with good intentions, might kill any bit of confidence they had. Best to wait a bit or until someone asked, even if it made Amelia's fingers itch to pick up the charcoal again.

'How's it going?'

She almost leaped out of her skin. Spinning around, she found Ben grinning at her, not in the least bit sorry he'd made her jump. 'What are you doing sneaking up on me like that?'

He showed her the bottle of champagne and jug of orange juice he was carrying. 'I come bearing gifts.'

'Ooh, lovely! This drawing lark is thirsty work,' said Bella, who, when Amelia turned, had actually made a really good start.

'Looking good, ladies,' Ben said, all charm and smiles as he made a show of pausing to examine each sketch in turn. 'You definitely deserve a drink.' He headed over to the table and they buzzed around him like bees around a flower as he chatted and joked and topped up their glasses. Amelia didn't miss that his hand with the juice was more generous than the one with the bottle.

Rowena came and joined them, bearing a tray of little snacks and pastries. 'How are we getting on over here?' she asked as she set the treats down on the table. 'Is Amelia taking good care of you all?'

'She's brilliant,' said Gill, tipping Amelia a wink. 'Though she needs a glass!'

'Oh no, I'm fine thank you!' Amelia held up her hands.

'But you're one of the gang now,' Gill protested.

'Honestly, leave the poor girl alone! She's trying to work,' one of the others scolded and Gill looked suddenly shamefaced.

Worried she was losing control of things, Amelia hurried to the other end of the room and grabbed a champagne flute from the table. Returning, she held out the glass to Ben. 'Just a spot.' He splashed a tiny bit of champagne into the flute and drowned it in orange juice. Amelia raised the glass and toasted the ladies. 'Cheers!'

'Cheers!' they chorused and Amelia was relieved to see Gill looking cheerful once more.

'Nice job,' Rowena said, low enough that the others wouldn't hear before she raised her voice and added, 'Well, I shall leave you in Amelia's good hands. Come along, Ben.'

As they left, Bella raised an eyebrow at Amelia. 'Friend of yours?'

'Yes.' Amelia hid her grin behind a sip of her mostly orange juice as the admission was greeted by a chorus of delighted oohs and aahs from the others.

By the time they took a break for lunch, the volume at their end of the orangery had risen quite a bit and Amelia was glad they were taking a break. The mist had lifted so Rowena was taking those who wanted to try a bit of painting *en plein air* out into the gardens. Only Bella wanted to join her, the others either heading to the spa for a massage or off to bed for an afternoon nap, so both Amelia and Ben decided to join in with the group that had gathered around a fountain.

The water had been switched off and the bowl into which the Grecian goddess was emptying an amphora had become a gathering place for fallen leaves from the nearby trees. It was a slightly melancholic scene and Amelia decided it would be an interesting spot to return to and see how it changed over the seasons. Only she wasn't planning on being there for another year, was she? Six months, for sure, but if she was still living on the estate in the height of next summer when the gardens were in full flower then something would've gone badly awry with her escape plan. It wasn't as if she intended to stay away forever, and hopefully her mother would get herself properly set with a full-time job and be earning enough to manage the cottage on her own.

She glanced across at Ben, who was chewing on the end of a brush, a deep frown etched between his brows. Would he still be around next summer? Or would he too have taken himself off to wherever he decided to set up his pottery studio? She wondered if he'd considered taking one of the units over at The Old Stable Yard, but maybe it was still too early for him to be thinking about making a more permanent connection with his new family. She peeked another glance over at Ben, who was now attacking his canvas with broad, decisive strokes. If he was still around then that would be another incentive to pay a return visit, wouldn't it? Tucking the thought away, she turned back to her own canvas and let herself get lost in the sheer joy of being paid for doing the thing she loved most in the world.

* * *

By the time they'd helped Rowena tidy up for the day and said goodbye to the guests, it was dark outside. As they made their way down the wide steps of the Hall, Ben offered Amelia his hand and she was happy to take it and snuggle up against his side. A chilly wind was blowing from the east, its fingers sneaking in under the edge of her collar and making her shiver. 'Here.' Ben released her hand and placed his arm around her shoulder instead, tucking her closer against him and they walked a little quicker. 'You had fun today,' he said as they crossed the sweeping driveway and began to follow the road.

'I did. I was worried I'd be too nervous to relax, but the ladies were such a blast I forgot all about it.'

'It's more than that, though. I was watching you this afternoon and you were practically glowing.'

Amelia laughed, feeling a little bit self-conscious. 'I think that was probably the cold wind making my nose red.'

He pulled them both to a halt and turned to face her. 'No, don't joke about it. I'm serious. When I looked at you, I could tell you were exactly where you were supposed to be and the reason I know that is because it's exactly how I feel when I sit behind my potter's wheel. You were born to hold a paintbrush in your hand.'

She closed the small distance between them and let her forehead rest against his chest. 'It felt so good,' she admitted. His arms closed around her and she let him hold her for a long moment before she pulled back enough to look up at him. 'Who knows, if Rowena is happy with how the rest of the weekend goes, maybe this can become a semi-regular gig for me.'

'Is it enough to sustain you, though?'

'It'll have to be, won't it?' Not everyone had family money to fall back on. She held that thought close because whatever lies Ben's father might have told him, she didn't doubt for a second that he'd pay every penny he was due to inherit if it meant getting his dad back. 'I don't want to talk about practical stuff; just let me hold onto the buzz of getting to paint again.'

Ben leaned down and kissed her softly. 'Of course.' His lips curled into a smile. 'Speaking of buzzes, you weren't tempted to accept Bella's invitation to remain one of her Besties tonight?'

They'd come back in from the cold of the garden to find the rest of the hens had rallied and were back on the bubbles again. They'd whooped with delight at spotting Bella and sent her hurrying off upstairs to get changed. She'd paused at the lift to ask Amelia if she wanted to join them for drinks and dinner. Amelia had been touched by the gesture, but she had something else in mind for the rest of the evening. 'I thought perhaps you might make me a better offer.'

Ben's hands slid from the small of her back to cup her bottom and pull her close against him. 'Oh, did you now?' Their lips met and soon Amelia forgot all about the worries of the past and her fears for the future. Nothing mattered in that moment but the man who held her safe and warm and cherished in his arms.

They lay in bed together later, Amelia's head pillowed on Ben's chest, his hand tracing soft circles at the base of her spine. The moon had risen some time ago and Amelia knew it was past time for her to go home. She could stay, she supposed, as she'd sent a text to her mum earlier saying she was having dinner at Ben's and it wouldn't take much for Daisy to put two and two together. But then she'd have to get up early in the morning and hurry home to change because turning up for the second day of the art retreat in the previous day's clothing was not going to happen. 'I need to go.' She forced the reluctant words out.

'I know. I'll get dressed and walk you back.' Neither of them moved.

'This is like the hot tub all over again,' Amelia said with a giggle as she snuggled closer.

'With less clothes.' Ben shifted suddenly, rolling Amelia onto her back and coming down on top of her, hands resting either side of her shoulders as his legs settled between hers. He lowered his mouth to hers for a long, slow kiss that turned her insides liquid once more.

'I really need to go.' Her last word ended on a little moan as he shifted his lips from her mouth to the sensitive spot beneath her ear.

'Are you sure?' Ben murmured against her ear as he traced the shell of it with tiny kisses.

She shivered against him. 'That's not fair.'

His low laugh contained just enough satisfaction that Amelia was determined not to let him get away with it. Raising one foot, she made a show of caressing it down the back of his calf, earning a hum of appreciation from Ben, who was still peppering her neck and shoulder with kisses. She hooked the quilt with her foot and dragged it down, exposing Ben's back to the cold air. 'Hey!' Ben exclaimed as he scrabbled in vain, trying to pull it back. Laughing,

Amelia kicked at the tangle of the quilt until it slipped to the floor, leaving them both fully exposed, although she had the advantage of Ben acting as a human blanket. 'All right, all right,' Ben grumbled. 'I can take a hint.' He swooped down for one final quick kiss, then rolled to the side.

Amelia immediately regretted her actions. 'God, it's freezing in here!'

She tried to cuddle close to Ben's heat but he pushed her away with a laugh and sat up. 'I thought you wanted to go home?'

'I might have changed my mind.'

He clicked on the bedside lamp, flooding the room with a light that felt harsh compared to the soft monochrome of the moon, and Amelia flung an arm over her face to cover her eyes. A few seconds later something soft landed on her middle and she lifted her arm to see Ben had tossed her top and underwear at her. Her jeans landed on the bed next to her before he started tugging on his own clothes.

Five minutes later they were bundled up in their coats, hats and gloves and Ben was pulling the patio doors closed behind them. 'You don't have to walk me home,' Amelia protested, though her heart wasn't in it.

'I'm not letting you walk back on your own,' Ben said, flicking on the torch on his mobile phone. 'And not just because I wouldn't be able to sleep thinking about you all alone in the dark.' His gloved hand tightened around hers. 'I'm just not ready to let you go yet.'

Amelia knew what he meant because she wanted to hold onto him for as long as possible as well. 'But how am I supposed to sleep when you have to walk back here from my place on your own?' she teased, though she knew she would worry about him even knowing Juniper Meadows was about as safe an environment as there could be. Well, now her father was behind bars and not around to cause any more mischief. The ugly reminder stole all the joy from inside her.

'I'll have to call you as I walk back and then I won't be on my own, will I?'

'That's true,' Amelia said half-heartedly, her mind to full of images she'd rather forget.

Ben gently shook her hand. 'Hey, where did you go?'

She didn't want to spoil what had been a wonderful evening by dragging up a load of old crap about her dad. 'Sorry, it's nothing, I was just daydreaming.' Ben's silence told her he wasn't buying it so she hunted around for something that might distract him. 'This might seem a bit left field and you can tell me to mind my own business, but I was watching earlier when we were painting outside and I was wondering if you'd given any more thought about where you might set up your pottery studio.'

'I hadn't really thought about it. I'll need to see how much I realise from my father's estate first as that will dictate things in terms of locations I can afford. I don't want to sink every penny I've got into buying somewhere and not leave myself a good cushion to support myself while I try and get up and running.'

'Prices around here are prohibitively expensive.' She knew from her own panicked property-hunting after Eric had given them notice of his intention to evict them. 'It's just a shame you don't know anyone who owns a huge expanse of land with lots and lots of buildings on it.'

Ben halted. 'You're talking about finding somewhere here on the estate, aren't you?'

'Like I said, you can tell me to mind my own business, but I was thinking how well something like a pottery studio would fit in with the other craftspeople who are already established at The Old Stable Yard. There's a few empty units and you'd have a ready-made customer base as it's already a popular place for visitors.' *And*

I'd still get to see you now and again. She kept that thought to herself. 'Look, it's just something that occurred to me so I thought I'd mention it. It's probably too soon for you to know if you want to be in such close proximity to the rest of the family.'

'I did like the set-up when Jason showed me around his workshop...' Ben fell silent and Amelia let him be as they continued to make their way out of the woods and onto the road. She assumed he didn't want to discuss it further so was surprised when he picked up the subject a few minutes later. 'I hadn't really thought about, or I hadn't really let myself think about it in case things didn't work out here, but it makes a lot of sense.'

Amelia was relieved he hadn't rejected the idea out of hand and didn't seem to mind that she'd suggested it. 'It's not something you have to decide about now. It'll be a while before everything's sorted with your dad's estate; by the time that comes through, you'll perhaps have a clearer idea about everything.'

He released her hand only long enough to curl one arm around her shoulders. 'It's a good idea, thank you.'

22

Ben sat at his desk on Monday morning. He'd logged into his work system with all good intentions of cracking on but instead found himself staring out of the window as he sipped his coffee and let his mind drift. He'd woken up with his arms wrapped around one of his spare pillows, the faint scent of Amelia's perfume still lingering on the cotton from Saturday night. She'd been tired last night after they'd finished the second day of the art retreat and he hadn't pushed her to come back with him. Though she'd enjoyed the weekend, he could tell it had taken a lot out of her to keep the hen party entertained. He'd definitely drawn the easier job of helping Rowena out with the rest of the guests. They'd been a much quieter bunch and much more focused, as learning or improving was really all they were interested in. The hens had come and gone all day, wanting to go for a walk, wanting to squeeze in another visit to the spa, wanting to celebrate and make the most of their time together. Amelia had done an amazing job keeping them happy and he could tell from the way Rowena had gushed over her as they were leaving on Sunday evening that she would have Amelia back in a heartbeat. He hoped it was something she would keep up.

It was a far cry, perhaps, from what she'd dreamed about doing when she was younger, but it was a stepping stone in the right direction. Maybe one day she would find a way to achieve those dreams of becoming an artist in the way he was going to try and fulfil his own desire to become a successful potter. They could work side by side over at The Old Stable Yard, even, because once she'd planted the seed in his head about setting up his studio there it had taken root. He gave himself a shake. No, he had to tread carefully there. No matter how much he was enjoying spending time with Amelia, he had to respect her wishes. She'd told him she wanted to leave once she got herself sorted out, and he had to respect that. That didn't mean he couldn't try and give her reasons to stay, but it would be her choice. He knew too well what it was like to feel pressured into going along with someone else's plans – he'd lived under the yoke his father had put around his neck after all. Ben had to look after himself, look after his own future and hope that somewhere down the line Amelia might want to align her future with his.

The phone rang, disturbing his reverie, and Ben pulled his attention back to the here and now. Thinking it was someone from work, he tapped the side of his headphones and answered without looking at the screen. 'Ben Lawson.'

'Ben. It's Dominic Proud.'

For a moment he thought about cutting the call off. 'What do you want?'

'I know I'm the last person you want to speak to, but can you please just give me five minutes of your time?'

Ben hesitated, then reminded himself he'd decided to deal with the devil if it meant he could get things moving with his father's estate. 'Things didn't go well the last time we spoke, so you'd better make it good.'

There was a long exhale of breath at the other end. 'I wanted to apologise for the way I handled things when we met the other day. You caught me off guard.'

'Caught you red-handed, you mean?' If this was some play for sympathy, Dominic was in for a disappointment.

A long silence followed. 'Indeed. I could make excuses to you for why I behaved the way I did, but I won't insult you by pretending there was any justification.' When Ben didn't respond, Dominic gave another of those world-weary sighs and continued. 'When I got home after you came to see me, I confessed all to Chessie. She was horrified, of course.'

'Discovering the person you're closest to has broken the law has a habit of doing that.' Ben wasn't sure if what Dominic had done was actually illegal or just unethical, but he wasn't going to let the man off without squirming a bit.

'Indeed. I can pretend I'm calling for purely altruistic reasons, but the bottom line is she's threatening to leave me and take the boys with her if I don't sort it out. I've spoken to Gary Dodds, our senior partner, and I'll be stepping down from the firm with immediate effect. He was equally appalled and wants you to know that if you haven't engaged someone else to assist you with the probate then he is willing to take it on – pro bono. Same with any conveyancing work if you decide to sell the house. Really, whatever you need for the foreseeable future in terms of legal representation.'

'And what's the catch? I sweep everything under the rug and forget what you did?'

'Not at all. Gary is willing to represent you regardless of any decision you may make about reporting me. If that's something you still wish to pursue, I'll self-report the issue myself.'

Ben couldn't help but feel sceptical. 'And what's brought on this sudden change of heart?'

'Chessie. When she said she was leaving it was like my whole world was falling apart. She and the kids mean everything to me.' There was something so simple and heartfelt about the way he said it that Ben actually believed him.

'I don't care what you do, to be honest; I just want to be done with the whole thing. Tell Mr Dodds he can email me about making an appointment and I'll deal with him going forwards.'

'Thank you.'

'Well, if that's it, I won't be a hypocrite and thank you in return, but I hope you and Chessie manage to sort things out.' His father had done enough damage to last a lifetime and the last thing Ben wanted was another family torn apart over this wretched business.

Dominic hesitated again. 'There's just one more thing.'

A lead weight dropped in Ben's stomach. 'Go on.'

'When I saw your father at the hospital to go over his final arrangements, he gave me a letter addressed to you. He didn't tell me what's in there, and I didn't ask him. He called me the next morning and asked me to destroy it. He also wanted me to hang onto the keys until I could gain access to his office and retrieve the files from his desk. I was going to put them both through your letterbox, but it didn't seem right not to speak to you about it first.'

Another letter. Christ only knew what it might say. 'If he asked you to destroy it, why did you keep it?'

Dominic gave a sad-sounding chuckle. 'Regardless of what you may think of me, I'm not completely without empathy. I never agreed with your father's decision to hide his diagnosis from you. My father died of cancer some years ago, and although some of my memories of those months are full of terrible pain, I wouldn't have given them up for anything. You deserved that time with him. To deprive you of what were some of his final words and feelings seems unbearably cruel.'

'Thank you.' It was all Ben could manage to say; his mind was in absolute turmoil at what was coming next.

'I could drop it through the door, only I wasn't sure when you were likely to be back. I have a scanner here, so I could email you a copy now if you'd prefer and the original will be waiting for you when you come home.'

Home. It wasn't his home, hadn't been for a long time. Was his flat in London? No, the stuff that had made it feel that way had fitted into a couple of cardboard boxes. Ben stared out of the window at the birds pecking at the feeder he'd hung on the patio, at the swaying trees beyond shifting into their autumn splendour almost before his eyes.

Was this home?

Maybe not yet, but there was a chance it could be one day. Maybe, just maybe this letter from his father would hold the answer to some of the questions that were holding him back. Hadn't he wished for just a few minutes with him so he could demand some answers? 'Send it.' He hung up before Dominic could say goodbye.

Less than five minutes later, a notification flashed in the corner of his laptop screen and Ben flicked his work messaging service to Do Not Disturb. With a click of his trackpad, he opened a new window on his browser and navigated to his personal email account. Taking a deep breath, he opened the message and scrolled straight down to the file attachment and clicked on it. The screen filled with his father's familiar handwriting.

Dear Ben,

I've tried to write this letter so many times, perhaps I'll make it past the first paragraph this time before I screw it up and throw it away. Perhaps I'll even have the courage to let you read it.

Perhaps not.

I don't know how else to say this other than to just come out with it. Your mother is still alive. I can't believe I've finally admitted that, even to myself. Did you know that if you tell yourself a lie long enough, you can actually start to believe it in the end? At least some of the time.

I know you'll be furious with me for keeping this from you and I won't try and make excuses for what I've done. All I can do is try and explain. Whatever happens, you must never blame her for any of this – it was and always will be my fault she left. I didn't know until I met Stevie that it was possible to love someone too much, but that's what happened with us. With me.

I can only liken it to an obsession. I loved her so much, I became convinced every other man would fall in love with her too. Worse, I believed she'd fall in love with someone else. How could she not when I wasn't worthy of her? The harder she tried to convince me that it was only me she was interested in, the more it fed my suspicions. I can make you all the excuses in the world. Tell you it was all my own parents' fault and that what I witnessed as a child had a deeply damaging effect on me. Maybe that's true, but I had other choices I could've made. Other paths I could've taken.

And so perhaps it was for the best that Stevie left me when she did. Before you were old enough to understand.

God forgive me if you'd ever had to witness what I put her through. At least she saved you from that. She saved me too in a way because her leaving was the catalyst I needed to try and sort myself out. I had counselling, which helped me to recognise that I was repeating the same toxic patterns as my father and do my best to break free of them. It was only a partial success, but I wanted to be the best version of me I could manage, for your sake. I couldn't trust myself with another relationship, not that I ever really wanted another woman. Only your mother.

I know I've let you down. That I tried too hard to control you. I kept telling myself when I pushed you to do what I wanted that it was for the best, but that was a lie too. I knew I was making you unhappy and I couldn't bear to lose you, not completely. That's why I didn't fight it when you told me you were moving to London. Buying you that flat was one of the hardest things I've ever had to do, but I knew the only way I could show you that I really loved you was to let you go. You taught me that at least, so thank you.

I don't know what else there is I can say because no apology will ever be enough to make up for what I've done.

I love you, son. If you find Stevie, tell her I'm sorry.

Dad xx

His mother's full name and address were printed in neat capital letters as though his father had wanted them to be as clear as possible. Below that were a final few scribbled lines in a different-coloured pen. Ben could barely make the cramped script out through his tears.

I've just read over what I've written and the urge to rip this up and throw it away is almost unbearable. I've been a coward for far too long. Please let the tiny burst of courage that enabled me to write this letter stay long enough to make sure it gets into your hands.

'Oh, Dad.' Ben closed his eyes and sank back in his chair. If what Dominic said was true, then his father's courage had failed him in the end. Would it have been better if the solicitor had obeyed his father's wishes and destroyed this final message to Ben? Only time would tell.

He got up from his desk and paced around the room, the walls of the lodge feeling like they were closing in on him. He went into the kitchen area, filled the kettle and turned it on. Five seconds later he flipped it off. Coffee wasn't going to help. He needed to think; he needed to talk to someone because what he'd learned felt like too much for his head to contain. Ben's first instinct was to message Amelia and tell her all about it. He opened WhatsApp and selected her name, then hesitated. She would be at work, doing a job she hated but needed if she was going to sort her life out. He hated the idea of her cooped up in that office. She should be the way he'd seen her on Saturday, happy and free and teaching other people to love what she loved.

Plus, she had her own shit with her father to sort out; she didn't need him dumping all his trauma on her shoulders as well. He would talk to her later, once he'd got over this initial shock. He paced again, that caged feeling threatening to overwhelm him and he knew he needed to get outside for a bit. He jogged upstairs and changed into his running kit. Tucking his key in an inside pocket on his shorts, Ben jogged down the patio stairs and around the side of the lodge.

He avoided the walking routes through the woods as the events company had already started building the light trails for the upcoming Halloween weekend. Setting up his running app, Ben made his way towards the Hall, planning on doing a long loop around the estate roads. Every slap of his feet on the hard surface settled the turmoil inside him. Every exhalation from his burning lungs expelled another bit of the poison that had been threatening to choke him.

The final part of the loop brought him back along the main drive from the entrance gate and Ben had slowed to a gentle jog, wishing he'd brought a drink with him. Spotting the farmhouse ahead, he decided on a quick detour. If no one was home, there'd be an outside tap at least where he could scoop a few mouthfuls of water and quench his thirst.

He knocked on the back door, but there was no answer. Hands on hips, he surveyed the building but there was no sign of a tap. Checking around the side, he spotted one under the kitchen window – well, he spotted the locked plastic cover someone had fitted to winterise the tap, and cursed their efficiency. Oh well, it wasn't too far back to the lodge; if he took things steady, he'd be fine. Or he could just try the door and see if it was open. The handle turned in his hand and Ben pushed the door ajar. 'Hello?' he called. 'It's Ben. Is anyone home?'

Silence. He stepped inside, trying not to feel like he was doing something wrong. This was his family's home, and he wasn't some random stranger. He toed off his trainers by the back door. He'd been on the roads so they were pretty clean, but still he didn't want to risk trekking mud across the tiles. A door opened and a voice called his name. 'Ben?' Ziggy walked into the kitchen. 'Hello! I thought I heard you. Sorry, I was on the phone.'

Though his uncle was smiling, Ben still felt awkward, like he'd been caught doing something he shouldn't. 'I was out for a run and I forgot my drink. I didn't mean to disturb you.'

'It's fine. I was ready for a coffee break anyway.' Ziggy picked up the kettle and used it to indicate towards the fridge. 'Help yourself to whatever you want. There's always a jug of cold cordial mixed up or there's some cans on the shelf.'

'Thanks.' Ben had been meaning to just grab a glass of water and be on his way, but a cold glass of cordial sounded too good to pass up. He lifted the jug out, then looked around the kitchen as though one of the cupboards would magically open and a glass would jump out for him.

'Cupboard above the fruit bowl,' Ziggy said as though reading his mind. 'Grab a seat and I'll be with you in a minute.'

'Have you got a towel or something?' Ben didn't want to sit on the cushioned chair when he was still sweaty from running.

'Yeah, of course. Hold on, I'll get you one from my bathroom.' Ziggy disappeared back the way he'd come and returned a moment later with a large striped towel, which he draped over one of the kitchen chairs. 'There you go.'

'Thanks.' Ben sat and poured himself a glass of cordial, drained half of it in one swallow then refilled the glass. 'I needed that. I underestimated how far a loop around the estate roads would be and by the time I spotted the farmhouse I was seriously flagging.'

Ziggy took the chair at the head of the table and set a cup of coffee on the mat in front of him. 'Do you run most days?'

Ben nodded. 'I try to, but it doesn't always fit in around work.' He winced, thinking about the way he'd just abandoned his work and headed out. Not that he'd have been any use if he'd stayed at his desk. 'Which is where I should be now.'

'Did something happen?'

Ben hesitated, wondering if it was fair to dump his troubles on his uncle like this. But he had asked, and God knows Ben could do with a sounding board. 'I just found out that my dad wrote me a letter before he died. He confessed about lying about Mum being dead and tried to explain what had happened between them. The solicitor just called me and admitted to having it. Dad gave it to him then asked him to destroy it the next day.' Ben shook his head, still too conflicted about the mixed messages of the letter and his father's subsequent actions to be able to make sense of them. 'He asked me to tell Mum he was sorry about everything that happened between them, and told me I must never blame her because it was all his fault. There's a load of stuff about his parents and how he loved Stevie too much and not passing that legacy on to me, but I don't know if I should even mention it to her.' The words tumbled out on top of each other. 'God, I wish he'd had the guts to tell me all this face to face, not leave me floundering around like this trying to clear up his mess. I hate him for doing this to me! I hate him for dying.' Ben pressed the heels of his hands into his eyes to ward off the burn of tears that were threatening to spill.

'Unfortunately it's the people we love the most who are often the ones who let us down the worst.' Ziggy took a sip of his coffee. 'Growing up, I was very close to my grandfather. Much more so than my father. He's been dead a long time now, but there are times I wish I still had him around to talk to. Whatever his faults, he knew more about the estate than anyone else. We had what you might term a complicated relationship, but I still find myself missing him sometimes. All I can suggest is that you give yourself time to grieve the person you knew and loved.'

'Loved?' Ben scoffed. 'He doesn't deserve my love after everything he's done.'

'He's still your father, Ben,' Ziggy said quietly. 'He's still the man who cared for you and raised you and did his best by you, however lacking that turned out to be. Don't turn your back on everything that's brought you to this point, because it's made you the man you are today. All of it, the good, the bad and, yes, the downright awful stuff too. You're too close to everything right now to see clearly. All you can do is live with the knowledge of what he's done, and remember that you are not on your own. We're here for you, Ben, each and every one of us in whatever way you need. Hopefully one day down the line you'll be able to come to terms with it, or at least find a way to live in peace with it and not let it spoil the many joys that life still has in store for you.'

'I'm surprised to hear you sticking up for him.'

Ziggy sighed. 'I've never been a man of violence, but in those early days when Stevie first came home I think I could've killed your father. But once Hope was born it was hard to hold onto all that hate. Whatever else he was, he was a part of her, and I didn't want my anger to taint her life in any way so I learned to let it go. Expecting you to turn your back on your father's memory would only hurt you more in the long run so again I'll have to find a way to forgive him for what he's done to you. And I'll do that by reminding myself that he kept you safe and he raised you well. What's important to me now is that you've found your way back to us. I know this probably sounds like an impossible ask but try not to let what happened between Stevie and your father poison all the good memories, because you bear none of the blame for their decisions.'

'Amelia said the same thing.'

Ziggy nodded again. 'And she'd know better than most.' He set his mug down and pushed it aside. 'Look, I'm not sure if this is the right time to mention it but I know from my own experiences that probate can be an absolute nightmare and it can't be easy for you trying to maintain things with your father's place and your flat in London on a single salary. So if the money side of things is something you are worried about then I promise you there's no need.'

Ben shook his head. 'I don't need your money. Not that I don't appreciate the offer,' he added quickly, in case Ziggy was offended by the blunt rejection. 'I mean, I have enough in my account to see me through. I'm hoping everything will be settled by the end of the year and then I'm planning on quitting my job and making a career change. Dad had substantial savings and there'll be the proceeds from the house once I sell it so more than enough to keep me going into the medium term at least. I'm going to hang onto the flat for now, because it'll be a good investment.' One thing that could almost be guaranteed was house prices in the capital would keep on rising.

Ziggy smiled. 'You misunderstand me, Ben. I'm not talking

about my money. I'm talking about yours. When we decided to turn the estate into a going concern, my siblings and I agreed that everyone would have equal shares. When Rhys was born, Zap decided to set aside a portion of his income for his son and Stevie decided to do the same for both you and Hope. When you turned eighteen and she thought you weren't ever going to come home, she stopped saving for you, but she never closed the account. I've been shifting it around every few years, so you've earned plenty of interest on top. I transferred everything into an instant access account when Hope decided she was going to try and meet you. There's the best part of a hundred and fifty thousand pounds ready and waiting for whatever you want to do with it.'

A hundred and fifty grand? 'You can't be serious?'

Ziggy folded his arms across his chest. 'Money isn't the kind of thing I tend to joke about.'

Ben shook his head, unable to take it in. 'I can't possibly accept. Not when I haven't done anything to earn it. I haven't contributed towards the running of the estate like Hope and Rhys have.'

His uncle smiled. 'Neither did they until after they were adults, but we still gave them both their savings accounts on their eighteenth birthdays. The fact they both chose to reinvest in the business was entirely their choice. We did everything we could to encourage them to look beyond Juniper Meadows.' Ziggy's focus turned soft as though he was suddenly somewhere else in his mind's eye. 'I was particularly concerned because I know what it's like to feel the mantle of responsibility being thrust upon your shoulders when you don't feel ready for it, and I didn't want that for either of them.'

'How old were you when you took over?' Ben wondered what had happened to his grandparents. He knew they were still around because he'd asked Hope about them. When he'd been here for supper, she'd shown him the colourful postcards from destinations all over the world pinned to the fridge and said Monty and Alice were off travelling in South America.

'I was twenty-two when my grandfather passed away, but he'd been preparing me for the role for as long as I can remember.' Ziggy's lips quirked. 'The joys of being the firstborn, even if it was only by five minutes.'

Ben's heart was suddenly hammering in his chest. 'How old is Rhys?'

Ziggy laughed. 'Don't panic, he's about four months older than you. So if you've set your sights on inheriting the title after me, then I'm sorry to disappoint you.'

Ben held up his hands, the relief enough to make him break out in a sweat again. 'Jesus, no! That's the last thing I want.' Realising who he was talking to, Ben pulled a face. 'Sorry, that was tactless of me. I'm sure you do a brilliant job, but I've never been ambitious.' He felt sad all over again. 'Which was a source of great disappointment to my father.'

'I was never given the choice. Family and duty meant everything to your great-grandfather. When it became clear that his only child wasn't going to do his bidding, he turned his attention to the next generation.'

Ben shook his head. 'But if your father didn't want to do it, why didn't he step in to protect you?'

'Guilt? Shame? Relief?' Ziggy shrugged. 'Take your pick. Monty always had a love-hate relationship with the estate. As in he loved his mother and hated his father. While Grandmama was alive, he did his best to stick around when he could. When things got too much for him, he and my mother would take off for a few months. My grandparents insisted they leave us here so our schooling wouldn't be interrupted, and they agreed with rather more alacrity than is good for a child's ego to bear.' Ziggy's smile was wry, but Ben could see the ghosts of that old pain still lingered. 'Monty and

Alice would flit in and out, bringing laughter and surprise presents and amazing stories of where they'd been and what they'd seen and then after a while he'd stop smiling and start spending hours alone tramping around the grounds. When that happened, we knew it wouldn't be long before they were off again. My grandfather always blamed my mother, said if my father had married the right sort of woman who understood our way of life and had been born to it then my father would've eventually come around and settled down. But it was easier to do that than admit some of the fault might lie with himself.'

'That must have been difficult for you.' Ben couldn't imagine what growing up would've been like without the strong, solid presence of his father.

'Yes and no. My grandparents raised us for the most part and you have to remember that Zap and I had each other from day one. Stevie came along less than two years behind us and Dylan was born just after Zap and I turned five. We were our own little gang, and the world was our oyster for the first few years. Then Grandmama became ill and we were packed off to boarding school, so when term ended all we wanted was to be back in the safety and security of the only place we'd called home. After she died, Monty and Alice came home less and less frequently and I grew very close to my grandfather. He lavished all his time and attention on me. If Zap had been less easy-going, it could've driven a wedge between us, but he never gave me even the slightest hint he was jealous. The complete opposite, in fact. I think he was just relieved that Grandfather left him alone to do his own thing.

'As he grew older, my grandfather became obsessed with what would happen to the estate after he was gone. He was worried my father would sell up before he was even cold in the ground, and he made me swear over and over that I wouldn't let that happen. I talked to Zap about it, and we made a pact to run the place together.'

'You've made a great success of it. Your grandfather would surely be very proud of what Juniper Meadows has become under your care.'

Ziggy nodded. 'Yes, but at what cost? He raised me to believe that duty came above all things. Your mother left because she felt like she had no place here, though I didn't realise that at the time. Then Dylan was gone, and I let my grandfather convince me it was because he'd inherited our father's wanderlust, and he'd be back. His obsession with living up to the legacy of five hundred years of history became my obsession too.'

It was hard to reconcile the man before him with the one he was describing. 'So what changed?'

'Grandfather died and a few months later your mother came home. I realised at once how badly I'd let her down, but it was only when your sister was born and I held her in my arms that the true impact of what I'd given up hit me. Family was everything, but not the ones in the dusty portraits hanging on the walls in the Hall. It's the ones that come afterwards that matter. Our children's happiness should come before everything. It was too late for me by then, but I was determined that neither Hope nor Rhys would feel the weight of legacy upon them. And now you've found your way home to us, I don't want you to feel it either.' Ziggy closed his eyes for a long moment, his face etched in heartbreak.

Ben didn't know what to say. He knew what he wanted to say, but was this the right time? Would it help Ziggy understand that whatever mistakes he'd made in the past, he'd helped to create a wonderful and loving family that Ben was already beginning to feel a part of, or would it make him worry more? He had to hope it was the former. 'You know I said I was thinking about changing my career at the end of the year? Well, I was thinking perhaps I could take over one of the units in the stable yard and base myself there.'

Ziggy's eyes blinked open, and his face settled into a neutral expression. 'What would you do with it?'

'I'd open a pottery studio. My father had very fixed ideas about what I should do with my life and, a bit like you, I did my best to please him. It's time to please myself and there's nowhere else in the world I'd rather follow my dreams than here.'

His uncle was quiet for a long moment. 'Have you spoken to your mother about it?'

Ben grinned. 'I mentioned it briefly and she didn't even blink, just said how exciting it would be and that she was sure I'd make a success of it.'

Ziggy smiled. 'That sounds like Stevie.'

'It was so different to how Dad would've reacted. I wish...' Ben cut himself off because wishing wasn't going to change the past. 'It helps knowing I can count on her for support.' They still had a long way to go, but he was starting to believe they'd find a way. 'Could you not mention to her about Dad's letter? Not that I plan on keeping it a secret from her, we just need a bit of time to get used to having each other around first.' He wasn't sure how Stevie would feel about what his father had had to say; she might not be interested but he would give her the choice and respect her decision either way.

'I won't say anything to her, but you can talk to me about it and about anything else to do with your father whenever you need to. Same goes for this new venture of yours. My door will always be open.'

'Thank you.'

'How far along with it are you?'

'Not very! I want to get everything sorted out with Dad's stuff first and then I need to work on a business plan, design the layout of the studio.' He laughed. 'I haven't sat behind my wheel in forever so I might find I've lost my skills when I try. I'll need to go and do some training courses, for sure. I'm not talking about opening up tomorrow. Maybe not even next year, but when I'm ready I want it to be here.'

Ziggy nodded. 'And what do you need from me to help turn your dream into a reality?'

'Nothing.' Ben smiled. 'Other than your blessing.'

'Well, you already have that.' Rising, Ziggy came around the table and placed a hand on Ben's shoulder. 'I'll never try to replace your father, but anytime you need to talk, I'm here. And I know Zap would say the same thing too.' Touched beyond words, Ben could only nod in thanks. 'And I meant what I said before. That money is yours to do with as you please.'

Ben was about to refuse it when the perfect solution came to him. 'I know what I'm going to do with it.' He didn't need it, but he knew someone who did.

23

The gloves and hat Ben had bought her kept Amelia toasty as she trekked to and from the bus each morning and evening the following week. Her boss, Caroline, had admired them on a chilly lunchtime walk around town and Amelia hadn't been able to resist telling her that they were a gift from a new friend.

'A male friend?' Caroline had teased.

'Maybe.' She'd refused to be drawn any further, wanting to keep Ben all to herself for now. It was all still too new to share and besides, she didn't want to make a big deal of it when she still wasn't sure what it was between them anyway. Things had progressed perhaps a little faster than either of them had expected at the weekend, but Amelia hadn't regretted a single second in his arms. Perhaps Ben was worried they'd rushed into it a bit because he hadn't asked to see her again when they parted on Sunday night, though they'd swapped lots of messages. When she'd asked him what he was up to, he'd been evasive and said only that he was busy with work. Since helping at the retreat, Amelia had become obsessed with her art and spent all her free time sitting on her bed hunched over a sketchpad. Her head was full of so many ideas it sometimes felt like her pencil would never be able to keep up with them. So while she'd hadn't minded not seeing Ben, it would have at least been nice to be asked. Pathetic, she scolded herself. A couple of mind-blowing orgasms and she was pining over the bloody man like he was the answer to all her prayers. They had been very good orgasms, mind. Besides, she'd be seeing him in the morning for the Halloween festivities and that would be soon enough.

Between work and her art, she was also trying not to neglect her mum. They'd been making good progress in their relationship and Amelia had felt guilty about how much of the unpacking and sorting of the cottage had been left to Daisy. So without the prospect of more orgasms, mind-blowing or otherwise, Amelia set aside Friday evening to help with the last of the boxes.

Even though they'd tried their best to downsize, they'd still brought too much with them. 'Shed or dump?' she asked her mum, holding up a hideous green and purple vase.

'My mother gave us that on our wedding day.'

'Definitely the dump, then,' Amelia said as she added it to a growing stack of items by the front door. 'Knowing Nan, it's probably cursed.'

'Amelia!' Daisy widened her eyes in shock before she burst out laughing. 'Actually, you have a point.' She rooted through the box in front of her and pulled out a pair of ugly brass candlesticks that had held pride of place on Amelia's nan's mantlepiece before she'd passed away. 'Add these to the pile.' Daisy rummaged in the box, then pushed it towards Amelia. 'All this rubbish can go.'

Amelia peered into the top of the box. It was full of her nan's things. 'You don't have to throw everything away, Mum.'

Daisy sat back on her heels. 'Why not? What's the point of dragging stuff I don't even like from one place to the next out of obligation? It's not like there's even lots of happy memories associated with any of it.'

She had a point. Amelia pulled out a floral teacup with a faded gold rim and a matching saucer. She balanced the saucer in one hand and raised the teacup with the other, extending her pinky finger as she glared at her mother over it. 'Only one biscuit, Amelia. You don't want to spoil your dinner.'

Daisy held her hands to her cheeks, laughing. 'Oh goodness, don't scowl at me like that, you look just like her!'

Amelia tossed the cup and saucer back in the box and shuffled across to her mother's side. 'We'll be all right, won't we, Mum?'

Daisy put her arms around her and held her tight in a way she hadn't since Amelia was a little girl. 'We'll be just fine, darling. Thanks to you.' She pulled back and reached out to brush a lock of hair off Amelia's forehead. 'I've let you take the strain for too long and I'm sorry.'

Amelia felt a knot unfurl inside her. It was only a little one in the messy tangle of feelings she held for this woman, but it was a start. 'It's okay, Mum.'

Daisy shook her head. 'No, it's not, but I'm going to make sure that it will be from now on.' She gave Amelia a wonky smile. 'There's a receptionist job going at the hotel. I thought I might apply for it. The money isn't brilliant, but it's full time. What do you think?'

Amelia threw her arms around her and hugged her close. 'I think that's a wonderful idea.' She sat back, not trying to disguise the happy tears in her eyes. 'Why don't you come with me tomorrow? I could do with an assistant.'

'I don't know the first thing about art.' Daisy shook her head. 'I don't know where you got your talent from because it's definitely not from me.'

'You can help me with organising the queue.' Queue! Nothing

like talking up her expectations. 'And if no one is interested in the face painting, we'll still be able to spend the day together so it's a win-win as far as I'm concerned.' Ben wasn't in any rush to see her again so showing up with her mum in the morning would make it clear she was happy to play things just as cool. Besides, it really would be nice to spend time with her mum doing something fun.

'That sounds lovely.' The way Daisy beamed at her, Amelia knew she'd done the right thing in suggesting it. 'Maybe we could have afternoon tea in the café,' Daisy suggested. 'My treat.'

It was on the tip of Amelia's tongue to suggest they could take a packed lunch with them but she stifled the words. A few pounds weren't going to make any difference and denying themselves constantly was frankly exhausting. 'We can celebrate your new job!'

'I haven't got it yet,' Daisy said with a laugh and a shake of her head.

'But you will.' Their luck had to start changing. As she hugged her mother, Amelia looked around at the fresh white walls and the last few boxes to be unpacked. Things were changing already.

* * *

Saturday morning dawned bright and clear. When Amelia went down to the kitchen to put the kettle on, Daisy was already there. There was no sign of her ratty old dressing gown, she was showered and dressed and had even put on a spot of make-up. Nothing too heavy, just a dash of mascara and a spot of blush, but she looked better than she had in months. She was wearing an oatmeal-coloured sweater that Amelia had given her for Christmas a couple of years earlier and a pair of jeans that looked like they were ready to fall down. 'You need a belt,' Amelia teased as she leaned over to kiss her mum's cheek.

'I know, but the ones I tried didn't have any holes that were tight enough to make a difference so I had to improvise.' Daisy hitched up her jumper to show she'd threaded a scarf through the loops and tied it at the waist.

Amelia smiled. 'Let's take one of your old belts with us and we can talk to Jason. I'm sure he'll be able to punch you a new hole in about two seconds flat.'

'Oh, that's a good idea. I'll go and fetch one now while I remember, and then I'll make us some tea.'

Amelia moved towards the toaster. 'I'll sort out breakfast. How many slices?' She waited for Daisy to make some excuse about not being hungry or that she'd already eaten.

'Two please. I found some peanut butter when I was unpacking and it wasn't even out of date.'

Amelia laughed because they'd found at least three cans of soup with use-by dates that even their tight finances hadn't deemed worth the risk. 'I knew our luck was changing for the better.'

Daisy not only ate both slices of toast, she also managed half a banana, which she split with Amelia. It was as if just getting out of their old place had been enough to give her mother a new lease of life and as Amelia hurried through her own shower, she hoped it was something that was there to stay.

By 8 a.m., they were ready to go. While Amelia had been getting dressed, Daisy had found a backpack in amongst the tangle of things they'd chucked in the understairs cupboard for sorting out later, and loaded in all the painting supplies. She'd also found a canvas holdall into which she placed a couple of insulated mugs, a small box of tissues, a couple of flannels and a packet of facial wipes. She held up a notebook and a handful of pens. 'I was thinking that if people didn't want to hang around in a queue, we could take their phone numbers and call them when their slot becomes available.'

'That's a great idea, Mum. See, I knew you'd keep me organised. Have you got room for these?' She handed her mum a pair of scissors and a roll of Sellotape. 'Hopefully there'll be somewhere to stick a couple of posters up.' In amongst all the other drawings she'd been doing, Amelia had knocked up a couple of advertising posters.

'I'm sure Sandra will let you put one up in the café window, and you'll have a table or something to work at; we can stick one to the front of that. What are you doing about taking payment?'

'I'm charging £5. Hope has made up a couple of floats and I'll also take PayPal as we can check that instantly on my phone. Jason said I can use his card terminal if we get stuck, but I'd rather not if I can help it.'

'Well, I won't mention cards and hopefully we can avoid it. Hang on a minute, I've just thought of something.' Daisy hurried into the hall and opened the cupboard. 'Now, where is it? I know I saw it earlier when I was looking for a bag... Ah ha!' She backed out of the cupboard, holding up what looked like a bum bag of all things.

'Where did that come from?' Amelia asked as her mother strapped it around her waist.

'I have no idea, but look, it'll be perfect for me to keep the money in.' Daisy pulled the zip open and shut. 'Much better than worrying about a cash tin lying around. Plus,' she said, tugging the strap around her waist to tighten it, 'it'll stop my jeans from falling down until I can get Jason to fix my belt.'

They set off soon afterwards, Amelia carrying the carefully rolled posters under her arm. Overhead, the sky was the pale ice blue of a husky's eyes. A thick frost layered the grass and cast a silvery sheen over the road. Double dark lines through the frost showed they weren't the first ones up and about. As they reached the main road through the estate, there were signs of life everywhere. Short orange bollards lined the verges on either side at regular intervals to discourage anyone from parking on the grass and they had to wait for a small convoy to pass them. The vehicle in front was one of the Juniper Meadows branded Range Rovers and as it slowed beside them, the window slid down and Hope grinned at them from beneath a white bobble hat. 'Morning! I'm just taking these guys up to the campsite car park so they can get set up, but I'll pick you up on the way back, if you like?'

'It's such a lovely morning, we don't mind walking,' Amelia assured her. 'You must have a million and one things to do.'

Her friend rolled her eyes, but her smile didn't slip and it was clear she was in her element. 'A million and two, but I'm heading back over to the stable yard after this so it won't be out of my way. Stick to the road and I'll find you!' And with a wave she was off, the two trucks emblazoned with 'Dazzling Displays' following in her wake.

True to her word, Hope was back in less than ten minutes and Amelia had to admit she was grateful for the sudden blast of warmth as they climbed into her car. 'I hope the cold doesn't put people off,' she said as she tugged off her hat and gloves and folded them on her lap.

'It'll be lovely once the sun gets a bit higher. At least it's dry. I nearly had a heart attack when I saw the forecast earlier in the week.' There had been early predictions of rain but a ridge of high pressure had pushed down from the Arctic, covering the country in a band of clear, cold air.

'I saw some predictions of early snow,' Daisy said from the back seat. She followed her words with a laugh. 'But then didn't they promise us a white Christmas last year and we didn't see a flake until late February?'

'Monty always used to say if I wanted to know what the weather was, I should stick my head out the window,' Hope said with a chuckle.

'How are your grandparents?' Amelia asked. 'Will they get home for Christmas this year?' Monty and Alice Travers were rare visitors to Juniper Meadows these days, seeming to prefer rattling around the world in their vintage VW camper.

Hope shook her head, keeping her eyes on the road. 'Nope. They've made friends with a couple who own a vineyard in Chile and Monty has decided he wants to learn everything there is to know about making wine.'

'Funny how Monty is interested in how everyone else runs a business apart from his children and grandchildren.' Daisy's sardonic tone was dry enough that Amelia raised her eyes to the rear-view mirror. Her mother shot her an unrepentant look before turning to gaze out of the window.

Thankfully, Hope took it in good humour and laughed as she said, 'The day Monty shows an interest in what happens here at Juniper Meadows is the day the devil gets frostbite on his arse.'

When they pulled up in the car park by the stable yard, it was already humming with activity. A tractor and trailer were parked on the field behind the café and half a dozen men were unloading hay bales and setting them out. A couple of others were scattering loose hay in between and a third team was unloading pumpkins of all shapes and sizes and placing them at random intervals. Amelia recognised both Rhys and Ben amongst the volunteers, each carrying a heavy bale of hay. Trestle tables had already been set up across the courtyard in front of the workshops and as they headed towards them, Jason raised his head from the pumpkin he was carving and gave them a wave. 'Morning! Looks like it's going to be a good one.'

'It certainly does,' Hope replied as she picked up a pumpkin

Jason had already carved. 'Wow, this is amazing!' She held it up next to her face and pulled her lips back in a rictus grin to match the pumpkin's garish smile.

'You could be twins.' Amelia winked at her.

'Ha! Remind me again why we're friends.' Hope's mobile phone buzzed and she set the pumpkin down. After frowning at the screen for a moment, she raised her head and gave Amelia a sunny smile, though there was no hiding the strain around her eyes. 'Right, I'm going to grab your float, and then I'm going to leave you in Jason's capable hands, if that's all right?'

Amelia gave her a quick hug. 'I've got this, and so have you.' She pulled back and met her friend's eyes. 'Today is going to be brilliant thanks to all your hard work.'

Hope shrugged but she smiled as well. 'It was a team effort.'

'And every team needs a leader,' Jason put in from the other side of the table. 'You've done a wonderful job pulling this all together, Hope. I can't tell you how grateful we all are.'

Amelia and her mum had the painting station up and ready to go by the time the others had finished setting up the fake pumpkin patch. Daisy had gone with Jason to sort her belt out so Amelia was alone when people started leaving the field. Ben made a beeline straight towards her table, a huge smile on his face as he pointed at the two posters she'd stuck to the front of it. 'Those look great, really eye-catching.' He circled the table and reached for her hand. 'I'm sorry I didn't see you arrive; you should've come and said hello.'

She eased her fingers free of his on the pretence of straightening something on her table. 'You looked really busy – besides, I needed to sort myself out. The field looks amazing; I'm sure the kids are going to love it.'

Ben frowned. 'Is everything okay?'

Amelia tilted her head to look up at him. 'I don't know, is it?'

'Well, I thought so, but maybe we're not on the same page, after all.' Ben moved closer and lowered his voice. 'Have I done something to upset you?'

'You haven't been in a hurry to see me after the weekend so I don't know...' Amelia glanced around, hoping her mother would reappear and give her an excuse to end the awkward conversation. 'I wondered if perhaps you felt like we'd rushed into things and wanted to slow down.'

Ben shook his head as he reached for her hand again. 'No, not at all! I'm very happy with everything that happened between us. I'm really sorry if I've made you feel disrespected or like I was pushing you away. It's been a weird week and I had some stuff I needed to sort out. I didn't want to unload it all on you when you've got more than enough on your plate.'

Oh dear. Guilt twisted her insides. She'd been so busy internalising her doubts, she hadn't given thought to the fact there might something else going on with Ben that had nothing to do with her. 'I'm sorry if you felt like you couldn't talk to me. That's the last thing I wanted.'

'No, that wasn't what I meant at all.' Ben gave a frustrated laugh. 'How are we making this so complicated?' He reached for her hand again and this time she let him take it. 'I received a letter that my dad wrote not long before he passed away and I just really needed some space to work out how I felt about it. I'm still not sure how I feel, but it's helped clarify a few things at least. It's not something I can resolve overnight and it felt more important to let you and your mum settle in properly. I didn't want to crowd you and I knew I'd be seeing you today.'

Amelia smiled, feeling a bit embarrassed for making a fuss over nothing. 'You seemed a bit distracted when you texted and I got all up in my head about it and managed to convince myself that maybe you were having second thoughts about us and just wanted to keep it friendly.'

Ben released her hand only long enough to place his arm around her waist and pull her close. 'I want things to be more than friendly between us,' he said, with a wicked glint in his eye. 'Much more.' His head ducked down as though he meant to kiss her and Amelia forgot all her earlier worries and went up on tiptoes to meet him.

'Hey! What's all this, then?'

Startled, they jerked apart to find Rhys glowering at them. Amelia opened her mouth, about to babble a load of excuses, and then just as quickly snapped it shut. 'What the hell business is it of yours?'

Glower turning to a massive grin, Rhys threw back his head and laughed. 'Nothing at all, but I couldn't resist. Besides, it was worth it just to see the guilty looks on your faces.'

Amelia gave him a thin smile while Ben looked like he might be considering the best place to land a punch on his cousin's smugly grinning face. 'Hilarious.'

Rhys gave them an unrepentant shrug. 'I thought so. Where's Hope, by the way?'

'I'm not sure. I think she was heading back up to the woods to check on the lighting team.'

'Okay, well, if you see her, tell her she owes me a fiver.' Rhys grinned again. 'I told her there was something going on with you two. I have a nose for these things.' He tapped a finger against it.

'You have a nose that's looking to get my fist on it,' Ben muttered. 'You've had your fun, now go away so I can kiss my girl-friend in peace.'

'Ooh! All right, big man.' Rhys held up his hands as he backed away from the table, still laughing. 'You've got five minutes and then we've got a hot date with a tractor and trailer!'

Amelia waited until he'd turned away before she turned back to Ben with a groan. 'He's never going to let us hear the last of this.'

Ben touched a finger to her cheek. 'Sorry, I didn't mean to come over all possessive just now.'

She smiled, wanting to reassure him. It must be odd for him, knowing what she and Rhys had once meant to each other. 'I like it when you call me your girlfriend.' She gave him a gentle nudge. 'And you don't have to worry about Rhys. I meant what I said before about that all being in the past.'

'Do you mind telling me what happened between you?' He still looked concerned and Amelia supposed she couldn't blame him under the circumstances. 'Lots of things. We were young when we got together and oblivious to anything other than that first rush of young love. Over time it became clear to me that we were never going to suit. Things with my dad were pretty bad at the time and Rhys tried to take over. He's always been so sure of himself and his place in the world that it makes him think he knows what's best for everyone else sometimes. We used to fight about it a lot, but the thing that really killed it was when I looked in his eyes and it wasn't love I saw there any more – it was pity.'

'I'm sorry.'

Amelia shrugged. 'Rhys has a bit of a hero complex and one day he'll find the right maiden to rescue, but that's not me.'

'No heroics. Got it.'

'No heroics,' she confirmed. 'Unless there's a spider in the bath.'

Smiling, Ben put his arm around her waist once more. He kissed her – nothing full on, just a sweet brush of lips that held a delicious promise of more later. 'I'd better go,' he said, regretfully. 'But will you hold my hand on the spooky trail later?'

She laughed. 'It's a date.'

24

Once the main gates opened at 10 a.m., Amelia didn't have time to worry about anything other than whether she was going to have enough paint to last the day. Shouts and laughter filled the air as children dashed around the pumpkin patch, looking for the perfect one to decorate. Those that didn't want to try their hand at carving could learn how to make other seasonal decorations with Carrie-Ann, who used the wire and tools for making wind chimes to string miniature gourds together. The queue for face painting was steady all morning and the system her mum had set up to take numbers and call people back worked well. Several parents had asked Amelia if she did bookings for parties and after she'd told the first couple it was a one-off, her mother had stepped in and asked them to leave their contact details and they'd be in touch.

'What are you doing?' Amelia hissed through her smile afterwards.

'Keeping your options open, darling. You never know, if this really takes off you could make some serious money.' Daisy reached into the bum bag at her waist and pulled out a sheaf of notes. 'There must be nearly two hundred pounds in here already.'

Before Amelia could respond, a woman with twin girls of about five or six stepped forwards. 'Do you only do Halloween designs?'

Amelia took in the stiff net tutus poking out between the girls' matching puffy pink coats and leggings covered in glittery stars and rainbows and smiled. 'Do you two like butterflies?'

By the time they stopped for lunch, Amelia's hand had started to ache from gripping a brush for too long. Everywhere she looked there were signs of her handiwork – a Spider-man here, a vampire there, an adorable little ghoul skipping along as she held her daddy's hand. The café was packed and they were about to give up when the woman with the butterfly twins waved them down. 'Here, we're just about to go. You can have our table.'

Amelia edged over to them with a grateful smile. 'Thank you.'

'You sit down and I'll get lunch,' her mum said. 'My treat, remember?'

It seemed really important to her that Amelia let her pay, so she held out her hands to take Daisy's bag and coat and didn't suggest splitting the cost. While she waited, she sent Ben a quick text.

We're having lunch. How's it going? X

It was a few minutes before she received a reply, by which time Daisy was back with a tray laden with sandwiches, two slices of cake and a couple of scones. 'We'll never eat all that!' Amelia protested as she accepted a miniature pot of jam to go with her scone.

'Well, at least we'll have fun trying,' Daisy said with a grin as she sat down and pushed up the sleeves of her jumper. 'Don't let me interrupt,' she added, nodding at Amelia's phone as it pinged.

'I was just texting Ben.'

'Of course you were. Tell him I said hello.' Daisy picked up a tuna sandwich and began to open the packet. 'I was thinking we could have him over for supper one night if you like? I could make a shepherd's pie.'

Amelia tried to hide her smile. 'I'll ask him.'

'What?' Daisy pointed her sandwich at Amelia, her tone accusing.

She shook her head. 'Nothing, I think it's a lovely idea.' It was so nice to be spending time like this, doing the normal, everyday things other mothers and daughters took for granted. Picking up her phone she read Ben's message, which said he and Rhys were still doing trailer rides between the stable yard and the woods and would probably be a couple more hours.

Mum wants to know if you'd like to come to dinner sometime. Nothing fancy, just shepherd's pie one night x

Sounds plenty fancy to me! Tell her I'm free any time xx

'Ben says any time for shepherd's pie,' Amelia told Daisy after setting her phone aside.

'Well, you work out what date suits between you and let me know.'

Amelia picked up her sandwich, then put it down. 'You don't think I'm making a mistake, do you?'

Daisy frowned. 'With Ben, you mean?'

She nodded. 'It all feels a bit sudden, and I wasn't expecting it at all.' She laughed. 'I don't think he was expecting it either.'

Reaching out across the table, Daisy rested her hand on Amelia's arm. 'Anyone who puts that smile back on your face is a good thing as far as I'm concerned.'

'You don't think I'm rushing things with him?'

Her mother shrugged. 'So what if you are? You're twenty-five, darling, not forty-five. You should be rushing into things. You should be running headlong at life, not wasting your best years worrying about me and... well, everything else.'

Amelia covered her mother's hand. 'I don't blame you for anything; it's just the way things turned out.'

Daisy shook her head. 'You might not, but I blame myself. I shouldn't have ever let things get as bad as they did. You deserved better and I'm sorry.'

She appreciated what her mum was saying, but Amelia didn't want to put a pall on what had been a lovely day so far. 'It's the future that matters, Mum, not the past. Let's just keep looking ahead because there's bright days coming. For both of us.'

There weren't many more customers after lunch, and they started to pack up just after three. The crowds had moved on from the stable yard for the most part and there was a steady stream of cars leaving the car park. Some were heading home, but a lot were moving up to the campsite car park to enjoy the walking trails. Amelia still hadn't seen Ben. She'd caught sight of the tractor and trailer a couple of times, but they stopped only long enough to unload and load the next set of riders.

Jason and Carrie-Ann were clearing up as well and Amelia went over to help them fold up the tables and carry them to where Zap and Ziggy were supervising the stacking of everything into the distillery, where they were being stored overnight. 'What else is there to do?' Amelia asked Jason as she knuckled the stiffness out of her back. 'I want to walk back with Mum before it gets dark.'

'I think we're just about done. We're going to grab a coffee and then head up to the trails. Thanks for all your help today.'

'It was so much fun, thank you for letting me join in at the last minute.'

A horn beeped and they all turned to see Rhys trundling across the now empty yard with the tractor and trailer. He jumped down from the cab while Ben clambered down from the back of the trailer. 'You've got straw in your hair,' Amelia told him with a grin as she plucked a piece that was caught in his fringe.

'I've got bloody straw everywhere,' he muttered. 'Including in my pants, I think.'

Amelia giggled. 'Well, I'm not helping you with that. Not here, anyway.'

'Right, I'm doing one last ride up to the woods if anyone wants a lift,' Rhys announced.

Ben raised his eyebrows. 'Fancy a ride?' She could tell by the gleam in his eye he was well aware of the double entendre and had zero regrets for making it.

'Much as I find the idea of getting straw stuck in my pants as well very tempting, I'm going to have to pass as I need to walk Mum home first.'

Daisy shook her head. 'Don't be silly. I'll be fine; go and have fun with your friends.'

'I can't leave you to go on your own, not with all that money.'

'I can walk back with you, Daisy.' It was Ziggy and he was staring directly at her mother as if there was nobody else but the two of them present. Whatever had gone on between them, it was clear to Amelia that Ziggy thought Daisy was more than good enough for him now.

'We can d— Ow.' Ben glared down at where Amelia had dug her nails into his palm. He opened his mouth as if to protest again, but she shook her head.

The silence seemed to stretch forever before Daisy finally dipped her head once. 'Okay.'

As the pair walked away together, Rhys looked like he might say something but Zap forestalled him with a low warning. 'Mind your business, son.' In a louder voice, he added, 'Go on, you lot. I'll lock up here.'

Rhys stared at his father for a long moment before shrugging. 'Are you and Mum coming up later?'

'And miss out on a chance to have the house to ourselves for a couple of hours? Not on your life.' Zap waggled his eyebrows just in case they hadn't all already got the drift of his romantic intentions.

'Ew, Dad, please.' Rhys shot his father a disgusted look and shuddered before his face broke out into a grin and he hugged him. 'I'll see you later.' He turned back to the rest of them. 'Right, you lot, all aboard!'

'I think it's nice your folks are still mad for each other after all these years,' Amelia couldn't resist teasing Rhys as both he and Ben helped first her and then Carrie-Ann onto the back of the trailer.

Rhys raised his eyebrows. 'And what if your mum and Ziggy are sneaking off together for a secret shag, eh? Would you think that was nice?'

She winced. 'I hate you.' Though she hoped the two of them could find some kind of reconciliation with the past, Amelia didn't want to think too deeply about where that might lead them eventually. Not that she didn't want her mum to be happy, she just preferred to fade the more intimate parts of her private life to black. Rhys roared with laughter as he closed the back of the trailer and locked it in place.

As she settled into one of the seating alcoves built with hay bales, Ben sank down beside her and slung an arm around her shoulders. 'Is there really something going on between your mum and Ziggy?' He kept his voice low though he needn't have bothered as Jason and Carrie-Ann were caught up in their own conversation on the opposite side of the trailer.

She looked up at him. 'They have a history together. That's all Mum has ever told me – well, that and that things didn't end well between them. I think maybe she and Keith got together on the rebound and then one thing led to another.' She shrugged. 'I'm going to leave them to it. Either they'll work it out or they won't, but I'm not going to push Mum either way.'

Ben hugged her close and kissed her cheek. 'I think that's probably a good idea. I wonder if it had something to do with his grandfather, though? We had a chat the other day and I got the impression he was very controlling of Ziggy when he was younger. It kind of reminded me of how things were with my dad, though his situation sounded a lot more intense.'

'I didn't realise you two were getting close.'

'It's a new thing, but it's good to know I have someone I can talk stuff over with.' Ben sounded reflective and a little sad, and she knew he was still thinking about his father.

'It's okay to miss him, you know?' The way his dad had behaved was beyond awful, but it was also clear he'd loved Ben in the best way he'd been able to. 'I think the hardest part about growing up is learning that our parents are only human.'

Ben swallowed. 'I was watching all the kids today and I realised for the first time that he'll never be around to meet his grandchildren.'

Amelia didn't know what to say to that so she just leaned her head against his chest and held him close as they finished the rest of the ride in silence.

Once they arrived at the woods, Ben seemed able to shake off his melancholy mood and was all smiles as they joined the queues of people already waiting to pay their entry fee. The five of them chatted easily across the two separate lines, neither Amelia nor Ben rising to the others' efforts to shame them into joining them on the scary trail. Their line moved a bit quicker and Amelia couldn't resist turning to give Rhys, Jason and Carrie-Ann a smug smile as she waved her hand to show them the pumpkin stamped on the back of it while they were still a few places behind. She looked around, but couldn't spot Hope anywhere. 'Do you think I should message her?' she asked Ben as they strolled towards an illuminated balloon arch that marked the start of the children's trail.

'She's probably busy sorting something out. Let's wait until we've done the walk and then we can maybe try and meet up for a drink after everyone's gone home,' he suggested.

'That sounds like a good idea. She'll definitely deserve one.' The temperature had dropped even on their short ride from the stable yard as the sun disappeared over the horizon. Amelia adjusted her red bobble hat and grinned up at Ben. 'You'll have cold ears by the time we're finished.'

'Not so.' Ben reached into the pocket of his coat and pulled out a light brown beanie, which he tugged on over his blonde hair. 'All set?' When she nodded, he held out his hand and they passed beneath the arch and into a veritable wonderland.

It was hard to know where to look first and they weren't the only people who had simply stopped in their tracks as they tried to take it all in. It was like walking beneath a blanket of golden starlight that stretched on as far as the eye could see. In amongst the trees, Amelia spotted shiny red toadstools and glowing orange pumpkins.

'Mummy, Mummy, look!' A little girl ran across in front of Amelia, pointing with delight at a tiny doorway in the trunk of a nearby tree, subtly illuminated by a light hidden somewhere in the branches above. 'Do you think a fairy lives there?'

The girl's mother came over to crouch next to the child. 'I'm sure one does, but it'll be past their bedtime, so we'd better not disturb them.'

Amelia had to turn her face into Ben's shoulder to hide a smile as the girl gave a solemn nod and replied in a whisper, 'Let's be very quiet and maybe they will come out.'

They left the family huddled by the door and Amelia hoped it wouldn't be too long before the little girl was distracted by all the other hidden delights. An owl hooted overhead, making her jump, and it took a few moments to realise it was a model of some kind as it turned its head towards her and one glowing eye disappeared and reappeared. 'Did that owl just wink at us?' Ben asked with a laugh.

'I think so. Oh look, isn't that sweet?' Amelia raised her arm to point at a chubby little goblin perched on another branch. It was too smiley to be scary. They spotted ghosts (very much of the friendly Casper type), a group of animatronic teddy bears who were having a night-time picnic and what looked like a dancing cloud of fireflies blinking in and out above one of the clearings, and all the while the glittering star canopy bathed the trail in a soft golden light.

'That was so much more than I expected,' Ben said later as they approached another illuminated arch marking the end of the trail. 'I can't wait to see what they do for Christmas.'

'It'll be spectacular for sure.' They exited beneath the arch to find themselves opposite the campsite car park. There was another exit point about fifty metres further along, from which a group of laughing teenagers appeared. A distant shriek sounded and Amelia jumped about a foot in the air. 'What the hell was that?'

Ben gestured to the teenagers, who were laughing and pointing as another group staggered out behind them. 'I'm guessing it's supposed to be part of the entertainment.'

Amelia wrinkled her nose. 'Rather them than me.' She checked her phone but there was no message from Rhys, who'd promised to let them know when they were finished. It was too cold to stand and wait so they began to stroll along the grass verge opposite the car park, from where they could keep an eye on the people streaming out of the exits and stay well out of the way of the queue of cars. Even with her boots and a warm pair of socks on, the cold was beginning to turn her toes numb. 'I hope they won't be too much longer.'

'While we're waiting, there's something I wanted to talk to you about. Something that came up when I was chatting with Ziggy the other day.'

'This sounds serious,' she said with a laugh. When he didn't answer, Amelia drew to a halt and turned towards him. Even with the bright illumination from the car park nearby, his face was half-hidden in shadows, making it impossible to read his expression. 'Ben?'

'I spoke to Ziggy about maybe setting up my studio in The Old Stable Yard.'

'You're really going for it.' Amelia tried to keep the envy out of her voice, but she knew she hadn't succeeded. She was happy for him and yet there was a little part inside that knew she was as far away as ever in achieving her own goals. The extra bit of money she would pick up from helping Rowena or doing some free-lancing at children's parties would be swallowed up by the never-ending gaping mouth of her father's debts.

'It was your idea.'

Her laugh sounded hollow to her ears. 'Well, yes, but I didn't think you were going to jump straight on it. All right for some.'

Ben sighed. 'I don't understand why this is a problem; I thought you'd be happy to know I'll be sticking around.'

'It's no skin off my nose what you do, Ben.' She knew she was being pissy with him, but she couldn't help it. He had no idea what it was like to worry about money.

It's not his fault. Guilt at her behaviour tasted sour and bitter on the back of her tongue.

Amelia stepped closer and put her hand against his chest. 'I'm sorry, I'm being horrible. I don't know what's got into me all of a sudden.' She did, but she didn't want to admit she was jealous of him. The last thing she wanted was to hold him back just because she wasn't in a position to move forwards with her own plans. 'It's been a long day and I'm just really tired. So what happens next?'

'Nothing until I get all the probate stuff sorted out. I spoke to the solicitor on Monday; that's how I found out about Dad's letter. He's stepping down from his firm and one of the partners there has offered to take everything on. He's sent me an email, but I haven't sorted out an appointment yet.'

'Do you want me to go with you when you see him?' It seemed like the least she could offer to do, having jumped down his throat just now.

'No, I'll be fine but thank you for offering. I'll sort something out with him in the next week or two. I need to start the ball rolling and I want to pick up all my other equipment from my dad's garage. I haven't sat behind my wheel for months. I might have lost the knack.' He said the last with a smile and Amelia was relieved he seemed willing to let her little outburst go with no hard feelings on his part.

'Rubbish,' she scoffed. 'Look at how scared I was to start painting again and what I managed to achieve at Rowena's art retreat, and again today with the face painting, and that's all with hardly any practice. I bet you'll find you're the same when you give it a go; besides, you'll have months to work on it while you get the studio fitted out.' Now she had recovered from her fit of pique, she couldn't wait for him to get started. It would be fascinating to watch the project unfold over the coming weeks and months, knowing he was finally getting to do what he'd always wanted to. Stretching on tiptoes, Amelia threw her arms around his neck. 'I'm so excited for you!'

Ben hugged her tight. 'Thank you.' He pulled back, keeping his arms hooked loosely around her waist. 'It's scary to think I might finally get a chance to do what I've always dreamed off, but I know if I wait any longer I'll regret it forever.'

'It's wonderful,' she repeated. 'Honestly, Ben, I'm so happy you're finally getting your chance.'

'And what about you?' His tone had turned serious again.

'What about me?' She tried to play it innocent, but she knew he must've sensed why she'd reacted negatively when he'd first tried to tell her.

'When do you get your chance to follow your dreams? Because I don't want to be the only one.' He let go of her waist and took her hand, squeezing her fingers through the soft wool of her glove. 'If I'm going to jump off the cliff into the unknown, I want you right there too.'

Amelia shook her head. 'It'll be a while, but I'll get there. I don't want you to worry about me, or feel like you have to wait for me because that might be a long time coming.' She tried to laugh to prove to him that it really was okay, but it was hard not to think about the millstone of responsibility around her neck.

Ben picked up her other hand. 'What if I said you didn't have to wait? What if I said there's a way for you to be free of your father's debts tomorrow.'

What on earth was he talking about? 'I don't think I like where this conversation is going. Did you ask Ziggy if he could lend me more money?' She didn't give him time to answer, her mind already picturing the two of them cosy at the farmhouse kitchen table as they decided what was best for her. 'That's it, isn't it?'

Ben shook his head. 'No, this wouldn't be a loan, it would be a gift to you. I found out the family have kept a savings account for me all these years, but with what I'm going to inherit from my dad, I don't need it. You do, though.'

'You just want to give me money? No strings attached and I can do what I want with it?' They should have stayed in the woods because this was some sort of ludicrous fairy story he was spinning her.

'Yes.'

'God, you're as bad as Rhys!' She tried to tug her hands free, but he was holding too tight. 'What did I tell you about not needing to be rescued? You really are a bloody Travers to your bones, whatever your surname is!'

'Amelia, please, don't do this. Let me explain to you properly.'

If he'd thought that was going to calm her down, he might as well have waved a red rag in front of a bull. 'Explain what? How you and Ziggy cooked up a plan to rescue poor, pathetic little Amelia and her mother, the local charity cases?'

Her explosion of temper seemed to spark his own. 'For God's sake, you're being ridiculous!'

Ridiculous, was she? She yanked her hands back again, sliding them free of the gloves he'd given her, so he was left clutching the mitten ends of them. Tugging off the matching hat, she tossed it at him. 'Have this as well! I don't need anything from you.'

Barely able to see through the angry tears stinging her eyes, she stumbled across the grass in the direction of the road. How dare he! How bloody dare he pop up in her life like this and think he knew the answers to everything. She marched along the side of the road, ignoring the slow stream of cars heading back towards the gate. The wave of righteous anger carried her all the way to the little junction that marked the road leading to the cottages. She could see the lights shining from the windows, and she slowed down to catch her breath. She couldn't go charging in and let her mum see she was upset.

'Your hands are getting cold.'

Amelia spun on her heel to find Ben standing not three feet

away, holding out those silly red mittens. As though just him mentioning it was enough to bring her awareness back to her body, she realised he was right, damn him. She shoved her hands in her pockets. 'I told you already, I don't need anything from you.'

Ben dropped his hand to his side. 'Answer me one question and then I'll leave you alone.'

It was on the tip of her tongue to tell him to get stuffed, but in the end her curiosity got the better of her. 'Go on, then.'

'Why didn't you take one of the estate bursaries when you had the chance?'

It was so far out of left field, she felt blindsided. 'What do you mean? You know why I couldn't take it; I had to get a job and help my parents.'

'You didn't have to. You chose to.' Ben held up his hands. 'I'm not judging your decision; I just want to know if you've been completely honest with yourself about your reasons for doing that.'

This was suspiciously close to what Hope had said to her before she'd offered her the use of the cottage. 'You're making it sound like I had a choice.'

'Didn't you?' He took a small step closer. 'Didn't I have a choice when my father kept pushing in the wrong direction?'

They'd already had this conversation. 'You were a child.'

'And so were you. He had so many expectations of me and it felt easier to go along with what he wanted. What if I'd pushed against him and gone my own way and made a complete hash of it? I couldn't let him down like that! Couldn't face him having to tell people his only child was a failure, not when I was all he had.' He closed the distance between them and rested his forehead against hers. 'And if I struggled with him wanting so desperately for me to succeed, how much harder was it for you with everyone expecting you to fail?'

She leaned back so she could look him in the eye. 'You think I chose to stay at home and put myself through all this heartache because I was afraid of what people would think if I messed up?' She didn't like the way the words tasted on her lips as she said them.

'I think you were in an awful situation, and I think you did what you thought was for the best.' Ben's voice was infinitely gentle. 'I think you grew up with parents who didn't support you properly because they were too focused on their own problems. I think you were surrounded by people like that awful bloke who screamed through your letterbox about how you were just like your dad.'

'Eric? He was just angry because Dad owed him so much money.'

Ben shook his head. 'There was more to it than that; I heard it in his voice. He sounded almost happy to be proven right.'

Amelia wanted to protest again but then she recalled all the times people had looked down their nose at her, had judged her because of her father's behaviour as if somehow she was responsible for it. 'Now you can understand why I'm so desperate to leave.'

'And I won't stop you if that's what you decide to do. There are no caveats on the money, Amelia. It was given to me to do exactly what I want with it and I'm passing it on to you with exactly the same instructions. It's not a bribe to try and get you to stay with me, no matter how much I might want that. It's about giving you the same freedom I now have. I want you to live the life of your choosing, not the one that's been dictated for you by the actions of others. I want you to be free.'

You should be rushing into things. You should be running headlong at life, not wasting your best years worrying about me and... well, everything else.

She shook her head. 'I can't just take your money.'

'Why not? I don't need it and you do.'

God, he made it sound so easy, and deep inside her a little voice cried out at her to take it, to set herself free from the chains of the past, from the terrible mistakes that were none of her making. 'It's not that simple.'

Ben tugged at her sleeve until she freed her left hand from her pocket and began to work one of the gloves down over her freezing-cold fingers. 'It really is.' His warm lips found her cheek. 'Let me do this for you, Amelia. Let me do this for us both so we can stop regretting and start living.' He traced a line across her cheek, and she couldn't help but turn into the warmth of it, to open her lips in welcome when his mouth reached hers.

'I'm scared,' she admitted when they finally broke the kiss.

Ben pressed his forehead to hers. 'I'm scared too, but it feels a little less scary knowing we'll be doing it together, don't you think?'

'What if it all goes wrong?' she whispered, still not ready to believe this was really happening.

'Then it all goes wrong, but at least we'll have tried. And we'll still have each other. Still have Juniper Meadows and the people who love us to catch us if we fall.' He kissed her again. 'What do you say?'

'Yes. Oh Ben, yes, please.'

EPILOGUE

'I might have known I'd find you in here.' Ben padded into what was now the spare bedroom of the little cottage since her mother had moved in with Ziggy over at the farmhouse. Amelia wasn't the only one who was making up for lost time, and she didn't care one bit what anyone else might think about the heir of the estate shacking up with the wife of the local criminal because she'd never seen Daisy so happy.

'I woke up and you were still fast asleep, and I just wanted to finish these last couple of paintings before tomorrow...'

Ben smiled as he handed her one of the two mugs of tea he was holding. 'I promise I didn't take it personally.' Leaning down, he brushed a kiss over her lips. 'Merry Christmas.'

'Merry Christmas.' She stepped back so he could see the painting she'd been adding the finishing touches to. It was one of a series she'd done of the Hall and showed it standing proud, surrounded by a blanket of snow. 'What do you think?'

'I think you've captured the moment perfectly.'

The weather gods – or an Arctic blast, for those of a less romantic nature – had decided to join in the festive spirit and had covered the entire valley in about three inches of snow in the past few days. While it looked beautiful, it had sent everyone who lived and worked at Juniper Meadows into panic stations to ensure the roads and car parks would be safe for the forthcoming Twelve Days of Christmas festival, which was kicking off on Boxing Day and would run through until Epiphany, after which the children would be going back to school. Amelia was running her face-painting stall again, but she'd also decided to exhibit and hopefully sell some of her paintings as well.

Since finishing at work at the end of November, she'd been painting like a woman possessed, the freedom to get up and do whatever she wanted each morning as heady as any drug. Though it had been scary to reach out, Amelia had contacted her old art teacher from school and with his help she'd explored possible options about how she could pick up her studies. He'd put her in touch with a friend who taught at the local college and, with a strong endorsement from her teacher, she'd been allowed to join his first-year A-level evening course for the rest of the academic year. Whether she could catch up enough to be able to pass exams in the summer, she would have to wait and see, but she'd been given the course materials for the first term to work through under her own steam so at least she'd have a fighting chance. And it was a much better option than having to wait nearly a whole year.

Ben was head and shoulders above her in terms of his academic qualifications and had been accepted on a summer school at the Royal Academy. It would mean them spending the summer at his flat, and though it was months away, Amelia had already made a list of all the galleries and museums she wanted to visit. Her life had become unrecognisable to her in a matter of weeks, and if she allowed herself to think too hard about it, the old fears would rise. She'd woken in a cold sweat more than once, expecting to find it was all a dream, but the warm reassurance of Ben beside her always grounded her back in reality.

Ben picked up the painting and studied it. 'How much are you going to sell it for?'

'I'm not sure, fifty pounds, maybe?' It sounded like an outrageous amount to her, but it was less than what she'd seen similar paintings on sale for in the local shops in Cirencester and Burford when she'd gone on a recce.

'I'll pay you double that if you'll wrap it up for me. I want to give it to Mum later as an extra gift.'

Amelia laughed. 'You don't have to pay me for it, Ben! You can have it with my blessing, although I'm not sure we should risk wrapping it until it's completely dry.' She'd only added a few little details, but now she knew it would be a present for Stevie, she wouldn't risk it being smudged.

Setting the painting aside, Ben put his arms around her waist and drew her close. 'We'll never make a businesswoman of you with that kind of attitude.'

She smiled up at him. 'What's mine is yours, Ben Lawson, because you have given me a gift beyond measure.'

After a lazy breakfast and a couple of hours watching children's cartoons on the TV and eating too many Quality Street, they bundled themselves up in their coats and boots and headed over to the farmhouse, where they would be joining the rest of the family for lunch. Their passage across the estate was made easier by the monumental efforts everyone had put in to clear all the roads, and though the sky was blue with barely a wisp of cloud, Amelia still sent up a silent prayer that the forecast would hold true, and they'd seen the last of the snow for now. The bare branches of the trees lining the main road had been strung with glittering, coloured lights and oversized baubles, providing a stunning display for what would hopefully be a rush of visitors the next day.

The company who had done such an amazing job with the illuminated trails at Halloween had been back to sprinkle their magic through the woods, and Hope had promised a preview of the display after lunch.

The back door of the farmhouse had been left open a little to let the dogs come and go as they pleased, and Ben pushed it wide, ushering Amelia in before him. Newspaper had been laid out beside the door and two pairs of boots sitting on it showed they weren't the first arrivals of the morning. 'Here you are!' Stevie cried as she took the two carrier bags full of presents Amelia was holding and set them on the kitchen table. She relieved Ben of his bags before leaning in to kiss him on the cheek. 'Happy Christmas, darling.'

'Happy Christmas, Mum.'

Amelia looked away, swallowing the sudden lump in her throat. It was so good to see the two of them so free and easy with each other after what had been a tough couple of months.

'We were just about to send out a search party!' Rowena said, waving at them with a spoon from her usual spot next to the oven.

Whatever she was stirring smelled absolutely heavenly and Amelia's mouth watered even though she couldn't possibly be hungry after the amount of chocolate she'd eaten that morning. 'We're not late, are we?' Amelia asked with a frown. 'I'm sure Mum said to come for eleven.'

'And so I did, darling,' her mother said, coming over to give her a kiss. 'Merry Christmas.' Daisy was wearing a cherry-red jumper and a splash of lipstick in the same bright shade.

'Merry Christmas. That's a lovely colour on you – is it new?'

'It was a present.' Daisy beamed up at Ziggy, who was all but plastered against her hip. It was as though now he'd finally won her back, he was terrified to let her out of his sight in case she slipped away from him again. From the way her mother's arm clung around his waist, Amelia knew the feeling was mutual between them.

It took another five minutes for them to take their boots off and get settled at the table, their progress impeded by myriad hugs and kisses as they were greeted and welcomed one by one by the rest of the family. Zap pressed a glass of something pink and fizzy on each of them as soon as they were seated. 'What's this?' Ben asked as he raised his glass to take a sniff.

'A champagne cocktail made with my new cranberry and ginger gin.'

Amelia took a sip. 'Gosh, that's lovely.'

Glowing at the praise, Zap took his seat next to Ben and moments later Hercule scrambled up to claim his usual spot sprawled across Zap's lap. 'I think it might be one of my best combinations yet,' he said, scratching the old dog fondly behind his ears.

'It's certainly a winner,' Ben said, reaching over to pet the dog.

Amelia glanced over at Stevie, and they shared a look before she turned back to Ben with a grin. 'I know we're not doing presents until after lunch, but your mum and I have something we wanted to give you.'

Stevie left the kitchen, returning a few moments later with a tiny bundle of black and white fur, which she carried over to them and placed into Ben's hands. 'This is Pepper.'

The little Dalmatian puppy squirmed in Ben's hands until he gathered it close against his chest and it settled down. 'Hello, Pepper.' He bent his head and nuzzled the top of the puppy's head. 'Aren't you a splendid little fellow?'

Amelia shared another look with Stevie, who was beaming with delight over her son's shoulder. 'I remembered you saying how much you missed your old dog, and I thought that now you were settled here you might like a new one.'

'He's amazing, thank you.' Ben leaned over to give Amelia a kiss, then looked up at his mum. 'I couldn't have asked for anything better.'

'He can stay with me when you go to London for the summer,' Stevie said, resting her hand on Ben's shoulder.

Overcome with excitement, the puppy licked Ben's chin, then peed all over his hands. 'Oh dear.' Amelia giggled, scrambling up to get a kitchen roll.

'Six months will give you plenty of time to get him house-trained,' Stevie added with a laugh as Ben mopped himself and the puppy up.

The other dogs came over to check their newest family member out and soon the kitchen was filled with their excited barks and little yips from the puppy. Carrying Pepper like he was as precious as a piece of the finest porcelain, Ben took him into the utility room, where a little crate had been set up with a cosy blanket and a bowl of water. Amelia followed him and watched as he placed the puppy inside and gently closed the gate. Pepper shuffled his bottom around to make a little nest in the blanket, curled up and was asleep in seconds. 'He's so adorable,' she murmured, not wanting to wake him up.

'He's perfect, but where did you get him from?'

'Denny told me his brother's dog had just had a litter and when he showed me a photo, I couldn't resist so I asked him if he'd save one for you. Well, for us.'

Ben put his arms around her waist and pulled her close. 'Us. I like that.'

'Me too.' She leaned up to welcome his kiss and for a moment the noise and laughter from the kitchen faded away.

'Might have known I'd find you two at it!'

They jumped apart at the sound of Rhys's voice, which of course had been his intention, and he bellowed with laughter. 'If you can put your girlfriend down for a minute, I wanted to have a chat with you about the lodge,' he said to Ben. 'I'm not booting you out, well, not yet, but I really need to get my arse in gear and do something with them and with the rest of the plans I've got for the campsite.'

'No problem,' Ben said as they followed him back into the kitchen. 'You've been more than generous to let me use it for as long as you have.'

'You can move in with me,' Amelia offered. It was perhaps a little earlier than either of them had expected, but she had no hesitation in making the offer.

'Are you sure?' Ben asked, taking her hand as they resumed their seats.

'Absolutely. Besides, you already spend more time at the cottage than you do at the lodge.'

'That's what I figured,' Rhys said with a wink as he sat down. 'I've had to accept I simply don't have the time to do it all myself, so I'm going to advertise for someone to come in and run the operation for me. I've warned Hope as well.' He nodded across the table to his cousin.

'Which is the kick in the bum I needed to get on with building my own place,' Hope said. 'I've got a meeting with Declan, our works foreman next week, to survey the new site we've chosen.'

Cam put his arm around her and smiled. 'Let's hope there's no ruins lurking under this one because I've got more than enough on my hands trying to make sense of the ones we've already found.'

'So many plans!' Rowena exclaimed as she placed a huge platter of sausage rolls, vol au vents and other tempting treats in the centre of the table. 'Eat up, everyone. It sounds like we're all going to need as much energy as we can get!'

ACKNOWLEDGMENTS

Welcome back to Juniper Meadows

I'm having so much fun exploring this gorgeous part of the Cotswolds, and I hope you all are enjoying it too! As the seasons turn, a setting like Juniper Meadows is just a gift that keeps on giving and as I get to know the Travers family better with every book they keep surprising me with their secrets, hopes and dreams. I can't wait to dive into the next book.

Thanks to Becca Allen (Copy Editor) and David Boxell (Proof Reader) for keeping me on the straight and narrow and doing their best to make sense of my (sometimes) nonsense.

None of this happens without the tremendous support I receive from my brilliant editor, Sarah Ritherdon. Thank you for believing I will get there even when I don't! x

Huge thanks to everyone at Boldwood Books. Simply one of the best teams I have ever worked with, and it is wonderful to be a part of something that feels very special.

Thanks to Alice Moore, cover designer extraordinaire x

I need to shout out the rest of the authors who make up #TeamBoldwood. What a brilliant, supportive group they all are x

Massive love to the best writing buddies in the whole world – Phillipa Ashley, Jules Wake, Bella Osborne and Rachel Griffiths x

Saving the best to last, all my love and thanks go to my husband x

ABOUT THE AUTHOR

Sarah Bennett is the bestselling author of several romantic fiction trilogies. Born and raised in a military family she is happily married to her own Officer and when not reading or writing enjoys sailing the high seas.

Sign up to Sarah Bennett's mailing list here for news, competitions and updates on future books.

Visit Sarah's website: https://sarahbennettauthor.wordpress.com/

Follow Sarah on social media:

- facebook.com/SarahBennettAuthor
- twitter.com/Sarahlou_writes
- bookbub.com/authors/sarah-bennett-b4a48ebb-a5c3-4c39-b59a-09aa91dc7cfa
- instagram.com/sarah_bennettauthor

Boldwood

Boldwood Books is an award-winning fiction publishing company seeking out the best stories from around the world.

Find out more at www.boldwoodbooks.com

Join our reader community for brilliant books, competitions and offers!

Follow us
@BoldwoodBooks
@TheBoldBookClub

Sign up to our weekly deals newsletter

https://bit.ly/BoldwoodBNewsletter